LONG DAYS, SHORT KNIGHTS

ROGUE ENTERPRISES
BOOK 1

JOHN WILKER

Rogue Publishing

Cover art by: Dan Voltz

V 1

ISBN: 978-1-951964-25-2

CONTENTS

Prologue   1

PART ONE
NEW ADVENTURES
Chapter 1   5
Chapter 2   16
Chapter 3   26
Chapter 4   35

PART TWO
BEING THE GOOD GUY
Chapter 5   45
Chapter 6   53
Chapter 7   64
Chapter 8   77
Chapter 9   87
Chapter 10   94

PART THREE
FAKE IT 'TIL YOU MAKE IT
Chapter 11   109
Chapter 12   117
Chapter 13   128
Chapter 14   137
Chapter 15   149
Chapter 16   162
Chapter 17   173
Chapter 18   185

PART FOUR
LIKE OLD TIMES

Chapter 19	201
Chapter 20	210
Chapter 21	218
Chapter 22	226
Chapter 23	238
Chapter 24	246
Thank You	259
Offer	261
Stay Connected	263
Acknowledgments	265
Other Books by John Wilker	267

For Nicole.
Our adventures mean the world to me

PROLOGUE

FOR THOSE JUST JOINING US...

The Rogue Enterprises team has been through a lot. They saved the Galactic Commonwealth once, maybe five times, but they stopped counting because no one was paying. They recently bought a warehouse to use as an official base of operations because living out of a starship was not as glamorous as the posters made it seem.

Wil Calder, the first human to leave our solar system and venture into the Galactic Commonwealth, and Cynthia Luar, a feline-featured ex-gangster, were recently married and are eager for some honeymoon time away from the rest of the team.

That leaves in charge Maxim and Zephyr, ex-Peacekeepers that Wil sprung from a prison transport. It's okay—they were framed.

Gabe is a simple engineering droid who became the figurehead of the Mechnoid Nation, and Bennie is a Brailack hacker who has been training to be a Knight of Plentallus.

There's more to all of their stories, so feel free to go read those and come back here. We'll wait. Or not. You don't have to be cool!

On a recent mission, the team was hired to be outside security consultants aboard the *Galactic Empress*, the most advanced pleasure cruise liner ever built. They met a young Olop girl named Nic, who bonded with Bennie, despite his best efforts. A few weeks ago, she showed up on the doorstep of Rogue Enterprises, looking to train with Bennie, and that is where we join our story...

Onward to the adventure!

PART ONE
NEW ADVENTURES

CHAPTER 1

WIL DROPPED the crate and stretched to rub his back. "Okay, this is the last one. Not sure why I had to unload them all."

Lounging in a folding chair near the *Ghost*'s cargo boarding ramp, Maxim looked up. "Because Zephyr and I gave you our share of the Moklan Pleasure Station credits we got from that cruise ship gig." He grinned. When Wil and Cynthia moved their wedding up, they also changed their honeymoon plans.

Wil sighed but nodded along. "Right. Seemed like a good idea twenty-two crates ago. Well, the client will be here to collect these in a week or so." The other man nodded. Wil continued, "While we're gone, you mind ordering a new gravsled or three?" In their haste to leave Nom Clamma to save Cynthia, they had left their gravsleds behind in a hotel.

"Sure thing." Maxim stood and walked to the crates. "These are what, again?" He rapped his knuckles against the plasticoid material. Kneeling down to look at the label, he read, "Fungal growth medium?" He stood and backed away. "You gotta stop taking jobs without telling us."

Wil waved his hands. "Hey, I ran this by y'all. I distinctly remember you were reading something on a PADD and said," he lowered his voice as low as he could, "'I'm not going, so do whatever you like.'"

Maxim rubbed his chin. "That does sound sort of familiar." He smiled. "You excited?"

Wil turned to his friend, beaming. "I am. Two weeks on what's supposed to be one of the most luxurious locations in the GC, all expenses paid. Can't wait." He nodded toward the front office. "What do you two have planned?"

From the door connecting the small front office space to the hangar that the *Ghost* occupied, Zephyr said, "I plan to keep him plenty busy."

Wil leaned to look past the deeply blushing Maxim to grin at Cynthia and Zephyr as the door to the front office closed behind them. He whispered, "I know what you think she means, but I bet she means finally painting the exterior of the building." He winked as Maxim frowned.

Cynthia's tail was swishing languidly as she walked toward Wil and the *Ghost*, a duffel bag slung over her shoulder. "You aren't packed."

Maxim released a sigh. Wil looked up at him, grinning. He turned to his wife. "I know." He pointed to the twenty-two crates haphazardly stacked against the near wall. "I was busy." He lifted an arm and made a face. "I'll shower and pack." He grinned. "I don't expect to need many clothes."

Zephyr blushed, looking at Maxim.

From across the hangar, Bennie shouted, "No! I told you, thrust, then parry."

"I'm trying!" a higher-pitched voice replied. "You suck as a teacher!"

"You suck more as a student!"

Everyone turned to look at the stairs in the opposite corner of the building. Bennie and his apprentice, Nic, the Olop girl he and Maxim had met while on their way to meet the others aboard the *Galactic Empress*, were coming down the stairs. The juvenile Olop had tagged along with Bennie when his and Maxim's shuttle, en route to the docking hub and waiting *Galactic Empress*, was hijacked by pirates looking for vengeance against the *Ghost* crew members.

During the incident aboard the luxury star liner, Bennie had forbidden her from getting involved, asking a massive Xelurian scientist to keep an eye on the young woman and her grandmother.

After the team saved the cruise ship and its passengers from certain doom, the young girl had hung on Bennie's every word as he told the story to anyone who would buy him a drink.

Nic had arrived at the Rogue Enterprises offices a week ago, with a note from her grandmother giving her permission to train with Bennie at a "special school," whatever that was.

Bennie tried to send her away that first night and several times a day since then. She continued to refuse, insisting she was ready to be a Knight of Plentallus, like Bennie.

When not fighting, the two were sparring and training. Bennie was doing his best, despite only learning what it meant to be a Knight himself not that long ago.

"Hey!" Wil shouted. "Give it a rest, you two!"

"She started it!"

"He started it!"

Wil sighed. He turned back to his other teammates. "I'm going to shower and pack." Cynthia grinned and followed him toward the nearer staircase.

As Bennie and Nic reached the two Palorians, Maxim said, "What's the problem now?"

Nic's mouth opened, but a green three-fingered hand moved in front of it.

"She doesn't listen," Bennie complained. "She never listens."

Nic slapped Bennie's hand away. "He keeps changing what he wants from me."

Maxim inhaled. "Look. If you're gonna continue down this path, you gotta figure it out." He pointed at Bennie. "Have you checked in with Nexum? Maybe there's a training program for Knights? Or a guidebook, or something?" Pointing at Nic, he added, "You need to realize you're the student. Be open minded. He's learning to teach. You need to learn to learn."

Zephyr leaned to the side. "Well. That's deep."

Maxim grinned. "I can do deep."

Gabe and Cynthia were standing on the *Ghost*'s cargo ramp. Maxim, Zephyr, Bennie, and Nic were a few meters away.

"Have fun!" Zephyr shouted over the growing rumble of the small warship's engines spooling up. Wil was already aboard, finishing the pre-flight checklist.

The ramp rose, and Cynthia shouted, "Have a good staycation!" She turned and ushered Gabe up the ramp with her as it sealed shut.

Gabe was returning to Arcadia, the homeworld of the newly minted Mechnoid Nation. The society created by droids from across the GC had been granted personal autonomy and civil rights. Gabe had helped to create this new society and, for several cycles now, had been fending off pleas to run for public office. He was returning to Arcadia to participate in some government stuff that none of the others really understood. Despite turning down public office, Gabe still held a lot of sway among his people.

The *Ghost* rose off her landing gear, the hydraulic pistons sighing as the weight of the ship left them. With clanks and whirs, the two powerful legs folded up into the body of the ship, armored panels closing over them.

"He won't..." Maxim started to say.

The *Ghost* was rotating to face out through the huge hangar doors.

Zephyr looked around, then turned, pushing Bennie and Nic toward the door to the front office portion of the building. "He might."

Maxim followed the others as the *Ghost* tilted, dropping her nose slightly, allowing the ship to drift forward on her repulsorlifts.

Once the *Ghost* cleared the large hangar doors, her atmospheric engines lit off with a boom, pushing the ship up and away from the building.

From the safety of the conference room, Bennie looked up at the two Palorians. "I thought he'd do it."

"Do what?" Nic asked.

Bennie turned. "Kick in the atmo engines while inside the building."

"Wouldn't that be dangerous?"

"Very," Zephyr agreed.

Bennie cleared his throat. "So, anyway, we're gonna be taking off."

Nic looked at him, her mouth hanging open.

Maxim looked down at his friend. "Oh? Where are you going?"

Bennie rocked on his heels. "Nexum. I spoke to C7K2 last night. He said there are lots of materials on the apprentice training program at the Tower of Plentallus."

"There's an apprentice training program?" Zephyr asked.

Nic made a high-pitched squeal, clapping her hands.

Bennie looked at her, making a face. "Do you even know anything about Nexum?"

She shrugged. "I like road trips."

Maxim smiled. "I'm glad you got some direction. If there were materials, why didn't C7K2 send them along when you told him about training her?"

"Well, I never really told him. I mean, I assumed I could do it."

"With what? Those training holos he sent when you left the Tower last time?"

Bennie nodded. "Yeah, that's what I've been trying to use on her." He hitched a thumb toward Nic. "I guess he curated that stuff for self-guided learning from a certain point in the training. C7K2 has a whole other, more in-depth set of records for how a Knight should train his apprentice. Apparently, once a Knight got to a certain level, they always found a kid to tag along with them. Do grunt work stuff and all that."

"Grunt work?" Nic murmured.

Zephyr said, "Booking a shuttle?"

Bennie clucked. "No. Not since that last time. I've decided that public transport is for losers." He looked at Nic. "No offense." She made a rude gesture but said nothing. Bennie said, "I rented a private shuttle. It should be ready by the time we get to the spaceport."

Zephyr shrugged. "Can't say I blame ya on the public transport thing. Private shuttle, though. Pricey way to travel." She raised an eyebrow.

Bennie smirked. "I may have hacked the rental company's reservation computer."

Zephyr groaned. "I didn't hear that."

Bennie turned to Nic. "Why are you still standing there? Go pack."

The hangar doors rattled as they rolled closed, sealing off the space from the dry, dusty surface of Fury. The Palorian couple watched first Nic, then Bennie, head back upstairs to the residential floor.

Maxim turned to Zephyr. "We're actually going to be alone for...well...a while." He grinned.

"Let's celebrate when those two are safely on a shuttle leaving orbit." She winked.

The shuttle Bennie hacked a rental for was spacious. It was about twice as long as the *Ghost*'s cargo hold, sleek and modern, unlike the aged Ankarran Raptor. Better still, it was almost entirely automated with a state-of-the-art sentient intelligence system for a pilot. Since Bennie didn't actually know how to fly a ship, that was welcome news.

The Brailack hacker and Knight of Plentallus tossed his duffel bag onto the bed in one of the three small single occupant berths near the front of the ship. He made sure his unwanted student took the berth furthest from him.

Bennie still wasn't sure about training Nic. For one thing, she annoyed the wurrin out of him. For another—if he was being honest with himself—the larger concern was that he didn't know if he was up to the task of training a potential future Knight. His own training was far from complete.

Her persistence had largely taken his second concern out of his hands. Since her arrival, he had tried time and again to send her home or really anywhere else that wasn't Fury. She refused, often vehemently, sometimes violently, to leave.

The speaker in the ceiling played a pleasant chime before saying, "We have been cleared for departure. Please secure for takeoff. We will lift off in five microtocks."

Bennie remembered how hard it had been for Wil to wrap his head around common Galactic Commonwealth units of time. Bennie never understood how twelve and sixty units made more sense to the human than simple base ten units. But, Bennie had learned over the years, from Wil and the humans he had met on Earth once, that humans were anything but rational.

Bennie walked out of the small berth to the seating area directly behind the cockpit. Nic was already there, seated and belted in. She was practically vibrating. "You've traveled before. Why are you so excited?" he asked.

"I've never been to Nexum."

"It's not that great, believe me." He dropped into a seat opposite hers. Fastening his belt, he added, "The locals are okay, the food is fine—"

"It's the home of the Knights of Plentallus!" she interrupted. "The Tower is a GC treasure!"

"It's okay." He nodded.

"How can you say that?" Bennie shrugged. She continued, "Built before the founding of the Commonwealth. Before, the, Commonwealth."

Bennie shrugged again. "Okay. So?"

"So? The Knights of Plentallus date back thousands of cycles. They roamed the stars dispensing justice and being good examples to others. Then they vanished." She leaned forward. "Don't you find that weird?"

Bennie looked up from his wristcomm. "Sorry, were you talking to me?"

Nic opened her mouth, but the ceiling interrupted her. "Prepare for takeoff."

It thrilled Bennie that the announcement distracted the young woman. He leaned back, letting the thrum of the atmospheric engines lull him into sleep. He had learned enough about the history of the order and its demise at the hands of the Tarsi in their creation of the Peacekeepers as galactic police force. He did not want to talk about it. He did not want to dash the dreams of his annoying young companion.

After cycles aboard the *Ghost*, Bennie was really liking letting a ship take care of flying while he focused on other things.

He had been tempted to dig into the pilot's core routines but decided against it since he wasn't sure a crash of the system wouldn't equal a crash of the shuttle.

He and Nic were sitting in the small cargo area at the rear of the craft. It wasn't what anyone would call spacious, mostly designed to hold the luggage of those traveling aboard the shuttle.

Given the relative size of both passengers and their lack of luggage, it made for an acceptable training space. Bennie was sitting cross-legged opposite his student.

"You have to keep a lot of variables in your head at one time: your physical surroundings, beings nearby, weather, vehicles, and more," he said.

Nic, her eyes closed, opened one eye. "Easy for you to say. You've got processor implants."

Bennie smiled, his eyes still closed. "It doesn't hurt. But I'm told that all the Knights could do it, and few, if any, of them, were enhanced."

"How?" the young woman pressed. She was struggling to keep her focus on any one thing, let alone holding multiple things in her mind.

"Meditation. Practice. Rinse and repeat. Close your eyes."

"They are," she lied, closing her eye. "So, you just sit here?"

Bennie shifted uncomfortably. Sir Jarek Ruus had never really been super clear on that point. C7K2 hadn't either. "I mean, sorta. Open your senses. What do you hear? What do you smell? Is there a breeze? From which direction? That sort of thing. The more you can train your brain to pick these things out, the more it becomes second nature."

After a pause that almost forced Bennie to open his eyes, his young charge said, "I hear the engines, the air circulation system. I can smell the...I don't know what it is, but something is in the air, pungent."

"Sorry," Bennie whispered.

"Gross!" Nic's eyes bolted open as she scrambled to get some distance from her teacher.

Bennie chuckled, getting to his feet. "Okay, enough sitting on our asses." He looked up at the chronograph display above the hatch connecting the cargo area to the rest of the small ship. "We've got time for one more lesson before lunch."

"What's for lunch?" Nic rubbed her stomach.

Ignoring her, Bennie reached for a small tool that was fastened to the bulkhead. Placing it in a pocket on his canvas trousers, he said, "Okay. Come see if you can get it."

The Olop girl stared at him. "Uh, no thank you, Grandpa Creeper. I am not putting my hand in your pocket."

Bennie's mouth opened. "Wha—? No, that's not..." He removed the small tool and the light over-tunic he was wearing, placing the tool in the shirt's pocket and hanging the shirt on a luggage strap hanging nearby. "Okay, here. Try to remove the tool from my jacket without rustling the fabric."

"Picking pockets? That's the next lesson?"

"Yeah." He pointed to the jacket hanging between them. "Go for it."

"That's a thing Knights of Plentallus do? Pick pockets?" She moved to stand in front of the garment. Wiggling her fingers, she gingerly reached into the pocket. The jacket moved and, before she could react to that, a thin wooden dowel slapped across her arm.

Jumping back, rubbing the stricken arm with her other hand, Nic snapped. "What the wurrin is that? Where did you get a stick?"

Bennie was leaning on a thin wooden cane. "Never mind where I got it. Rustle the over-tunic, get a whack." He motioned to the hanging jacket. "Try again."

"Why are you teaching me how to steal?" she complained.

"How much do you think being a Knight of Plentallus pays?"

She shrugged. "I dunno. A lot, probably."

After collecting himself from laughing hard enough that his stomach hurt, he said, "Nothing. It pays nothing."

"What?"

He held up a finger. "That's not the point, though. I'm not teaching you this so you can rob people."

"Let's circle back to the pay thing." She scowled.

Bennie waved a hand. "That pocket won't pick itself. Try again." He tapped the end of his stick on the deck.

CHAPTER 2

BENNIE AND NIC spent the rest of the shuttle trip practicing. Sometimes it was mental exercises, sometimes physical. In between the training, they argued.

By the time the rented shuttle was entering orbit, the young Olop girl was moderately proficient lifting things from pockets. Bennie had explained that it wasn't so much about robbing someone as being able to liberate evidence or other vital findings. The role of a Knight was always ambiguous, and it paid to be flexible.

To his surprise, she'd taken to code slicing quickly. Still far from his skills, but no slouch.

Her swordplay needed a lot of work still.

The ceiling speakers chimed. "We have received landing clearance. Please secure all loose items and prepare for atmospheric entry."

Bennie took the training sword from Nic. "You'll get it. I wasn't that awesome with a sword at first, either. I mean, who uses swords?" He smiled.

"Right? Will mine be a blaster like yours?" She followed

him into the seating area. "Speaking of, when do I get my laser sword?"

Snapping the harness around his waist, Bennie smirked. "Beam saber, and not any time soon." He held up a hand to stop her protest. "When the time is right, you can make your saber however you like."

The shuttle's pilot intelligence did a remarkable job traversing Nexum's atmosphere. It brought the vessel to a gentle rest on a small landing pad in the Tower's rear property where the public wasn't permitted.

After the conversion to public museum, most of the Tower had become a tourist trap, open sun up to sun down under the guidance of C7K2, the matte black caretaker droid. Bennie was never sure what the GC Council or Peacekeeper's thought about that. He honestly did not care.

Once the two passengers stepped off the boarding ramp, it rose as the pleasant computer voice said, "Thank you for using Aldon Shuttle Services, a subsidiary of the Draplin Combine." The shuttle was impossible to see with the naked eye by the time Bennie and Nic reached the rear entry to the Tower. C7K2 and DV-o were waiting for them.

Bennie smiled. "Hi, guys. This is Nic." Before either droid or the Olop girl next to him could say anything, he added, "Show her around, get her situated. Bye." He waved as he headed straight for one of the lifts, his wristcomm beeping as he neared it, allowing him access. The lift doors closed behind him, leaving the stunned trio staring at the closed doors.

The two droids turn in unison to Nic.

C7K2 said, "Hello, I am C7K2, and this is DV-o. I am the caretaker of the Tower. DV-o handles training when Sir Ben-Ari Vulvo is in the Tower."

"I'm Nic'ole Thot'la. You can call me Nic." She offered a small furry hand.

Each droid took the offered hand. C7K2 said, "We would be happy to show you around." He extended a hand toward the lift Bennie had just taken. "You may leave your bag here with Sir Ben-Ari Vulvo's. We will collect them later."

The heavy door slid shut, cutting off the landing area. Nic followed the two droids through a twisting maze of rooms and floors, some open to the public where she had to fight through crowds, and others for official use only.

"What's this?" Nic asked upon entering a dimly lit room lined with holograms of worlds and beings, most of which she didn't recognize.

C7K2 said, "This is one of the Halls of Remembering. The Knights believed that it was important to not only celebrate their wins, but acknowledge their losses. Each of these displays is such a loss." The droid pointed to a blue and green world covered in clouds. The holographic planet was slowly rotating. "Vimdash Three. Destroyed by a plague."

Nic leaned closer to the holographic world. She turned to the droid. "Everyone died?"

"Three thousand cycles ago. Yes. The Knights of Plentallus were unable to help them."

"The whole planet?"

The droid inclined his head. "Several dozen Knights were there to help. Several of the best minds among the order did everything they could."

"Why doesn't the GC talk about this?" Nic asked, leaning in to gaze at the hologram.

"The Tarsi are not fans of history that predates the formation of the Commonwealth, particularly history that highlights the good the order did. All but the most prestigious schools have stopped teaching it entirely." He pointed to the ceiling. "The historical archives contained in the Tower are some of the most complete in all the Galactic Commonwealth."

While Nic was getting a tour, Bennie was in the beam saber lab, his saber hilt taken apart on the Brailack-height workbench and a cracked power cell casing off to the side, discarded. "That explains that," he whispered to himself, pulling a new power cell from a bin of similar units. After ensuring it was unblemished, he inserted it into the housing and connected a few leads. A PADD next to him, connected by wires to the main control unit of the beam saber, scrolled a diagnostic across its screen, finally settling on "Diagnostic Complete. No Warnings."

Bennie was disconnecting the PADD and reassembling his weapon when C7K2 entered. "Sir Knight."

"Hey, CK." Bennie didn't look up from his work. "Get my annoying new problem settled?"

"Yes. She is...remarkably curious. She has retired to guest quarters on level 18. Would you like me to provide her quarters on the residential floors?"

Bennie clipped his beam saber to the loop on his belt. "Not yet, not until I know what I'm doing with her. I tried meditating. On what I should do about her."

C7K2 stepped far enough into the room to allow the door to slide closed. "And?"

Bennie sighed. "And nothing. I sat there for an entire tock in the dark. I finally had to stop when I couldn't get a song I heard the other day at the office out of my head." He shrugged. "How did the others do it? Find answers in meditation, I mean."

"Many used drugs."

Several tocks later, after Bennie got his belongings settled in his room on the 38th floor of the Tower, he was knocking on the door that was assigned to Nic. "Open up. We're going to dinner."

"Hold on," came the muffled reply.

The guest quarters on level 18 of the Tower were nicer than most hotels and far nicer than the budget stateroom Nic and her grandmother had shared aboard the *Galactic Empress*.

The luxury cruise liner, the biggest pleasure ship ever built, had run a GC-wide contest, and her grandmother had won. The entire trip had gone sideways when some of the ship's investors hired mercenaries to destroy the ship in order to get their investment back through the insurance payout.

The door slid open. "Where are we going?" Nic was wearing an outfit similar to Bennie's earth tone tunic and trousers. Where his outfit was pale browns and off whites, hers was all darker browns and blacks.

"Dinner." Bennie waved toward the lift at the center of the Tower. With the exception of the floor that separated the Knights-only floors from the publicly accessible floors, a central pair of lifts ran up and down the center of the building.

"What? No comment on my outfit? CK gave it to me." She fell into step next to him, fidgeting with her belt as they headed for the lifts.

Bennie glanced over. "He shoulda asked me first."

Nic was silent the rest of the way out of the Tower. She knew she was capable of being a Knight of Plentallus. She didn't understand why Bennie was so against it.

The doors to the restaurant swung open. "Sir Knight!" The hostess beamed as Bennie and Nic entered the restaurant. "We have missed you!"

"Hello, Gertrude," Bennie said, walking up to the podium.

"Is there something wrong?" Nic asked, glancing from Bennie to the woman behind the host podium. "Your voice is all low and gravelly. You need a glass of water?"

Bennie waved a hand, shushing her.

The Trollack woman looked up from her podium. "We have

your table, of course. Just you and your," she looked at Nic, "assistant?"

"Apprent—" Nic started to say.

"Thank you," Bennie interrupted.

The restaurant was as busy as usual. When Bennie had first discovered the place, he used the clout that the Tower offered to convince the owner to leave a table open for when a Knight was in the Tower, knowing full well he was the only Knight.

"This is so fancy. I thought you said we didn't get paid?" Nic said, looking around. Tables were scattered just far enough apart that their well-dressed occupants had privacy. Nexuu occupied most of the tables, but here and there, Nic saw other GC races.

She'd never seen Nexuu before. Their lidless blue eyes were entrancing.

"Who's we? You got a turd in your pocket? You're not an anything, yet," Bennie retorted.

She beamed. "'Yet.' Not 'never.'"

Bennie scowled. "Anyway. Part of being a Knight is that we rely on the kindness of those we serve."

She looked around at all the well-dressed Nexuu and other beings. "Who in here do we—

you—serve?" She cocked her head. "Is that why you do that thing with your voice?" She leaned in. "Does it hurt? Should I do that, too?" She cleared her throat. "How does this sound?" Her voice was thick and deep.

Bennie scowled and was about to answer when the server came to take their orders. Nic ordered a pasta dish with Nuflonog and a fizz-pop. Bennie said, "I'll have jerlack steak and qorrum fries."

The server left and Nic said, "You did it again! Your voice is all deep, like Maxim's." Her eyes went wide. "You've conned them into comping your meals here!"

Bennie shushed her and whispered, "Don't ruin it! Did you see the prices on the menu?"

The pair ate in relative silence until Nic asked, "So, what's the deal with all this?" She pulled at the sleeve of the outer tunic she was wearing. "Why is mine all browns and blacks?"

Bennie set his fork down. "I haven't read all the manuals yet, but I guess that's what they did way back when. Apprentices." He held up a hand. "I'm not saying you're an apprentice yet. They dressed that way to make it clear they were part of the order but not Knights. You might as well dress the part." He looked around. "Plus, it ensures they comp your meal, too."

Nic sighed. "Is it supposed to be scratchy?"

Bennie nodded. "Supposed to keep us humble or some dren. It helps if you run them through the clothes refresher a dozen times."

"Good night, Sir Knight," C7K2 said as Bennie and Nic entered the lift. He nodded to Nic. "And you, young miss."

Nic waved. "'Night, CK." The lift doors slid closed. "So, what now?" She looked up, a little, to Bennie.

He turned. "You go to bed. I do some work. That's what's next."

"Boring. I'm not even tired. I want to see more of the Tower."

Bennie said, "There's plenty of time for sightseeing." The doors slid apart on the level where the young Olop's quarters were located. Bennie shoved her out. "Bye."

She turned in time to scowl at the smiling Brailack as the doors closed.

As far as she knew, she was the only resident of the entire

floor. Turning a slow circle, she headed off in the direction directly opposite her room. He didn't say she *had* to go to bed.

The public areas of the guest room floor were pretty sparsely decorated. Hallways branched out in four directions from the central lift column. Each hallway had four doors, two on each side. The first set of doors was smaller, leading to more triangular rooms, without windows—at least, real ones. C7K2 had mentioned that they had large display screens to simulate the view from the direction the room faced. The second pair of doors led to larger rooms with floor-to-ceiling windows. Her room was one such room. She was sure that if Bennie had been consulted, she'd be in one of the smaller rooms.

She stopped at a door. Each had a control panel set next to it. Hers had been keyed to her wristcomm. She waved the device near the reader on the off chance that all the doors on the guest floor had been keyed to her wristcomm or left blank. The panel beeped and flashed a red light. She should have known a droid wouldn't be lazy enough to just assign all the doors to one wristcomm, even if no one else was using them.

Well, that was okay. This wasn't the first locked door in Nic's life. She looked around to ensure she was alone and pulled the access panel from the wall. A few microtocks later, the door lock clicked, allowing the door to slide open. She wasn't useless, even if Bennie thought so.

The room was one of the interior ones, a wedge with a large —but not floor-to-ceiling— display where the window would be if the room were on the exterior of the building. She looked at the view. "Not bad, really." She rested a hand on the display. Turning, she said, "There you are." Above the door to the small refresher was a grate covering what she assumed was the air duct—an air duct that connected to every other floor of the Tower, including the non-public floors. She grinned and moved a chair over to the wall so she could reach the grate. The chair wasn't enough. She hated how many things were designed around "talls." She spent a few microtocks dragging the dresser across the room, then hefting the chair up to precariously balance on top of the dresser. Olop were natural climbers, so the wobbly furniture tower wasn't an issue. She was prying the grate off the wall in no time.

The ducting was a tight fit, but doable. It took very little time to work her way to the center of the Tower where the horizontal ducts met the larger vertical ones.

"Okay, I'm on 18. Let's start at the first Knights-only floor, I guess." She braced her feet against the opposite side of the large vertical duct and climbed.

The 27th floor was one large open space, a gym of sorts. More weapons than she could even identify were racked along all four walls. The floor, and oddly, the ceiling were all padded. She peeked out into the space but didn't see any reason to leave the ducting for that room.

The 28th floor was interesting. The lift lobby was larger than on the lower floors, with several doors leading off of it and only one corridor leading to more doors. After walking around the floor to get the lay of it, Nic was back in the ducts thanks to a large planter that she was able to drag under the vent. The first room she peeked into on the next floor was some type of media room. "This looks fun."

The room was about twice the size of her guest room. Several overstuffed seats designed for different physical configurations faced a blank wall. There was an older model holoprojector mounted to the ceiling. Resting on the arm of one of the chairs was an equally dated PADD. Nic hopped into the seat and began browsing the options.

On the nightstand, Bennie's wristcomm beeped. Then it beeped again. Then it said, "Sir Knight. Wake up!"

Bennie rolled over and pushed the talking device onto the floor.

"Sir Knight, we have an issue," the voice from the wristcomm said.

Bennie opened his eyes. "What?"

"Your not-an-apprentice is missing."

"CK?"

"Yes, who else would it be?"

Bennie sighed. "Where are you? I'll be right there."

"The command center."

Bennie frowned. "We have a command center?"

"Level 29."

CHAPTER 3

"DREN," Bennie whispered, stepping into the command center. "How did you not tell me about this place?" He looked around the room. It took up most of the entire 29th floor. Screens lined the wall, and the floor was covered in workstations, each with a few displays mounted on it. There was a raised platform in the center with what looked like a gaming table on it. He was pretty sure it was not a gaming table.

C7K2 and DV-0 turned. The former said, "It did not come up."

Bennie made a face. "So, where is she?"

DV-0, the training droid, said, "We are scanning floor by floor. As with most things in the Tower, the floor sensors are a bit dated. We have to scan each floor versus the entire building at once."

"Efficient," Bennie griped.

"There," C7K2 said, pointing at the flat display on the wall, a wireframe of the Tower on it. "Level 28, the archives."

"I thought the archives were up on 42?"

"We have many archives," the matte black droid said. "That room is dedicated to longer historical archives and stories."

Bennie rocked on his heels. "Okay, whatever. Let's go."

The door to the archive viewing room slid open with a *swoosh*. Nic was curled up, watching something projected on the wall before her.

"What the wurrin? Are you trying to give me a reason to ship your ass back to your grandmother?" Bennie stormed in, two droids behind him.

She looked up, the fur around her eyes dark and wet. She pointed at the image being projected.

On the wall, rendered in grainy holographic particles, a Multonae Knight was leaping between a group of Trollack, cutting them down. The Knight landed in a crouch, spun, and stabbed his beam saber blade into what looked a lot like a juvenile Trollack. An unarmed juvenile Trollack.

Bennie's mouth hung open. He turned to the droids. "What the wurrin is this?"

Before the droids could answer, Nic said, "There's more." She tapped the PADD, then wiped her nose on her sleeve. The holo image shifted to a recording that looked a bit more recent than the previous one. A young Olop man was jumping and dodging through a crowd of Ruknak, his beam saber slashing through their rock-like skin like it was paper. It wasn't clear from the footage, but it looked like the Ruknak were fleeing the knight.

Bennie spun on the droids. "Explain. Now."

C7K2 stepped forward. "The history of the Knights of Plentallus is...complicated."

Bennie flapped his arms. "What do you mean, complicated?" He pointed to the flat image. "He's cutting people down! Isn't that Gelflux Prenta?" The holographic Olop Knight of Plentallus slashed his blade across a Ruknak, dropping it.

"Sir Gelflux Prenta, yes," C7K2 replied.

"Those people are running from him!" Bennie screamed.

"How did I not know about this place? What else have you not told me?"

DV-o inclined his head. "We thought it best to not overwhelm you early on."

Bennie stood there. Nic hopped out of the chair. She snuffled, wiping her nose again. "I'm going to bed." She pushed between the two droids.

Bennie stared after, then turned his attention back to the droids. "Was all of it a lie? Jarek Ruus? Was he just a drunk grifter? Did he kill people?"

"Sir Knight." C7K2 spread his arms. "All Knights kill people. It is the nature of things." He held up a hand to forestall Bennie's retort. "There is much history, not all what we would like it to be."

Bennie ran his hands over his head, moving to collapse into one of the chairs.

The caretaker droid said, "Would you have us believe your history is all altruism, Ben-Ari Vulvo? Wanted in five systems for computer crimes. Wanted in two others for felony assault, wa—"

"Those assault charges were bogus!" Bennie waved a hand.

"And the inciting revolution and vote tampering?"

"Well..."

C7K2 approached the chair and put a hand on the back, looking down at Bennie. "The Knights of Plentallus were not perfect. No being or organization is."

Bennie exhaled. "I get it." He looked up at the two droids. "No more secrets."

"Agreed," the two bots replied in unison.

He sighed, wriggling in the chair. "I guess I should bone up on the history of the order." He made a circular motion in the air. "Roll it."

C7K2 exchanged a look with DV-0, then said, "The remote is right next to you."

The two droids left, and Bennie settled in to watch some of the more uncomfortable stories of the Knights of Plentallus.

The cafeteria in the Knights-only section of the Tower had been closed for cycles. After the last Knight left the Tower, C7K2 shut it down and reassigned resources. Bennie met Nic in the public cafe on the second floor of the wide circular base of the Tower.

"Morning," he said, putting a cup of chlormax down as she arrived. "I got your breakfast." He pushed one of the two plates before him over to a seat on the opposite side of the table.

"Thanks." She dropped into the seat, not making eye contact. She poked at the pastry absently. "I think I'll—"

Bennie held up a hand. "Wait. I know last night was crappy. I didn't know that stuff, either, and it's really screwed up. I get it if you want to leave, but I thought about it last night while I watched more of that stuff than I ever want to see again. I think you should stay." Her head snapped up. "I'm not saying you're an apprentice yet." He stuck his tongue out. "But I think it's possible, and I think it's my responsibility to make the Knights of Plentallus an organization that I'm proud of."

"So, like, more criminal?" She took a big bite of her pastry.

"'Like more criminal,'" Bennie mocked in a high-pitched voice. "No. Not that. I was going to say you show a lot of promise, but now...no." She opened her mouth, but he held up his hand again. "Come on, we're heading into town." He stood and headed for the open archway of the cafe.

Nic hopped out of her seat, snatching the remains of the pastry as she did, trotting after Bennie.

The Tower of Plentallus sat at one end of the mid-sized city of Aqu Var. While the local Nexuu loved having the Tower and the Knights around, their society operated like any other. Gleaming towers full of businesses of all sizes, doing all sorts of things...boutiques, restaurants, and more packed the city center.

"Where are we going?" Nic asked for the third time. They'd been walking, seemingly without destination for several tocks. Bennie would occasionally stop and talk to someone that flagged them down, accepted some snack or trinket when offered. They didn't seem to have a destination.

He turned to her. "Does it matter? You got someplace to be?"

"Back to Cranky Grandpa, I see."

"Don't make me leave you at an orphanage." Bennie turned down a side street. He looked around, mumbling. "Supposed to be right here somewhere."

"I was thinking I could visit the workshop where you assembled your beam saber when we get back to the Tower."

Bennie paused. "What? No. No beam saber for you."

"Oh, come on."

"No."

She sighed. "Fine. What're we looking for?"

Bennie pointed. "There."

Nic followed the gesture. "What? That weird symbol on the wall?"

He frowned. "Weird symbol...yeah. It marks places under the protection of the local syndicate."

"I thought you said you and Maxim shut that down last year."

Bennie nodded. "We did, but I heard some rumors that someone had moved into this place. Figured we should check."

"And what if they did?" a voice asked from behind them.

Bennie looked at Nic. "You weren't watching the alley opening?"

"Did you tell me to?"

"I told you to train your senses. Make it like second nature to hear everything, smell everything."

Nic made a face, planting a hand on her hip. "You didn't."

"Excuse us," the large, well-dressed Nexuu man said from the entrance to the alley. He was wearing a tailored charcoal gray suit that complemented his darker-than-average green skin.

Bennie held up a hand, palm out. "We went over this on the shuttle," he scolded.

She pointed at the man and his small contingent. "You didn't smell them. Or hear them."

Bennie scoffed, "I was distracted."

"Grab 'em," the man growled, motioning to his two flunkies.

Two red-skinned, four-armed men moved out around their boss, followed by a pair of Harrith men, all four blocking any route out of the alley. One of the bigger four-armed men cracked first one pair of knuckles, then the other.

"Oh," Bennie said. He pushed Nic back behind him with one hand, while the other unclipped his beam saber.

"What're you doing?" She slapped at his hand before producing a wicked-looking blade half as long as her forearm. The same one she had when Bennie met her. She darted around him, teeth bared, blade held at the ready.

The nearest multi-limbed thug screamed in surprise a moment before a small furry terror, armed with sharp teeth and a knife, landed on his face.

Bennie, slightly more used to the savagery, didn't miss a beat. The screams of Nic's opponent drowned out the *snap-hiss* of his beam saber activating. He charged the two Harrith toughs, letting a battle cry escape his lips. Unlike their colleague, the two Harrith weren't as easily shocked. Both dropped to a knee, pulling pistols free of holsters under their arms. Both drew down on the charging Brailack.

"Dren!" Bennie shouted, changing course, swiping frantically to deflect those plasma rounds that came closest to him as he dodged behind a small trash bin.

Nic was aggressively biting and stabbing one man, who then grabbed the back of her tunic. "The wurrin is this?" He tossed her down the alley with one of his upper arms as one of his lower hands pulled a pistol from a holster on his thigh.

Bennie shut off his energy blade, twisting the selector as he took aim. A bolt of purple energy shot from the end of the hilt, striking one of the Harrith men in the chest, burning a hole through him, igniting his suit jacket. The body hit the ground, flames engulfing it.

"Gross!" one of the thugs shouted, stepping away from the conflagration that was rapidly filling the alley with the smell of burned flesh and fabric.

"Give up now and no one else...gets lit on fire!" Bennie shouted from behind his trash bin. The answer was several plasma bolts striking the thin metal, melting holes through it. Bennie leaped out from behind his diminishing cover, firing randomly.

While the remaining criminals were distracted by Bennie's fire, Nic emerged from the back of the alley, screaming. She darted past Bennie to leap onto the head of the nearest Harrith man. The lanky man screamed, his long thin arms pinwheeling. *What is it with her and heads?* Bennie wondered.

He used the confusion to ignite his beam saber and dive into the fray. Two quick swipes turned one of the four-armed goons into a two-armed goon. Over the screaming, Bennie shouted, "This only ends one way."

The leader of the group raised his wristcomm. "Get out here. We've got trouble!" He took a few steps back as Nic's opponent fell to the ground, his face a bloody mess and his flat nose conspicuously missing. She looked up, growling, blood soaking the fur of her face, her pink streak nearly invisible amid the gore covering her.

The door that Nic and Bennie had been looking at earlier opened, slamming against the alley wall. Three Trollack rushed out, each with a pistol.

"Okay, two ways," Bennie said over the hum of his beam saber.

Nic looked over her shoulder. "See, I should have a beam saber."

"You look like you're doing okay without," Bennie said.

"Ahem," the Nexuu man said.

Bennie sighed. Snapping off his beam saber, he laid the hilt on the ground. Looking at Nic, he shook his head. She scowled first at Bennie, then the leader of the group, before tossing her blood-soaked knife to the ground.

"Lock 'em up inside," the leader told the three new arrivals. Turning to the rest of his original group, he ordered, "Clean all this up. Get Holvaro to a medical facility."

Bennie handed his beam saber to one of the Trollack men. Nic followed suit, dropping her bloody knife into the man's webbed hand.

Bennie and Nic followed the three Trollack back inside the building, down a series of steps that gradually angled back under the alley and the building next to the one the door was set in. "So, who are you guys?" Bennie asked.

"Shut up!"

After a few more microtocks of walking, the nearest Trollack said, "Stop." He reached past them to open a door. "In."

The cell, such as it was, was closer to a root cellar. "Cozy," Bennie quipped, making a slow circle.

"Now what?" Nic asked.

Bennie made a patting motion in the air, then pointed to the door and the sound of the three Trollack walking away. Once the sound of their footsteps and banter couldn't be heard, he said, "Now we escape."

CHAPTER 4

"OH, you got a lock pick up your butt?" Nic replied. She had dropped down onto a crate that, according to the label, was full of tubers.

Bennie frowned. "No, I don't have a lock pick." He turned to look at her, smirking. "I do have a plan, though."

"Well, I'm reassured."

Bennie made a rude gesture that she ignored.

"So..." she continued.

"We need to wait a bit. Let them get settled."

She sighed. "Oh. Great." She picked at a piece of loose adhesive tape. "So, how did you meet your friends?"

Bennie had turned back to the door and was now slowly looking at every detail in the room. "Huh? What friends?"

"What do you mean, 'What friends?' How many do you have? The ones you work with!" the girl snapped.

Bennie stopped investigating the room. He inhaled. "Well, I met Wil a cycle or two before the rest. He had made it to Fury after his crew was killed, and he wanted a clean registration for the *Ghost*. Well, it was the *Raptor* then."

He rubbed his chin. "I did the job and sent him on his way,

never gave it another thought." He shook his head at the memory, smiling. "I wonder if I'd still have my shop...?"

"Then what?" Nic was leaning forward on the crate, her hands cradling her chin.

"Then nothing. A cycle or two later, these two pushy drennog PKs show up at my door, saying Wil sent them. I knew I shoulda just left them standing there."

"Not very noble."

Bennie clucked. "Anyhow. They needed new idents and wristcomms to match. No sooner had I gotten them set up and was about to push them out the door, more PKs came knocking on my door. All downhill after that. My lab was burned, then actually exploded. That last part was my safety feature more than the PKs. We scrambled through sewers until we met up with Wil at the ship. I didn't have any place else to go and figured my identity was burned, too, so..." He shrugged.

"Wow."

Gathering himself up, he said, "Yeah. Well. Okay, let's get out of here." He nodded to her. "Pretend you're having cramps or something."

Her light brown fur rippled. "What? No. Why me?"

"You're the girl."

"I'll save clawing your eyes out for later. You want a distraction?" She hopped off the crate. "Hey, out there! I think my grandpa is dying!" She turned and winked at Bennie's scowl. "Hey! He's puking all over the place! Hey! It's probably old age or a hearts problem."

Bennie growled, then hearing the footsteps, he fell to the floor and began convulsing.

Nic whispered, "Can you throw up?"

He glared. "Not on command!"

"What's going on in there?" one of the Trollack gangsters demanded.

Nic shouted, "Your Harrith friends—I think they hurt him up in the alley. He needs a doctor!"

The door opened. "Back up!" the thug urged, pistol held at the ready, pointed at Nic.

He moved to kneel next to Bennie's still shuddering form. "What's wrong with you?" He put a webbed hand on Bennie's shoulder, shaking him.

"Oh, nothing," Bennie said before a tiny green fist jabbed straight up into one of the unsuspecting gangster's eyes. Before the man finished falling, he had a small, brown-furred attachment on his back, and it reached around to claw at his face and remaining undamaged eye. Bennie rolled away and got to his feet. "Don't eat him. Just knock him out!"

"I'm try—" Nic started to say but was hurled from her opponent out into the corridor.

The Trollack gangster got to his feet, his remaining eye roaming the space to find Bennie. He lunged the moment he spotted the Brailack.

"Ah!" Bennie shouted, barely dodging the tackle. He kicked at the other man, moving to get some space between them. Before he could turn, Nic was sailing through the air to land on their jailer's back, small fury fists raining blows on the back of his head.

When the Trollack staggered, near collapse, Bennie waved. "Wait, wait!" He grabbed the man's collar. "Where's our stuff?"

The Trollack man stammered, "Upstairs...Mr. Lugo's...office."

"Thanks." Bennie punched him as hard as he could, square in the face between both eyes.

Nic leaped from their jailer's back before he hit the floor. "Now what?"

"Like I said—we get out of here." He held up his hand, waving it and wiggling his fingers. "Search him."

Other than a base model wristcomm and a few hard currency credit chips, the Trollack had little on him. Bennie stomped on the wristcomm after deeming it worthless.

Creeping through the hallway, Nic asked, "What about Gabe? Was he with Maxim and Zephyr when they came to you?"

Bennie slowed, looking over his shoulder. "What? Oh, we stole him later."

"Stole him?"

They reached the stairs, the same ones they had come down earlier. Bennie made a shushing sound, then pointed away from the door they had come through. Nic nodded.

They crept through the hallway, checking the few doors they came across until they found one that looked right. And was locked.

Bennie looked at the door, then Nic. "I can't pick locks without my wristcomm."

She sighed. "Not very useful without gadgets, are you?" She smirked and reached for the access panel. "Keep an eye out, Gramps."

"I really dislike you." He turned and crept back down the hallway. He had gone only a few steps before being summoned back with a hiss and the snapping of tiny fingers. "Okay, you're pretty good. Explains how you got around the Tower so easy."

Nic smiled and stepped aside.

"Hear anything in there?" Bennie asked.

She shook her head.

Bennie pushed open the door. The office was empty. Sitting on a desk that looked to be carved from a single piece of pale blue rock were their wristcomms, Nic's savage little knife, and Bennie's beam saber hilt.

"Huh. This wasn't so bad," Nic whispered from behind him.

Bennie scowled. "Are you trying to jinx us?" He motioned to the office. "See if there's anything we can grab to give the authorities." He moved around the desk, pushing the chair aside. After slipping his wristcomm back on and clipping his beam saber to his belt, he tossed Nic her wristcomm, noting that it was not a child's unit but a model only a few levels below what his had started at before he improved upon it. *Not shabby,* he thought to himself.

He made a note to himself to check out what mods she had installed on the device later.

The desk drawers were mostly empty except for the one with a prodigious amount of pornography and a half empty liquor bottle in it. Bennie thumbed through the reading material before noticing that Nic was looking at him. Dropping everything back into the drawer and sliding it closed, he said, "What've you got?"

She clucked. She was next to a half height file cabinet in the room's corner, which for an Olop, made it a full height unit. She held up a folder. "I think these are time tables and a chart of accounts."

"Chart of accounts?" He held out his hand for the folder.

She handed him the folder as she said, "I took banking for beginners in primary school. I know a chart of accounts when I see one."

He pulled a face and nodded. "Okay. Let's go before they get back."

"Too late," the heavyset Nexuu man—*Mr., what? Luigi, loogie? Lego? Lugo.* Bennie was pretty sure it was Lugo—said from the doorway.

Bennie turned to Nic. "Seriously? He snuck up on you twice?"

"Uh, you too."

"Not this again," Mr. Lugo groaned.

Bennie moved his hand to his hip as slowly as he could. "Any chance you're in the market for an assistant? I mean, you've seen what she can do. Fair warning: she's a pain in the ass."

Nic spun. "You wouldn't—" Her hands were flapping anxiously. "How dare you—"

Bennie raised his beam saber, activating it as he did. A magenta glow filled the small office. The move was fast enough that Lugo didn't react until the blade was pointed at him.

"Okay, look, man. This can go two ways. We fight our way out, or you let us walk out."

"And then?" the crime boss asked.

Nic edged over to stand next to Bennie, doing her best to look intimidating.

Bennie waved his free hand. "You find a new place to set up. We'll call this a wash."

The Nexuu squinted. "You don't act like I expected a Knight of the Tower to act."

"I'm a new breed." Bennie smirked.

The other man didn't seem impressed, but he remained silent as he thought it over. Finally, he huffed, "Very well." He raised his arm, speaking into his wristcomm. "Our guests are leaving. Don't bother them. Start packing things up, we're finding a new base." He turned to Bennie, eyebrow ridge raised.

Bennie smiled, his beam saber clicking off. He looked down at Nic. "Let's go."

Thankfully, she didn't say anything. She edged past the big Nexuu man, who made no move to stop her. Bennie followed, throwing out a salute as he passed.

They made their way back to the door in the alley. Pushing it open slowly revealed the alley was empty, all signs of their earlier scuffle scrubbed away.

Bennie looked around, impressed with the cleanup. "Let's head to the local security office. I think it's a few blocks this way." He pointed. "We can drop off this," he patted the folder he had tucked into his outer tunic vest, "on our way back to the Tower."

After dropping off the folder to the local security office and providing a full statement, Nic said, "So, you stole Gabe?"

Bennie rubbed his chin. "Oh. Well, yeah, sorta."

"Sorta stole?"

"Well, we definitely stole him, but it was more like liberating him. They crated him up to be sold or destroyed. We don't really know." He smiled. "Once we opened the crate to take a peek, I don't remember who turned Gabe on, probably Wil. Once we did, and he told us his story, we knew we couldn't hand him over to Xarrix."

"Xarrix?"

"Yeah, bad guy and all around drennog. He hired us to steal the crate Gabe was in. Wil did jobs for him off and on for a few cycles. We finally killed him a while back."

"What?"

Bennie waved a hand. The Tower was in view now, a few blocks away. "Another time." He walked a few more steps, watching her from the corner of his eye. "So, I'm thinking if we're going to make a go of this whole apprentice thing, both of us should take it more seriously." He stopped walking and waited for the excited squealing and dancing around ended before continuing. "Done?" She squealed one more time, bouncing on the tips of her toes, then nodded. "I don't think it's gonna be easy. There's a lot of weight and baggage on our shoulders here." She nodded, her head bobbing up and down. "Okay, then. Let's go get started." He resumed walking toward the Tower.

"Does that mean I get a—"

"No."

"But I'm your apprentice?"

"I didn't say that."

PART TWO

BEING THE GOOD GUY

CHAPTER 5

"THAT HURT!" Nic was on the padded floor, rubbing her hip.

"It would not hurt if you had blocked my attack," DV-o said, offering his metallic hand.

Nic got to her feet and picked up her training sword, a wooden thing whittled and shaved into the shape of a beam saber blade. She eyed the training droid. "Ya think?"

"I do." It backed up and assumed a ready stance. "You may try again."

Since Bennie's and her return to the Tower after their run in with the gangsters, she'd officially begun the process of becoming an apprentice Knight of Plentallus. Bennie still refused to call her an apprentice, or let the droids do so, but she knew he'd cave eventually. This was her first training session with DV-o, the droid that acted as Master at Arms and head of swordsmanship training for the Tower. Having trained hundreds of Knights and studied all available materials, the humanoid-shaped droid was the best, and only, teacher available to would-be Knights.

Nic struck a ready pose and nodded. Her opponent wasted

no time stepping in, sword held high. She stepped back, her own sword moving into a horizontal position to block the attack.

"Good. Be ready," the droid said, bringing his sword down, his torso pivoting to allow his wooden blade to swoosh sideways past her upraised block. His wooden sword whistled.

Nic twisted into the move, dropping her arm to pull the training sword down as quickly as possible to deflect the strike she saw coming. She was partially successful, deflecting much of its power but allowing a glancing blow against her leg.

"Very good," DV-o said. He spun in a fluid motion, recovering from the attack to begin his next move.

While the droid was moving into his next attack, Nic stepped in close, wedging her sword up into the droid's elbow. With a twist, she had the arm pushed back and out of position.

Straightening to show that he was no longer sparring, he said, "Interesting maneuver. What was your follow-up move?"

She tilted her head. "Uh..."

DV-o nodded. "It is important to plan several moves ahead. As you practice more, it will come naturally."

"Hey," Bennie shouted from the edge of the training area. "How's she doing?"

"I'm definitely ready for a beam saber," Nic said, leaning on her wooden sword.

"She is not." DV-o held up a hand. "She shows great promise, however." Nic stuck out her tongue.

Bennie nodded to the droid, holding his hand out as he walked toward the pair. The droid offered his training sword and moved to the edge of the space. Bennie spun the sword a few times. "Ready?"

Nic assumed the ready position. The moment Bennie matched her, she struck. He parried, spinning backwards to slash at her side. Unable to parry, she jumped back, barely avoiding the attack.

"Good job!" Bennie complimented.

Nic smiled, her sword lowering a bit. Bennie kicked her legs out from under her. She hit the ground with an *oof*. To punctuate the win, he bonked her on the back of her head with his sword.

Bennie grinned. "Never let your guard down."

"Unconventional," DV-o said in a low voice.

Nic got to her feet, rubbing the back of her head. "Cheater."

Bennie shrugged. "Come on. We need to help C7K2 decide which archive recordings to move to the public viewing galleries."

DV-o asked, "Are you certain, Sir Knight, that is the best course of action? Those archives could be damaging to the public image of the order."

Bennie shook his head. "Only way to clean the slate. If we're," he gestured to Nic, "building the next generation of Knights, we're doing it our way." He turned to Nic. "No, still not getting a beam saber."

It took the rest of the day to select archival footage that was truthful but not overly traumatic to view. The early trial and error had proven too much for Nic, who took dinner to her room. Bennie tried to be as intentional as possible in selecting footage that showed the difficulties that the Knights of Plentallus faced in being the adjudicators of justice.

By morning, the caretaker droid had moved the files to the public viewing galleries and crafted a warning for those who chose to view them.

Bennie and Nic were in the lower-level cafeteria for breakfast when an alert trilled from his wristcomm.

Nic looked at the device. "That's a new noise."

He nodded. "Yeah. Oh, dren." He dropped his utensil. "Come on."

"What?"

Bennie's answer was to forward the details from his wrist-comm to hers. Trotting along behind him, toward the lifts, she read the screen. "Oh."

Level 26 of the obelisk-shaped Tower was the transition between publicly accessible areas and those reserved only for Knights. The public lift opened out onto a floor devoid of any walls. A few scattered clusters of seats were the only features of the floor. It was meant to be a space where a Knight could meet someone without leaving the Tower, giving the visitor the thrill of being a guest of the Tower above the normal publicly accessible spaces—while also not permitting them into the more secure areas.

Bennie and Nic wasted no time moving to the set of lifts that serviced the Knights-only floors. Access to the upper levels was granted by using the hilt of a beam saber as a key. The setup had impressed Bennie. Each saber had an embedded secure enclave chip that connected to the Tower's systems.

Level 29 was the command center. From the layer of dust on everything, and the canvas coverings still adorning most of the consoles, Bennie was pretty sure no one had used the space in a couple of tens of cycles, at least. He patted a console, sending a cloud of dust into the air. "This is reassuring. You didn't even tidy it up from the other night?"

C7K2 turned. "What would be the reason? As you can imagine, the need for this space diminished over the cycles. At one point, a dozen Knights would be on duty day and night, monitoring hundreds of nearby worlds in addition to Nexum, directing Knights in actions across what is now the GC."

Nic whistled.

"Neat," Bennie said. "So, a building collapsed?"

The matte black droid inclined its head then turned to a display on the wall. On it, a plume of smoke was rising from a pile of rubble, the remains of a residential tower. "The Dfelponun Tower collapsed a half a tock ago. Civil authorities are, of course, responding, but the local governor requested your help."

"To what? Lift rocks?" Bennie said. Nic punched him in the arm.

"Ow." He turned. "Cut it out."

C_7K_2 said, "While you are not physically impressive, and thus of no use in clearing rubble, your presence could be inspirational."

"No offense taken," Bennie said. He turned toward the door. "Okay, come on, lackey."

Nic grumbled but fell in behind him.

The scene of the Dfelponun Tower collapse was utter chaos. Nexuu were scampering everywhere, barking orders, asking questions, screaming, and wailing. Rescue vehicles were flitting about like insects. Heavy construction vehicles were only just beginning to arrive on the scene.

Nic was trailing behind Bennie. "This is horrible." She waved a waft of smoke away. The smell of pulverized duracrete and blood assaulted her nose.

Bennie nodded and looked around. "Hey!" A nearby Nexuu in a civil security uniform turned. "We're here to help."

"Sir Knight." The woman nodded, her narrow, lidless eyes impossible to read. "We appreciate you." She pointed toward a trailer that had seen better days. "The local commander is in there."

Bennie nodded and motioned for Nic to follow him. The trailer was just as chaotic as the scene outside. The local commander was a haggard older Nexuu man. After thanking the Knight of Plentallus and his not-an-apprentice for coming, he asked them to help with crowd control.

Bennie was guiding a crowd of curious onlookers to a spot further from the rubble, using his beam saber as a visual aid to keep their attention, careful to not slice off any limbs.

Nic was helping a group of security officers nearby. "This would be a lot easier if I had a—"

"No!"

"I'm going to bed," Nic said. Grime and dust covered both of them. Her quarters were still on the publicly accessible floors. She had begged for access to the upper floors, but Bennie continued to refuse.

He nodded. As the doors slid closed, he said, "You didn't suck out there."

To the closed lift door, the Olop girl said, "Thanks?"

The door to Bennie's quarters opened, and the lights came on automatically. Unclipping his belt and letting it fall to the floor, he said, "Call Wil."

The desk in the room's corner faced a window that looked out onto the city beyond. The computer terminal built into it came to life. A moment later, a tired-sounding Wil said, "What do you want?"

"Good to hear from you too, drennog." Bennie slipped his tunic off.

As he was dropping his dirt-crusted trousers, Wil said, "This is a video call, you freak!"

Bennie turned too quickly, his feet still in the trousers, and lost his balance. After crashing to the floor in a tangle of under-garments and limbs, he shouted, "Audio only."

"Too late, I'm scarred for life," Wil quipped. "Gimme a second. It's early here. I'll go out on the patio."

Bennie untangled himself and found his night clothes. "Sure."

"Okay, so what's up? You kill that kid and need to stash the body? Or just calling to flash me?"

Bennie smiled. "No, to both. She's still pushing to be an apprentice."

"Is that a problem?"

Bennie sighed. "I don't know. Feels like if I make it official, then I'm responsible for her or something."

"Yeah, I feel like you're already responsible." In the background, some type of party was going on.

"Is that a party?"

"Our room is over the adults-only pool. There's always a party. So...you called to tell me you weren't ditching the kid? She's not going on Rogue Enterprises payroll, just so you know."

Bennie made a face. "No. I wanted to see what you thought. I mean, she'll be here with me for a bit, but then we'll back with everyone else."

"There's plenty of room in the warehouse, but aboard the *Ghost*, she'll have to bunk with you."

"What? There's two guest berths!" Bennie shouted. He stomped over to the desk, dropping into the seat.

"Yeah, and they're for paying customers." A sound came over the channel. "Yeah, babe. Be right there, talking to Bennie." A pause. "Cyn says, hey. So, look, it's cool with me if you bring her on. She's a cool kid, but she's just that, a kid. Don't get in over your head on this."

Bennie rubbed his chin. "We can revisit the berth thing later. Thanks, loser. Appreciate it." He reached for the control as Wil was shouting about paying customers.

Nic was in the cafeteria the next morning when Bennie walked in. "Pack your gear. We're heading out," he shouted, then turned and left.

"Where are we—" She saw he was gone and jumped up from the table. Catching him at the lift, she repeated, "Where are we going? Do I get a laser sword? What should I pack?"

The lift door slipped open. "Multon. No. Your apprentice getup should be good." He stepped in.

She pumped a fist. "Yes!" She jumped in before the door closed.

"This one is going down," Bennie said. The lift shifted as it began its descent.

Nic looked at the control panel and hissed. "Ruined the moment."

CHAPTER 6

THE TRIP to Multon was shorter than the trip from Fury to Nexum, so Bennie let C7K2 book them on a regular commuter shuttle.

"My seat is sticky," Nic complained.

Bennie looked up from the PADD he was reading. "Did I give the impression I cared?" He hated to admit it, but she was right. C7K2 had booked them on a dilapidated rust bucket that looked like it was held together with hope and adhesive. He was going to have to talk to the droid about budgets.

He set the PADD down. "First principle of the Knights?"

Nic's furry face scrunched at the sudden change in the conversation's direction. "What?" When he said nothing but continued to stare at her, she coughed. "Uh...to...uh, serve the public trust."

Bennie nodded. "Second?"

Feeling more confident, she said, "Protect the innocent." Before Bennie could ask, she added, "The third? Uphold the law."

"And the fourth?" He smiled.

She scratched her head, the streak of pink-dyed fur sticking up at odd angles. "There isn't a fourth."

Bennie clucked. "Bennie is always right."

Nic sighed. "Whatever, Grandpa." She stuck her tongue out, baring her teeth.

She looked out the window of the shuttle. "So, what's Multon like? Why're we going there? You know anyone there?"

Bennie looked around. They were alone in the small seating area of the shuttle. The other occupant, a Harrith woman, had left half a tock ago to visit the snack bar.

He said, "C7K2 keeps a history of where every Knight is from. Several came from Multon. He suggested a visit might reinvigorate the Multonae's interest in the order."

"So, like a PR thing?"

"More or less. Plus, I've never been so thought it would make for some interesting training opportunities. See someplace new. Get out of our comfort zones."

"Yay," the young Olop girl drawled, then tilted her head, smoothing the fur around her neck and small furry ears as she said, "So, like, we just go where we want?"

"No...well, yeah. More or less."

"Then we should go to cool places."

Bennie made a series of high-pitched noises, mimicking what she said. He then said, "Go work through the forms I showed you." He made a dismissive motion with one hand.

She made a face, then hopped off the seat and started working through a series of moves that Bennie had shown her back at the Tower.

Bennie watched for a second before looking at his wrist-comm. Did he know anyone on Multon? No, but he knew someone from Multon. He scrolled through a list of contacts. After selecting one, he watched as custom routines in the communication software automatically began routing the call through comm nodes near and far, once even changing communication protocols for two hops before reverting. Finally, the screen flickered and a familiar face appeared.

Not the familiar face Bennie was expecting.

"What do you want?" asked Tah'tu, Rhys Duch's Brailack major-domo, smiling unkindly. The Multonae crime kingpin was a friend, after a fashion, of the Rogue Enterprises crew. His Brailack assistant was less of a fan.

"To talk to him, not you," Bennie retorted.

The blue-skinned Brailack scowled. "One moment." The screen went blank.

Bennie looked up. "No, no. Plant your feet, right angles. There you go. Smooth motions, imagine a blade in your hand. You don't want to cut your leg off."

"Hey, Bennie!" his wristcomm shouted. A blonde-haired man in what Wil would call a Hawaiian shirt was looking up from Bennie's wristcomm screen. "What's up, my friend?"

It amazed Bennie how much Multonae resembled Humans. When he first met Wil, he assumed he was a Multonae. When Wil had told him about Earth, he thought maybe it was a long lost Multonae colony. As far as anyone could tell, that wasn't the case.

Bennie put on a fake smile. "Well, my app—" he looked up to spy Nic watching him, "friend and I are going to Multon for a public relations thing."

The blonde kingpin smiled. "Oh, neat. For your club? With the swords?"

Bennie growled. "It's not...Never mind. We'll be in Sentullo for a bit. Figured you'd know the places we should see and the places we should stay away from."

The other man never stopped smiling. "The capital is a busy place with a lot of competing interests, if you know what I mean."

"Any of them yours?"

He shook his head. "No, which should tell you something. I keep my interests far from Multon."

"Anything specific or more of a 'watch our backs' thing?"

"Well, the Bol Naar syndicate more or less runs the place. I mean, obviously from the shadows and all that."

"Obviously."

"They're not people I like to engage with. But they follow the rules more or less. They let the politicians do their thing, etc., etc." He waved a hand barely visible on the small screen.

Bennie made a face. "Aren't you, like, orders of magnitude more powerful?"

"Well, yeah, but I don't like to flaunt it," the man who looked more like a surf bum than a crime lord said.

"You live on a private island," Bennie said, then waved his other hand. "Anyway, steer clear of the Bol Naar. Should be easy. We're just there to remind folks the Knights of Plentallus are a thing. Try to drum up some interest."

The other man nodded. "Sounds like a plan." He looked off screen. "Oh, gotta go. Zash says Grell just set the new hedge maze on fire!" The screen went black.

Bennie sighed. He looked up. "Hold your right arm straighter."

"Ugh," Bennie said after the third Multonae slammed their hip into his head. "I hate giants."

Nic smiled and held a hand up, one claw poking from the tip of her stubby finger. A pedestrian was angling toward the pair, likely on a collision course, until she jabbed their thigh with the tip of her claw. The offender yelped and steered away, rubbing their hindquarter.

Bennie made a face. "Nice technique." He guided them out of the flow of foot traffic.

They had landed in the municipal spaceport on the outer edge of Sentullo. From orbit, the planet Multon looked like any other. Forests, oceans, plains, and deserts. Cities spanned multiple ploriths, sometimes merging with the next nearest city, all surrounded by sprawling suburban developments. On their way down from orbit, they watched massive freight and pleasure vessels ply the single ocean on the planet.

Bennie's homeworld of Brai had little in the way of ocean-going pleasure craft. There were a few inland seas scattered around the globe, but they were so full of predators that the Brailack never really took to the water.

"So, where are we going?" Nic asked when they reached a transit hub of the spaceport. It was still crowded, but there were fewer hips slamming into them.

"C7K2 booked us rooms at a place downtown. The Galactic Suites, I think he said it was called. Sounds fancy." He hoped it was nicer than the shuttle the droid had booked them on. He pointed to a doorway that exited out onto a series of platforms for public transport vehicles to pick up passengers. Checking his wristcomm, he added, "We've got an appointment with the mayor before dinner. Pick up the pace."

"The mayor? Of Sentullo?"

Without looking back, he said, "No, the mayor of Pickled Doorip town. Yes, Sentullo." He motioned her up onto a hover bus.

Their hover bus rose silently and began its trip into downtown Sentullo. Nic looked around. Except for an elderly Trenbal woman, she and Bennie were the only non-Multonae on the bus. The other woman saw Nic looking around and smiled, her pale scales dull from age. The trip wasn't very long. Seemingly at random, Bennie reached out and tapped the button on the seatback in front of them, indicating that they were ready to disembark.

The downtown area was a forest of metal and transparisteel. Towers rose into the scant cloud cover: reds, oranges, deep blues, and greens. Bridges and skyways linked them all in a pattern that made sense to someone. Buzzing between it all were hover cars and vans moving the wealthier citizens and cargo around.

Nic was trailing behind Bennie, her mouth hanging open. "This place is huge."

He looked over. "Olopnal has cities, right? One of my exes is Olop. She used to go on and on about her hometown."

"Well, sure. But, not this big." She gestured to the buildings. "Our cities are more...natural. We have skyscrapers and all, but they're covered in growing things, and...I dunno...they have a different feeling." After a few microtocks of silence, she said, "So, we're hoping us being here will make people want to become Knights?"

Bennie took a deep breath. "I mean, not just our being here, but yeah, that's the hope. Really, I just wanted to get away from the Tower, let you see more of the GC, explore your training on the road. C7K2 suggested the public relations angle and our destination."

"Like show dolies."

"Whatever the wurrin that is."

"Tiny herbivore creatures. My ancestors hunted them. Now we make them pets."

They turned a corner and Bennie said, "I think that's it." He pointed up ahead of them.

"That doesn't look fancy," Nic said, squinting against the bright sunlight.

Bennie looked up at the Galactic Suites. The building was tall, fitting in with the buildings nearby. That was about as close to luxurious as the building got. Unlike its neighbors, it was not shiny metal and glass. It was some type of spray duracrete-type material with windows wedged in at regular intervals.

"Very un-fancy," he agreed. "Definitely gonna have to talk to C_7K_2."

"Maybe there's another Galactic Suites?" Nic offered.

"We should be so lucky." He approached the matching double doors. One slid away, the other made a grinding noise but remained where it was.

Next to the dilapidated reception desk was a bar with three mismatched stools. One stool was occupied by what might have been a corpse. A Multonae woman well past retirement age looked up. "Checking in?"

"Well, we're not here for the bar," Bennie said. He swiped on his wristcomm, eyeing the body at the bar.

Her terminal beeped. "Says a lot that you came for the rooms." She tapped her screen a few times, then pressed a button, causing both Bennie and Nic's wristcomms to beep. "Elevator 2 is broken. Take 1 or 3." She pointed past the three-seat bar to a short hallway with four lift doors, two on each side.

"And 4?" Nic asked.

The woman looked at her. "Don't ask about 4."

Nic poked the occupant of the bar stool once, jumping when he or she twitched.

Bennie shouted, "Come on, leave the dead body alone."

Nic glanced at the stool occupant, then rushed to join Bennie at the bank of lifts.

Their rooms were on the 73rd floor, facing out into the forest of buildings. If he pressed his head against the window, Bennie could see a large park off in the distance.

Sighing, he said, "Well, it's not as gross as—" He turned to the chair near the bed, spotting several stains. "Never mind."

The announcer panel next to his door beeped. The door

had not even fully slid into the recess when Nic barged past
Bennie. "There is a..." She was flapping her arms. "I don't even
know what it is, on my bedcover."

She looked at Bennie's bed. "Taking yours is out of the
question."

Bennie said, "Okay, so it's not a five-star hotel. Knights don't
seek such base comforts."

She squinted. "Uh huh."

He waved a hand. "After our meeting with the mayor, we
can stop at a store, pick up some clean sheets." He looked
around. "And a flamethrower."

"So, uh, you know the mayor?" Nic asked.

The Sentullo mayoral office was a short walk from the
Galactic Suites, fronting the park that Bennie saw from his
room. He and Nic were both in their traditional Knight of Plentallus outfits. Hers were the darker colors of an apprentice; his,
the light browns and tans of a Knight.

"No. Why?"

"How'd you get a meeting?"

He smirked. "People don't say no to Knights of Plentallus."

She made a rude noise but said nothing.

The walk was pleasant enough. Their outfits helped the
much taller Multonae notice them and not run them over.
Beings from across the GC packed the streets: an occasional
Palorian, likely an off-duty Peacekeeper, a gaggle of pint-sized
Durbrillians, and a few other assorted races.

The mayor was a portly older man, bald and sweaty
despite the temperature-controlled office that looked out over
the park.

After exchanging handshakes, the mayor said, "Thank you,

uh, both of you, for coming. It's a pleasure to see Knights of Plentallus on Multon."

Nic opened her mouth, but Bennie beat her to it. "She's an apprentice, sorta."

Nice looked up. "Sorta?"

The sweaty mayor chuckled. "I see. A new generation of Knights is born." He reached over to pat Nic's head. The girl dodged, growling.

The mayor gestured to a seating area on the balcony. "Please."

After an anonymous assistant delivered beverages, the mayor asked, "So, the Knights of Plentallus are back?"

Bennie nodded. "We are." His voice was a couple of octaves lower.

Nic turned in her seat. Leaning away, she whispered, "What's wrong with your voice?"

Bennie scowled at her but turned back to the mayor. "We're rebuilding the order from the ground up. There's much to live up to, and more to improve."

The mayor nodded slowly. "Well said, Sir Knight, well said. I'm sure you know that many a Knight came from Multon. Our people were always proud to be a part of something so special."

Bennie nodded. "That's why we're here." He gestured to the park, city, and planet beyond. "It's our hope that the Multonae will once again be a part of the order."

Another of the mayor's seemingly endless supply of assistants came over. "Sir, perhaps the Knights," she glanced at Bennie, "would be willing to join us at the rally?"

Nic perked up. "Rally? Like a big party?"

The mayor wiped his bald head, smiling. "Yes, sort of. Tomorrow, in fact." He turned to Bennie. "I'm announcing my candidacy for governor on a platform of cleaning up the organized crime in Sentullo and, more widely, the planet."

Bennie's eyebrow ridges rose. "Bold position. The Knights don't back candidates, though."

The mayor frowned fractionally. "Oh, no, no. Of course not. I'm simply thinking you could take advantage of the press and audience gathered. Tell the people about your order, the history that my people share with the Knights. Remind them what your order stands for. That kind of thing."

"Well, C7K2 said to do the PR stuff," Nic said.

Bennie turned. "I suck at speeches." He hitched a thumb toward the mayor. "I was just hoping he'd donate some funds or resources or something."

Nic shrugged. "This is what's on the table." She waved his objections away. "I'll help you. Come on, it'll be fun."

The mayor bobbed his somehow—again—sweat covered head. "Indeed. If your visit here is to be fruitful, tomorrow's event will be the perfect opportunity. I'd be surprised if you didn't leave Multon with a few candidates signed up and waiting to join you on Nexum."

"Hopefully less annoying ones than the one I've already got." He glanced at Nic, who made a face and bared her teeth.

The mayor and his assistant exchanged looks, the young woman finally saying, "I can...add you to the agenda?"

Bennie sighed. "Sure." He looked at Nic. "Guess we better get back to the Galactic Suites to work on my speech."

The mayor clucked. "You're staying at the Galactic Suites, are you?" His face made it clear that not only was he familiar with the establishment, but also, he had a low opinion of it.

Bennie flushed a deep green. "The brochure was a bit misleading."

"We would be happy to provide better accommodations for—"

"Yes, please." Nic nearly leapt from her seat.

Bennie put a hand on her arm. "We're fine. Thank you."

The mayor stood. The meeting was over. "Very well. I am truly looking forward to having you with us tomorrow. I can see a bright future for your order and Multon."

"Come on, apprentice. We've got a speech to write." Bennie scowled. "Don't look so happy."

CHAPTER 7

"THIS IS SO EXCITING!" Nic was skipping along the sidewalk ahead of Bennie. "You're going to give an address in front of the entire city!"

"Calm down." Bennie was trying his best to not think of the size of the crowd.

The pair was walking along the park, nearing the end closest to their hotel, when two Tleb and a Multonae woman stepped onto the sidewalk from the park. The two canine-featured beings bared their teeth, each clutching a small blade.

The Multonae woman said, "Hand over your wristcomms and any hard currency you're holding. No need to get hurt." Her ink black hair was cut into a bob. One eye was blue, the other green.

"Unless you want to," growled one of the Tleb, a woman, as she twirled first one blade then the other.

"Want to what?" Bennie asked, holding up both hands, palms out.

"What?" the other Tleb said, baring his teeth.

Bennie waved a hand. "Never mind. We don't want any trouble."

Nic glanced over. "We don't?"

He shook his head. "We don't." He looked at Nic. "We don't get into fights for no reason."

"They're trying to rob us. That's a reason. A good one."

"Excuse us," the Multonae woman said, "but we are."

"Are what?" Nic asked. Bennie coughed to hide his chuckle.

The much taller woman scowled and nodded to her friends. The two Tleb strode forward.

Bennie sighed as he assumed a fighting stance. He motioned for Nic to mimic him. He glanced over. "Straighten your back foot. There you go."

While her companions focused on Nic, one Tleb woman snarled and lunged for Bennie. He dropped to a crouch as his attacker reached him, using her momentum to push her up and over him.

The Tlebs crouched and came in low, charging Nic. She growled, baring her teeth. In a swift motion, her own blade appeared in one hand. A split second before the pair reached her, she dropped into a roll that, with a normal opponent, would take their legs out from under them. Against an opponent even shorter than she was, she bowled into the Tleb man's midsection. He tried to stab her, but a quick slash of her blade severed the tendons in his arm, forcing him to drop his blade with a scream and a whimper. The woman was just out of reach as she got to her feet and darted to the side.

Bennie spun before his attacker hit the ground. He stepped in and let loose a kick as the woman landed. It connected with her hip, sending her spiraling head over feet before she hit the ground.

The Multonae woman got to her feet. "You little green drennog. I'm gonna gut you," she growled. She leaned in and swung; her right hook aimed right for Bennie's head—no small feat for someone twice his height.

Bennie leaned forward and to the side, a move she wasn't expecting, bringing him inside the arc of her punch. Her fist passed within a millimeter of his head. As it continued past, he grasped her arm, pulling her further off balance. She stumbled right into his small fist, which struck her squarely on the nose. He rained two more quick blows on her before twisting out from under her. She reeled back, blood flowing freely from her ruined nose.

Nic spun on her heel, kicking the Tleb man in the jaw, sending him sprawling to the ground, his ruined arm splattering blood on the sidewalk. She ducked a punch from the other canid being, but not fast enough, the small woman's blade catching her shoulder.

The Tleb woman winked as Nic clutched her shoulder, blood oozing between her fingers.

The Multonae woman wiped her face with her sleeve. The move left blood smeared across her face and a fresh trickle running down her chin. Bennie glanced over to Nic and her opponents. "You attract trouble!"

"You're making this my fault?" She leaped at the Tleb man, landing on him, knife ready to strike. His one good arm flailed at her.

"Don't kill 'em!" Bennie shouted, just as she struck. Her hand stopped halfway to the canine-featured man's chest. The man whimpered something before she punched him in the face with her free hand. The pair collapsed to the ground, Nic rolling off her opponent.

Bennie looked back just in time to see the Multonae woman rushing him. She collided, tackling him to the ground, shouting obscenities. Blood and spittle splashed across his face.

"Gross!" he shouted as he hit the ground, two much larger and more powerful hands around his neck. "Shut...gah...up!" he shouted between thuds of his head hitting the ground. He looked up. "Ouch!" He thrust his hands up, clapping the woman's ears. She roared, rearing up enough for him to get his feet under her. Pushing with all his might, he forced her up off of him.

Bennie was rolling back to his feet when Nic leaped onto the back of the Tleb woman. With several quick blows to the growling woman's head and a final yelp, Nic rode the unconscious woman to the ground. Nic stood up and pointed. "Can you at least take care of the big one?"

Bennie turned just in time for a fist to strike his face. "Gah!" he shouted, a hand to his face as he staggered backwards. "Otay, now I'm mad," he growled. He leaped into the air with a scream. The Multonae woman's startled yelp died out as he sunk his teeth into her cheek.

By the time Nic walked over, the Multonae woman was sprawled at Bennie's feet. "She dead? You said no killing." He shook his head. "Is that some special Knight thing? Biting people?"

Bennie wiped his mouth. "What? No, Brailack can secrete a powerful sedative when we bite people."

"You just run around biting people?"

His eyes bugged. "What? No." He turned to look at each of their would-be attackers. "I mean, not all the time." He stuck his tongue out. "You never know where someone's neck has been."

The idea of speaking in front of a crowd turned out to be something Bennie was not at all comfortable with. After handing off the three would-be muggers to the local authorities, Bennie and Nic grabbed a meal and worked on his speech. Every sentence they crafted filled him with more and more dread.

As a kid growing up on Brai in one of the most powerful families around, he had avoided public outings, letting his sister, already an outgoing personality, shine more. He had much preferred computers and activities that benefited from a distinct lack of attention being paid to him.

The pair worked late into the night, finally calling the speech they had cobbled together done, barely five hours before sunrise.

The next morning in the lobby, Nic looked at Bennie as he exited the lift. "Are...are you drunk?"

Bennie frowned. "No. I mean, that's not a bad idea." He ran a hand over his head. A sheen of sweat was already covering it. "That would actually have made more sense."

"Than?"

Benne squinted. "Never mind."

"Your beam saber is tucked into your pants."

He grabbed the hilt and fumbled, clipping it to his belt. "Turns out, public speaking kinda freaks me out. I might have self-medicated."

"Because that should go well."

Bennie walked to the exit. "Come on."

At Nic's urging, they hired a cab to take them to the rally. She didn't think they'd have a repeat of the previous night's action but figured it was better to be safe than fighting small canids for pocket change before the rally.

The rally was in the park they'd walked by twice already. At the far end was a massive semi-natural amphitheater that was packed with thousands of Multonae plus a few hundred other beings mixed in.

"Oh, wurrin," Bennie mumbled as the cab pulled along the curb. "That's a lot of people." They exited the cab and headed for the check-in area.

Nic turned to him. "You'll be fine. Or flop horribly. Either way, you're never gonna see them again, so..." She shrugged.

"If that was meant to be reassuring, you suck at it." Bennie walked to the security entrance. Reaching the guard, he said, "We're...I'm a Knight of Plentallus. She's a street urchin I found on my way here. We're expected."

The big man nodded and stepped aside, holding out an arm to welcome them into the security zone back stage.

One of the mayor's assistants met them, one they hadn't met previously. "The mayor and his chief researcher will start the rally. You'll be the closing speaker." She didn't wait for a reply, pointing toward the stage and a row of chairs behind the lectern.

"Thought he said we'd open it?" Nic grumbled.

Bennie shrugged. "Guess he changed his mind."

The pair watched as the crowd in the park grew. By the time the mayor stepped up to the lectern, the crowd had filled the amphitheater, the park beyond, and if he wasn't mistaken, Bennie thought it had spilled out into the streets bracketing the park. He absently wondered if the three toughs that tried to mug him and Nic were in the crowd. Probably not out of the hospital yet.

The mayor spoke, and spoke, and spoke some more. He seemed to jump from topic to topic: first a history of the city and the park, then crime, then his plans to fight crime, then something about the planetary system. Nic's eyes were hard to keep open by the time the mayor finally arrived at his plan to eliminate organized crime, first in Sentullo, then across the planet. Nic didn't know much about the planet or how it worked, but the idea of less organized crime seemed to appeal to the crowd. The cheering drowned out whatever it was the mayor just said. She did see more than a few angry faces in the crowd, which seemed odd, given the topic.

She turned to Bennie. "This is boring."

"Shut up."

"We've been here a hundred tocks."

"It's been half a tock."

"Are you sure?"

"Your wristcomm tells time, same as—" The crowd roared again. "Now I missed what he said." She made a face that made it clear what she thought of that.

The mayor gestured to the side of the stage where a blonde-haired woman was fidgeting in the last seat in the row along the back of the stage.

Bennie and Nic both turned. The latter said, "Who's that?" Bennie leaned over and pinched her. "Ow!"

"I don't know. Maybe he said it when you were flapping your gums."

She crossed her arms, saying nothing further.

The crowd erupted in applause as the middle-aged woman made her way to the lectern. The mayor took her hand, pumping it vigorously. He leaned in and said something to her, causing her to nod. The mayor turned back to the crowd. "Miss Adel has spent the last three cycles sequestered in a secret research facility, pouring over data from sources all over the city, the planet, and throughout our system." He turned to her, smiling. "We have more than enough data to shut down all Bol Naar syndicate operations, not just here in Sentullo but across all of Multon and beyond." He paused for the roar of the crowd.

Nic leaned over. "So...She's—"

"A giant target? Yeah," Bennie said.

The mayor spent another half a tock outlining how his administration would dismantle organized crime, first in

Sentullo, once he was elected, then across the globe and to the GC beyond. By the time he got around to inviting Bennie to the lectern, the crowd was thinning, and when there was applause, it was far less uproarious than earlier in the day.

From her seat, Nic could see the sweat forming on Bennie's hairless head. She tried counting the beads as they rolled down his neck but lost interest around two hundred.

Bennie stepped away from the lectern as the dwindling crowd, most of it, politely clapped.

Nic stood and met him halfway to the row of seats. "That... wasn't horrible. Mostly," she whispered.

The mayor passed Bennie, patting him on the head, then making a face as he wiped his palm on his slacks. Bennie swatted the sweaty hand away and pushed Nic back toward the chairs.

Dropping back into their seats, before Nic could say anything, Bennie said, "Okay, clearly I need to work on my pitch."

"You do."

"Shut up."

"Maybe C7K2 can hire an agency?"

"I can do it."

"I don't think you can. You were really bad."

"You said it wasn't all bad."

"I was being polite."

"I can leave you here." Bennie scowled.

The mayor thanked everyone for coming and ended with his campaign slogan and a round of thank yous: the audience, the organizers, the security forces, the Knights of Plentallus, and a bunch of others. It did not thrill Bennie that he thanked the Knights, implying that they supported his candidacy, but short of jumping up and rushing the lectern, there wasn't much he could do about it.

Nic and Bennie were walking back out of the park. The security checkpoint that they came through on the way in was already gone.

"Sir Knight!" someone shouted.

The pair turned to see the mayor, his assistant from before, and the woman from the end of the row approaching. "Mr. Knight. Would you join me and Miss Adel for dinner tonight?" He beamed, rubbing his forehead dry. "I want to celebrate how well my campaign kickoff went." He draped an arm around the mystery woman: *Ankle? Abscess?* Bennie had already forgotten.

"I could eat," Nic offered.

Bennie looked at her, growling. "I could eat you," he said under his breath. He turned to the mayor and his entourage, sighing. "It'd be our privilege." Behind him, Nic pumped her fist, licking her lips.

The mayor nodded to his assistant. "Call the Starlight and update my reservation." The young woman nodded and hurried off, working her wristcomm.

The mayor turned to the other woman: *Abstract? Alabaster?* Bennie decided that he really needed to work on remembering names. "This is Lyral Adel."

The woman smiled, a polite but disinterested smile. "Hello."

Bennie grasped the woman's forearm. "What's your deal? You his secret weapon?" The woman's eyes darted to the mayor, who grinned.

The young assistant returned. "Sir, I've updated the reservation."

"Very good, Vivi. Go ahead and get the car." He turned to Bennie and Nic. "I'll see you both tonight." He turned, guiding the other woman away.

"Now what?" Nic asked. "Back to the hotel?"

Bennie grinned. "Oh no. You've been so helpful today. I

think you've earned some training." He bared his teeth in a grin. "Lots of training. Lots."

"Why are you grinning like that?" She took a step back.

"Because I'm going to enjoy this." He pointed back into the park. "And you won't."

She sighed.

"I think we might be under dressed," Nic whispered as she and Bennie exited the hover cab. She looked up the ornate stone pathway to the Swal Drogona. The building sat alone on an outcropping overlooking downtown Sentullo.

Bennie lifted an arm, inhaling. He wrinkled his nose. "It's fine." The pair were in the same clothes they were wearing at the rally: Bennie in his light-colored tunic and trousers, beam saber clipped to his belt, Nic in her matching but darker-colored outfit.

"You know, my outfit would look more official with—"

"No," Bennie interrupted as they reached the front door. The Swal Drogona was a two-story building made mostly of glass or some other transparent material. Rich, dark woods made up the supporting structure. Well-dressed Multonae and assorted other GC races filled almost every table that Bennie could see. The second floor was actually a series of semi overlapping half circle levels, lined with tables. According to the Zelp reviews, the upper tiers provided an outstanding view of the city.

The mayor and the woman from the rally—*Avril Lavigne?* Bennie still couldn't recall her name—were seated at a table in the middle of the first floor. Guess the mayor's pull wasn't that good.

"Bit showy," Bennie mumbled. Nic shushed him.

The mayor spied the two Knights and stood, urging his guest to follow suit. Waving, he said. "Sir Knight, young... almost-a-Knight. Over here!"

Nic whispered, "Almost-a-knight." Bennie looked over at her but said nothing.

Once the wait staff deposited everyone's orders and retreated, Bennie spoke. "So, you—

what? Have a dossier or something on the Bol Naar syndicate?" he asked around a mouthful of seared Nuflonog.

The blonde-haired woman's blue eyes twinkled in the lighting. He was certain her name was Abbi, *or was it Alibi?* She smiled. "Pretty much. I've been auditing planetary records for months now. Banking, real estate, trade, shipping, and more. I developed algorithms that pieced together the entire network."

"Sounds dangerous," Nic said around a mouthful of jerlack. She had ordered it as raw as the health code would allow, to the chagrin of everyone at the table.

Mayor Dardle bobbed his head, doughy cheeks wiggling. "Indeed, quite dangerous, but we took precautions."

Bennie raised an eyebrow ridge. "Precautions? Like what? You just broadcast to the entire planet, your whole system, that you had the means to end crime by taking down, well, the biggest syndicate here." He took a bite. "Not sure there are that many precautions in the galaxy."

The mayor took a bite of his own meal: jerlack steak, well done. He had drizzled a condiment more suited to a sandwich, all over it. "We have the Knights of Plentallus."

Bennie's mouth fell open. "Come again?"

Lyral raised a hand. "Actually, you don't play into the precautions the mayor and I have taken." She sipped her Palorian spirit wine, then added, "All of my work is off-planet. We set up an encrypted data core in an undisclosed location. Write only. A data broker manages the data flow, and the algorithms work on separate data cores." She took another sip. "Hack proof."

Nic looked around at the adults surrounding her, all quietly chewing and staring at each other. "So, what's it like being so tall?"

Everyone turned to her.

Lyral shook her head, swishing her drink. "The data core accepts data packets and algorithm updates. It sends the results of queries through three relays before my terminal receives them."

Mayor Dardle waved an arm. "Yes, of course, our data security is top notch. We hired a renowned data security expert out of Tro Ella to set up the core and the relay system. The Bol Naar syndicate can't hack it, or even gain access via one of us. Only our contractor has physical access." He pointed to his chief data scientist. "In two weeks, we'll trigger the release of the collected data. The syndicate will topple. In the meantime, your presence today lent legitimacy."

Bennie stabbed a piece of Nuflonog. He looked at it, then shoved it in his mouth. "I told you we don't endorse candidates. You tricked me." The mayor opened his mouth, but Bennie waved him off. "You don't think warning them was a bad idea? The syndicate, I mean."

The mayor starred at Bennie blankly.

Bennie opened his mouth to explain the foolishness of alerting your enemy that you were coming for them, when the front door crashed open. Without turning, he groaned, "Of course." He sighed, taking a bite of his meal.

Two plasma pistol shots rang out, followed by screaming. A lot of screaming.

Bennie wiped his mouth on the back of his hand, then turned to Nic. "Get them to the kitchen or coat closet or something. Hide 'em."

She opened her mouth, looked at him, and turned to the terrified mayor and data scientist. "Come on, you two." She grabbed a roll from the table, holding it in her mouth, and pushed the mayor out of his chair. The scientist woman followed.

"Where's the grolacking mayor?" someone shouted.

Bennie turned to see four well-armed Multonae men in black suits near the front door. He hopped out of his chair and crawled from their table to the one next to theirs. Huddled together underneath was a pair of Harrith. He looked back to see the mayor and the data woman crawling toward the opposite side of the building from the front door, Nic behind them, poking them to move faster.

Bennie shushed the couple under the table with him. "I'm a professional."

"A...a professional what?" one of the men asked.

Bennie made a face as two more energy rounds struck the roof, eliciting more screams.

"Mayor Dardle and the woman, and you all live," one attacker shouted.

CHAPTER 8

"GO FASTER!" Nic hissed, pushing the mayor's backside, eliciting a choked yelp.

"Young lady, I am going as...fast as...I can," the portly official complained.

"Shh," the woman crawling next to him urged. "They'll hear you and kill us."

Ahead of them, Nic spied the door to the kitchen. "Hurry up," she urged.

"You're quite rude for an apprentice," the mayor complained.

Nic growled. She slowed, peeking over the top of a nearby table. She had no idea where Bennie was but could see all four goons: two were moving through the dining room, pulling people up from under tables and off the floor, urging them toward the other two goons who were keeping them corralled near the front door.

"My wristcomm isn't working," Dardle said, pushing the door to the kitchen open slowly to not attract attention.

Lyral sighed. "They're using a jammer. As far as anyone outside knows, we're all in here enjoying our dinners."

Nic looked at the two of them. "Stay put. I have to go help Bennie."

"He said to keep us safe," the mayor protested.

"Getting rid of these drennogs will keep you safe," she retorted, then pulled the kitchen door closed.

She peaked over a table again and set off back into the middle of the dining room.

One goon of the roaming pair, a bald-headed man, shouted, "The authorities aren't coming! Give us the mayor, and this ends!"

"Where's the mayor?" someone shouted, followed by a scream as the bald man and his colleague grabbed them and pushed them toward the front door and the growing group of people who weren't the mayor. Someone else shouted, "Turn over the mayor so we can leave!"

Bennie poked his head up over the table to see that he was one table, give or take, away from the roving attackers. He looked around; Nic and her charges were nowhere to be seen. Good. Leaping up from cover to land on the table, Bennie said, "Hey, guys!" He activated his beam saber as he kicked a bowl of bread at one of the pairs. Bennie wasn't sure who screamed louder, the crowd of restaurant patrons or the two men waving their hands to deflect breadsticks.

The bald man's friend, a skinny, dark-haired man half a head shorter than his friend, swung his pistol toward their attacker. Before he could squeeze the trigger, a magenta beam of solid energy sliced through his arm. The pistol, still gripped in a hand attached to a stump of arm, fell to the floor.

Bennie didn't wait. He took two steps and leaped at the bald-headed man. While in the air, he snapped off his beam saber, thumbing the selector on the side. The moment he landed on the man's chest, he pushed the end of his beam saber hilt against his opponent's chest and pressed the activator. A bolt of purple energy burned through the man in a split second. Bennie rode the corpse to the ground, jumping off to land in a roll under the nearest table.

Weapons' fire and screams made it impossible to hear anything, but Bennie was pretty sure he knew where the other two were.

"Whoever you are, surrender!" someone shouted.

"Why?" Bennie shouted back. "Seems like I'm winning."

Several plasma rounds slammed into the top of the table that he was next to, sending splinters flying in all directions. Scampering as fast as he could to the next table, Bennie came face to face with a Brailack woman.

"Who are you?" she whispered.

He grinned. "It's going to be okay. I'm a professional."

She blinked. "A professional what?"

Bennie scowled, hissing, "Unacceptable!" He crawled to the next table. Popping his head up to look around, he shouted, "Can't catch me!" He dropped and scampered while frantic weapons' fire shredded the table he just left.

"We just want the data the mayor said he had! No need to drag this out!"

Bennie eased over the top of the table. He was five tables from the remaining gangsters. Whether due to intelligence or not, the remaining pair was still next to the corralled restaurant patrons. He ducked back down and looked at the table with the Brailack woman under it. "Psst." She looked over. "Hand me that roll."

"What?" She looked around.

He gestured with his beam saber hilt, causing the woman to

flinch. She followed the gesture and retrieved the roll. She rolled it toward him. Snatching it, he winked and took a bite.

"Hey."

Bennie nearly jumped. Instead, he tipped over, screeching an expletive. "What the wurrin are you doing?" he hissed.

Nic smiled. "You need backup."

"I do not." A plasma bolt struck the table next to him. He growled at her, then stood and aimed his beam saber hilt. He fired once, then dropped back to the floor, pushing Nic along before energy weapons' fire shredded a table nearby.

"You go that way. Distract them."

"See, you need me."

"Just...just go do that and don't get shot." He didn't wait for her. He turned and crawled under a table directly toward the two gunmen.

"He totally needs me," she whispered to herself as she crawled in the opposite direction. After a few tables and worried exchanges with patrons, she stood up. "Hey! You two!" She waved her arms.

Both men turned, firing as the Olop girl ducked back under the table and crawled away. The table exploded behind her.

"This is getting us nowhere," the gunman with a mohawk said. He checked the charge on his pistol, then turned to the crowd, grabbing a well-dressed Multonae woman. She screamed as he put the pistol to her temple. "Come out, you bobble-headed little drennog, or I burn her skull out."

People under tables, and in the crowd behind the gunmen, screamed. A man in the crowd by the door fainted, dropping like a bag of stones.

From the table next to the crowd, Bennie stood. "Fine. You got me."

The two men turned to him, shocked expressions on their

faces, no doubt assuming they'd have to kill a hostage or two before their opponent gave up.

From across the room, Nic popped from behind a table. "Hey, grolackers!" She leaned back and hurled a roll as hard as she could toward the two men. The baked projectile sailed through the air, arcing high overhead, to land at least three meters short of its target.

Bennie sighed and rubbed his face with his free hand as swung his beam saber hilt toward the nearest gangster. The bolt of energy caught the gangster square in the chest, pushing him back against a well-dressed Harrith man in the crowd.

The sole remaining gangster spun, firing wildly as he did. Bolts of plasma stitched across the room, shredding tables and igniting linens. A Multonae woman who had stood was struck in the chest. Bennie dropped to the floor as plasma bolts raced over head. Bennie glanced over, meeting the woman's lifeless eyes.

Nic looked around, spotting a plate on the table next to her. She snatched it, drew back, and threw it with all her might.

Bennie heard a loud thud, followed by the sound of breaking ceramic and a new round of screams. Standing, he looked around. "Why do you all keep screaming?" His gaze fell to the prone form of the last gangster, a shattered dinner plate on the ground next to him.

Behind him, Nic was leaping up and down. "Yes!"

Bennie looked around. The entire first floor was a ruin. Tables were on fire; overturned chairs littered the floor. The diners on the rings above were beginning to peak over the railings. They had wisely kept out of sight up until now.

Nic trotted up to him. "That was so cool! Did you see? I got him right on the forehead!" She mimed throwing the dish.

Bennie tried his best to keep a straight face. "Where are the mayor and the auditor?"

Nic's face fell. "Kitchen." She turned to lead the way.

Bennie put a hand on her shoulder. "We have to get them out of here. When these krebnacks don't check in, the syndicate will send more." She turned and walked with him. He looked over. "That was a pretty great throw." She turned, a grin splitting her face.

Bennie found the mayor, his data scientist, and the kitchen staff huddled together in the walk-in freezer. He hitched a thumb over his shoulder. "We gotta go."

The mayor stood. "Wh-what? Wh-where?"

Bennie shook his head, sighing. "Right now, not here." He met Lyral Adel's eyes. "They want you more than him."

The data scientist looked at her boss and stood. Bennie nodded. "Good call."

The mayor followed them to the back of the kitchen. "Now what?"

Bennie rubbed his chin as he looked around. Spotting a wall panel, he trotted over and pulled the panel open. "Yes," he whispered, finding bundles of wires inside.

The mayor looked down at Nic. "What's he doing?"

She shrugged. "Beats me. He doesn't tell me anything."

"Aren't you his minion?"

She shrugged again.

Bennie spent a few minutes connecting his wristcomm to various wires inside the access space. Several times, the mayor opened his mouth to be cut off by a look from Nic or Lyral Adel.

Finally, Bennie said, "Got it." He looked down at his wristcomm, clucking to himself. "Okay, so they didn't send any back up, yet, and it looks like enough patrons have gotten out and called the authorities that they're not likely to." He looked at the two Multonae. "But, you're not safe yet."

The mayor made a slow circle in place, running his thick fingers through what was left of his hair. "Sir Knight. You must protect me...er...her."

"Who?" Lyral Adel asked, turning to look at the mayor.

"You," he retorted. "As long as they don't have the data, they won't risk killing me. Too public." He coughed. "I hope." He pointed to Lyral. "Take her somewhere safe until after the election."

"After?" Bennie, Nic, and Lyral repeated before glancing at each other.

"Jinx," Nic whispered to herself.

The mayor nodded. "What are our options? The Bol Naars know we have the data to close them down." He looked at Bennie. "Perhaps you were right. The only hope now is to release it. I'll do what I can to delay them. Maybe if I suspend my candidacy?"

Bennie squinted at the heavyset man, who was sweating profusely, despite having just come out of a freezer. He nodded. "Okay. Come on." He held out a hand to the blonde-haired woman.

Her pale green eyes sent daggers at the Brailack. "I can walk on my own." She pushed past the mayor and Bennie toward the exit in the back of the kitchen.

Nic fell in behind her. Bennie hung back, turning to the mayor. "You sure about this?" The mayor nodded. "Okay. We'll be in touch." He trotted off after the two women.

The mayor let loose a long sigh, looking around the kitchen. The staff had long since vacated, fleeing through the dining room. He gathered himself up and marched through the door, back into the dining room. As the doors swung closed, he shouted, "Ladies and gentlemen! Non-binary citizens! It's going to be all right!"

Bennie caught up to Nic and Lyral just outside the restaurant. Looking around, he said, "We'll go back to our hotel, regroup."

"Hotel is a strong word," Nic said.

Bennie thought about arguing but didn't have it in him to defend their current lodgings.

"So..." Lyral looked around. "How do we get there? I don't have a car."

"How did you get here?" Bennie demanded.

"Rode with the mayor." She looked around the parking lot. "You two?"

Nic grumbled. "We took a cab."

The much taller woman threw her hands up above her head. "I'm doomed. Maybe I should just turn myself in to the syndicate."

In the distance, Bennie could hear sirens. He turned a slow circle, then stopped, smiling. "Come on."

"I'm not walking from here to the hotel," Nic complained. She pointed past the restaurant over the bluff's edge, the glittering core of downtown Sentullo beyond it.

Bennie waved his hand. He stopped next to a sleek sedan.

"Whose vehicle is this?" Lyral asked.

Bennie smiled. "Ours..." He pulled two wires from the end of his wristcomm. "...In about a microtock." He moved to the front of the vehicle, running a hand along the surface as he did. He stopped and slipped the two wires into a recessed section of the bumper. Next to Nic and Lyral, the driver side door slid up to allow entry.

"To do!" Bennie bowed. Moving to the passenger side, he pushed the control to open the door. "Get in."

Nic hopped in without a word, clambering over the seats into the back.

Lyral Adel just stared. "You're just going to steal someone's car?"

Bennie nodded. "We don't have a lot of choices. We'll do our best to leave it in the same condition it is now." He pointed to the driver's side. "You're driving."

She shook her head, more to clear it than anything else. "What? Why? No, I'm not. Isn't stealing some sort of violation of your code or oath or something?"

Bennie leaned down and pointed into the vehicle at the large seat, set quite a way from the controls. "Not designed for Brailack." He stood and looked past the stunned data scientist. "We really have to go." He dropped into the passenger seat, the door sliding silently closed behind him.

From the backseat, Nic said, "Come on, Data Lady."

Sighing, Lyral eased herself into the driver's seat, the door closing behind her. "Where to?"

"The Galactic Suites," Bennie supplied. He tapped the center console, bringing the onboard computer online.

"You're braver than I thought. They should have condemned that place cycles ago." She eased the hover car out of the parking lot. In the rear-view display, a well-dressed Quilant woman waddled out of the crowd of restaurant patrons, arms waving.

The trio sat in silence for a while, the mayor's data scientist guiding the vehicle through traffic. Finally, Bennie said, "Technically, yes."

"What?" the two women in the vehicle with him asked in unison.

"Stealing. Technically, Knights of Plentallus aren't supposed to run around stealing things."

"But?" Lyral pressed.

"But," Bennie repeated nasally. "We didn't have a choice."

In the backseat, Nic recalled the archive videos she'd seen, certain that those Knights had said something similar before committing their atrocities. She hugged herself.

After another round of semi-awkward silence, Nic asked, "So, uh, what now?" She was distracting herself by pushing buttons on the console that separated the two small rear seats. The entertainment system blared to life, then turned off. The interior lighting came on, cycled through a handful of colors, then shut off.

"Cut it out," Bennie snapped. "I need to think."

"Don't hurt yourself," Nic said.

"Your assistant, or whatever, isn't very polite." Lyral turned the car down a street alongside the park. All signs of the rally earlier in the day were gone. She couldn't believe it had only been a couple of tocks.

"You just ran a traffic signal."

Lyral shook her head. "What?"

Bennie pointed behind the car. "Traffic control signal back there."

"Is that important?" She kept her eyes on the road.

Bennie shrugged. "Not the worst crime I've committed today."

"Aren't the two of you supposed to be heroes or something?"

CHAPTER 9

"IT'S AS gross as I thought," Lyral said, taking in the room.

Nic walked past, jumping onto the bed. "You get used to the smell."

"Doubtful."

The rest of the ride had been quiet. No run-ins with city security or syndicate goons. They ditched the car a block from the hotel and came in through the back security door, the lock no match for a beam saber.

Bennie was standing at the window, tapping his chin absently. "We're safe enough for now." He turned to the data scientist, still standing at the door. "Get some sleep. We'll figure out our next steps over breakfast."

"Over breakfast?" Lyral repeated, venom in her voice.

Bennie shrugged. "Most important meal of the day." He pointed to the bed. "You two stay here. I'll be next door." He reached for the door that connected the two rooms.

Nic propped herself on her elbows. "Bed's mine." She pointed at the small love seat opposite the bed.

Bennie looked at her. "You're the one that's couch sized. Let her have the bed."

"Why?" the young Olop complained.

Bennie's brow ridges furrowed. "Because I'm the Knight and you're not." He stepped through the door before either woman could say anything further, closing the door behind him. Despite the closed door, he could hear the shouting.

He took a deep breath, looking around the room. He grabbed a PADD from the small desk and climbed up into the bed. He tapped a few icons, routing a communications request through a handful of relays on- and off-planet, before sending the comm request to its final destination.

Maxim's face appeared on the screen. "Hey, Bennie. What's up?"

Bennie smiled at the sight of his friend. "Need some advice."

"Don't tell them where you live or what you make," the big Palorian replied.

"Wha—? Oh. No, not that." He smirked. "I know how the game is played." He shook his head. "I'm on Multon."

"So many Wils."

"Right? It's worse than Earth. They all just look like him. Anyway. Me and the kid are..." He looked around the darkened room. "In it."

On the screen, Maxim shifted, sitting up straighter. "You need us? Wil and Cyn have the *Ghost*, but we can hop a shuttle."

Bennie shook his head. "Thanks, no. We're gonna be off-world by tomorrow night. We've got a civilian with us now."

"You're a civilian."

"Whatever. You know what I mean. Now I've got the kid, and this data scientist woman. The Bol Naar syndicate is gunning for her, thanks to the fat Wil mayor. I'm thinking I should leave Nic here."

"No."

"No? Why?"

Maxim looked off screen. "Be right there, my love. Helping Bennie with something...No, he doesn't need bail...No, I don't think it'll blow back on us." He turned back the camera. "Zephyr says hi."

"Uh huh." Bennie smiled.

"So, anyway. You can't leave her. You agreed to train her."

"Technically—"

"No 'technically' about it. You took her with you. She's your responsibility. If you leave her behind, you'll never mend that wound. She's your apprentice now. Use her." Bennie opened his mouth to object, but his friend continued. "She survived the whole *Galactic Empress* thing and then found you. She's not useless."

Bennie inhaled. "Yeah..."

"You learned to work with us. You'll learn to work with her." Maxim looked up from this screen. "Yeah, I gotta go." The screen went black.

Bennie laid the PADD down, sighing. He stayed in bed for a while, unable to sleep, until he finally gave up and got out of bed. Leaning against the shared door, he heard nothing on the other side. The two women must be asleep. He grabbed his beam saber hilt and left the room.

The lobby of the Galactic Suites was deserted; even the reception desk was empty. Someone had stuck a vellum sign to an empty brochure holder, reading, "Back in three." It wasn't clear to Bennie if that meant three tocks or microtocks, or when the sign had been stuck to the display. Shrugging, he pushed open the door and walked outside.

The street was empty, the morning commuter rush still a

few tocks away, and the night-out-on-the-town crawl-home rush had ended a tock or two earlier. It was that weird time of night turned early morning when cities were truly silent.

Which was why the sedan parked across the street caught Bennie's attention. Four well-dressed Multonae men were stepping out of the vehicle. He kept walking, making sure he was heading for the opposite corner of the block from where they'd abandoned the car from earlier. He made a show of playing with his wristcomm as he rounded the corner out of sight. He thought about calling Nic, but was sure her wristcomm would be off if she was sleeping, and he didn't have the other woman's contact details.

He leaned back around the edge of the building. The four men were crossing the street. How did they know where they were? The mayor? Bennie hadn't expected the doughy politician to fold so fast, but it was the only thing that made sense.

He waited until the last man entered the hotel, then rushed to follow. Outside the doors, he unclipped his beam saber and took a deep breath. Then he stepped into the lobby. The four men were standing around the reception desk. Two were on the non-public side, working on the terminal, presumably trying to locate Bennie's and Nic's entries. He was glad that old habits from working with Wil and the others had kept him from booking under their real names.

Bennie stood there, watching the four men for what felt like forever. When he realized they weren't likely to notice him, he said, "Excuse me."

The two nearest men spun, pistols in hand. Bennie yelped as he dove behind a ratty old sofa. Pulse pistol blasts ripped into the furniture, sending flaming stuffing into the air. Bennie crawled to the end of the couch, flipping his beam saber into blaster mode. He popped up, pressing the activator switch repeatedly, sending purple bolts of energy flying across the small lobby.

"Where'd it go? Was it the Brailack?" Shouts filled the space.

"Keep looking for their rooms!" another voice ordered.

Bennie scurried away from the ravaged sofa as quietly as possible. He got to a chair and leaned out to get his bearings.

The two men behind the reception desk were still there, one busily typing while the other kept a weary eye on the room. The other two were now one, fanning out along the wall opposite Bennie, pistol out, scanning side to side.

When the man along the opposite wall was aiming as far away from Bennie as possible, the Brailack popped up over the top of the chair and fired. The first bolt struck the wall, sending flaming bits of plaster everywhere. The second shot struck the suited gangster in the chest. He slammed backwards against the wall before slumping to the floor.

By the time the man standing watch behind the reception desk could return fire, Bennie was scrambling the other direction.

"I've silenced the automatic alarm. Just so you know," one of the remaining men shouted. "Just give up and give us the woman."

"No thank you," Bennie shouted, on the move.

"Your funeral, you little green dren."

The *snap-hiss* of his saber announced Bennie's location a split second before he leaped up and over the reception counter. "Or yours," he said. He swung his blade in a wide arc through both men. Their suit jackets showed a still glowing line across the front as the bodies hit the floor.

Bennie looked around and made a face. The lobby was in shambles; the sofa was still burning; the air had a distinct burnt flesh smell to it. He hurried to the elevator.

Nic's eyes snapped open. She sat up, her small ears twitching. Something was wrong. She looked around the room. The annoying blonde-haired woman was snoring loudly in the bed. *Stupid Bennie, giving Data Lady the bed.* The couch, like everything else in the Galaxy Suites, was ratty and in ill repair. A piece of spring or something else structural had poked her in the back all night, no matter how much she shifted.

She turned to the door. Someone was outside. "Stupid Grandpa, not giving me a beam saber," she grumbled, reaching over to the coffee table for the knife she always carried. She grabbed it and rolled off the couch onto the floor between it and the coffee table.

The door to the room slid open, flooding it in light from the hallway. Nic took a deep breath, stood, and hurled her knife at the lone figure silhouetted in the doorway.

"Grolack!" the shadow hissed, stepping into the room.

"Are you trying to kill me?" Bennie hissed. He grabbed the knife, yanking it out of the wall opposite the door. He stepped into the room and passed a hand over the sensor inside the door. The lights came on; the door slid closed.

"What...what's going on?" Lyral Adel mumbled, sitting up in bed.

"Oh, sorry," Nic said.

"What's going on?" Lyral repeated. She turned to Bennie. "Ben-Ari, what is happening?"

Bennie looked at the ceiling, exhaling. "We gotta go. They found us."

"What?" both women asked.

"I'm never going to survive this," Lyral said, rising from the bed. She had slept in her clothes. She made a half-hearted attempt to smooth the wrinkles from her clothes, then groaned and gave up.

"I gotta pee before we leave," Nic said, heading for the bathroom.

Bennie moved to the window, looking outside. The gangsters' car was still parked opposite the hotel. People were on the sidewalk, cars moving up and down the street. The morning commute was beginning.

He looked at the bathroom door. "Hurry up!"

"I can't go if you rush me!" the muffled reply came back.

He rolled his eyes.

Finally, the sound of the toilet flushing came through the door.

"Okay, we can go," Nic said.

"Did you wash your hands?" Bennie asked, smirking. He moved to the door, pressing the button to open it.

CHAPTER 10

BENNIE LEANED out into the hallway. "Clear." He motioned for the two women to follow him and left the room. The hallway was in the same state of disrepair and neglect as the lobby and rooms.

"They're going to kill us, aren't they?" Lyral asked.

"They'll try," Bennie said from up ahead. He had absolutely no plans to die anytime soon. If nothing else, his dying on a solo gig would give Wil far too much pleasure at Bennie's expense.

"And what? You'll just kill them?" the Multonae scientist retorted. Her eyes were wide, and she was moving between looking ahead and quickly looking behind them.

Nic looked up. "I mean, better than the alternative."

"But aren't you two supposed to be, I don't know, heroes or something?" She stumbled, resting a hand against the wall. "Isn't that what you said at the rally earlier today...yesterday? Whenever? That you're rebuilding some old peace keeping group or whatever."

Bennie looked over his shoulder. "The Knights of Plentallus."

"Plumbus?"

"Plentallus." He waved a hand. "The Knights were keepers of the peace and warriors for justice. The Tarsi came around and created the Peacekeepers and did their best to erase the Knights from the collective memory of the GC."

Stepping into the elevator, the scientist asked, "And they ran around killing people?"

Nic growled, but Bennie put a hand on her shoulder. "Yes." He held up the other hand to stop further questions. "The Knights did a bunch of dren that was really horrible. I don't like killing people. These syndicate goons aren't giving us much choice." The elevator doors parted. Bennie grimaced.

Lyral gasped, her hands covering her mouth, her eyes as wide as small dinner plates. "Oh, my gods." She took a tentative step out into the ruined lobby. The sofa was still smoldering, and the bodies were exactly where Bennie had left them a few microtocks ago.

Bennie followed. "Oh, see. He's still alive." He pointed to one of the men near the reception desk. He was dragging himself toward the lobby doors. Having only one working arm was keeping his pace slow.

"It's not a points system," Lyral grumbled.

"Where's the reception person?" Nic wondered.

Bennie shrugged. "Wasn't here when I came down."

"Why did you come down?" Lyral asked, taking in the tremendous amount of damage the lobby had taken. Her gaze lingered on the remains of the sofa.

"I couldn't sleep" was all Bennie offered as he looked through the transparent sliding front doors. "I don't see any others. We can take their car."

"More stealing?" the Multonae woman complained.

Bennie turned. "You'd rather walk? We need to get off this stupid planet."

"My cousin could take us in. She said—"

"She said? You called someone?" Bennie snapped. His gaze shifted from the woman he was supposed to protect to the younger woman who was supposed to be his apprentice.

Nic put her hands up in a defensive posture. "I didn't know." She pointed a small hand at their charge. "You didn't say I had to watch her the whole time."

The taller woman shook her head. "I called her while Nic was in the restroom. She has a place in Hartcol Pines."

"I don't know where that is," Nic said.

Bennie made a face. "They almost certainly had a tap on your comms." He pointed to her wristcomm. "Chuck that."

"What?"

"Ditch it. We'll get you another," he insisted, looking up and down the street. "Okay, come on." He reached over and slapped the access plate to open the doors. The sun was just lightening the sky now.

The vehicle was right where the four men had left it. Bennie found the small recessed access port and connected his wristcomm. Nic was bouncing from foot to foot, looking up and down the street. The street was decidedly busier; several hover buses were working their routes as private vehicles zipped around on their way to jobs all around the cluster of downtown buildings.

"You're making me nervous. Cut it out," Lyral snapped.

Before Nic could reply, Bennie shouted, "Done," over the sound of a passing delivery vehicle. He stood, sliding the data cables back into his wristcomm.

"I think I should stay here," Lyral blurted out, stepping onto the sidewalk and backing away from the car. "My cousin can pick me up." She raised her arm. "I can call her, then toss this."

"That's not a good idea. The syndicate obviously knows everything about you by now. There isn't a square plorith on this planet that's safe for you."

"But—"

"No buts. Come with me if you want to live."

"Us," Nic added.

Bennie scowled and pointed to the car. "In." Everyone piled in, tossing the guns and knives they found on the back seat onto the sidewalk. Bennie was in the driver's seat this time, adjusting the seat and control surfaces as best he could in order to accommodate his much-smaller-than-the-average-Multonae physique. After plugging the nearest spaceport into the auto drive system, he released a long sigh. The vehicle rose from the ground and merged into the early morning traffic.

Nic, sitting next to Bennie in the car's front, turned to look at the data scientist in the back seat. "It'll be okay. He's a mean old krebnack, but he's a hero. He saved my gran and me and a bunch of people on a shuttle before saving the entire cruise ship we were on."

Bennie turned. "I am not old."

Nic waved a hand. "Yes, you are." She stayed focused on Lyral. "We'll keep you safe. I'm almost a Knight, too."

"No, you aren't," Bennie retorted, frowning.

"This doesn't fill me with hope," the scientist said, sighing. "If the syndicate is so powerful, what chance do you two have? No offense, but so far this hasn't been that impressive of a rescue."

"You're still alive, aren't you?" Bennie said, turning to face forward and noticing that the car was no longer on a course for the spaceport.

Bennie clawed at the center console. He glanced over to Nic. "Help me find the release."

"Um...the release?"

Bennie gestured at the display. "They hijacked the car. We're not heading for the spaceport. We have to disable the remote-control unit." He looked around and spotted the small camera pickup in the ceiling, likely a security feature. He glared into the lens, then ripped the small unit from the ceiling.

From the backseat came a loud moan.

Bennie spared a glance, frowning, before turning his full attention on the console. He fumbled around a bit more before finding it. He looked at Nic. "There should be a matching release on your side. Just up under the lip." He gestured with his chin.

"Got it." The console came free with a click. Bennie pulled it out as far as it would go. He looked up. "Your knife?"

Nic smiled and offered the blade hilt first. Bennie looked through the jumble of components until he spotted the remote-control unit. Thankful that most hover car makers used industry standard parts, he pulled the unit out enough to give the blade clearance and sliced through the connectors. The car immediately came to a stop. He pulled the offending device from the jumble of wires and components, handing it to Nic. He then pushed the console back into place.

Lyral looked out the windows. "Now what?"

"We take the long way," Bennie replied, re-engaging the auto drive function. "They can't track or control the car now. I don't remember if these units," he took the unit back from Nic and held the disconnected piece of tech up, "interface with the auto drive to send our programmed destination or not."

"What if it did?" she pressed, voice trembling as she wiped her palms on her pants.

"We deal with that situation if it arises," Bennie replied. He looked at the console. "We're half a tock from the spaceport. Try to get a little rest."

To illustrate his point, he closed his eyes. Rest was definitely off the menu, but closing his eyes helped him focus his thoughts. He was in way over his head; he knew that. He also didn't know what to do about it. Calling his friends to come bail him and Nic out was out of the question. For one thing, Wil and Cynthia were on their honeymoon with the *Ghost*. Max and Zephyr would have to book public transport, which would take a while. Gabe was on Arcadia doing whatever he did there. For another, it'd be embarrassing. He sighed.

Rest did not come for any of the trio. In the backseat, eyes closed, Lyral Adel wondered how her life had taken such a dramatic and dangerous turn. Four cycles ago, the mayor, fresh off his election win, had come to her. The news had been carrying a story about a research project she had been the team lead on that used one of the largest data sets on the planet. The team had written an algorithm that could parse data from multiple disparate data sets, find commonalities, and build a model. They had successfully run it against planetary weather data, intra-system shipping, tax systems from across the Multonae realm, and more. Every time, the software created a foolproof model, showing the relationship between seemingly disparate data points.

That was what the mayor wanted, to use her software to root out organized crime. Multon had a long, long history of organized crime being the primary business of the planet. Long before the Multonae left their homeworld, organized crime had its hooks in everything. The mayor had thought he'd taken all the necessary precautions to ensure the syndicate couldn't stop the project. In hindsight, Lyral realized that the mayor was naïve in his assumptions. Killing her would ensure that the model was never released. Whether or not it was destroyed mattered less, so long as it was never seen.

"We're here," Bennie said, breaking everyone out of their respective reveries.

They ditched the gangsters' car a block from the entrance to the spaceport, near the private hangars, hoping to confuse any pursuit. The spaceport was busy. The commuters, making their way to the moons and orbital stations for work, had already lined up to make their way through customs.

"Okay, now what?" Lyral asked, looking around the main hall that bustled with beings heading to work. She turned to Bennie. "You have a ship?"

"You really should buy something," Nic said, not turning to look at Bennie, her eyes fixed on a food stall along the far wall. "You know. I'm kinda hungry."

Bennie rubbed his forehead. "Okay. You two go get some food." He made a show of saying the next part loud enough to draw Nic's attention. "Get something for me, too."

"Where will you be?" Lyral asked, her shoulders bunched as she looked the room over for the second or third time.

"Getting us a ride." He turned to head off, then turned back. "Don't attract attention." He turned, then turned again. "Get me something!" He headed off in the opposite direction.

Nic looked up at the woman towering over her. "You heard him. Don't attract attention."

The scientist clucked. "I'm not the one that looks like a child's stuffed toy." She left before Nic could reply.

The food stall was moderately busy, commuters grabbing chlormax and various types of baked goods for their trips across the globe or into orbit. Nic and her charge found a small table in the corner. Nic tapped in an order on the tabletop interface. When she finished, she pressed a control for the display to rotate to the other seating position. Lyral placed her order and looked at Nic.

"What?" the smaller woman said.

"Payment."

"Go for it."

"Why should I pay?"

"We don't charge for our services, it's not the way. Relying on the kindness of those we help, however, is the way." Nic made a *go on* motion.

The other woman frowned and moved her arm only to stop. She smiled. "No wristcomm." She waved the naked arm to punctuate the statement. Bennie had made her toss it out of the moving car on their way to the spaceport.

Nic frowned, raising her own arm. "This, is not, the way." She paid for the meals.

Across the wide main hall, Bennie was standing in one of the rentable retail units that small spaceport-related businesses often filled. This one was a ship broker called Ships! Ships! Ships!

"No, I don't want a freighter," he growled.

The Burzzad salesperson bobbed their head, long neck bending in a way that made Bennie a little nauseous. "We have many sizes and classes of freighter that—"

"Listen, you long-necked drennog. I don't want a freighter. I want something small, fast, and if possible, armed." Bennie made eye contact with two out of the salesperson's three eyes. "No freighters."

He looked over his shoulder, toward the food stall. Nic and the Multonae woman were seated, eating something, engaged in what looked like a conversation that wasn't an argument. He turned back to the Burzzad, looking at the display between them, flipping images quickly. "What about this one?"

On the screen was a craft that looked like someone had taken a box of crackers and strapped engines and stubby little wings to it. Minimal cargo capacity. Atmosphere capable, no weapons. High FTL rating.

The Burzzad bobbed their head. "A nice choice. We have it here at the port, even. It is unarmed, however."

Bennie nodded. "Yeah, I can work on that problem later."

The salesperson leaned down, their neck bent in a wide arc to bring their head near Bennie. "We do have a sister company that can add a wide array of armaments to this class of vessel."

Bennie waved a hand. "No time."

Nodding, the salesperson said, "Very good. You have funds?"

Bennie looked at his wristcomm, picking one of his aliases. Gergbert Bluffy had more than enough credits in his account. At least on paper. By the time anyone noticed that no actual credits were moving around, he'd be long gone. He swiped on his screen, the sales terminal beeping a happy tune. Sure, it was technically theft, but he was certain this shady Burzzad was charging at least twice what the ship in question was worth.

The Burzzad smiled, pointed ears twitching. "Very good." Their three eyes blinked in a pattern of two, then one. "Very good." They handed a data chip to Bennie. "Please be careful. That is the only copy of the command codes."

Bennie nodded. "Where is it?"

"It will be on private pad 12 in about ten microtocks. It will take that long to walk there. Do you need directions?" Bennie shook his head. "Very good. Very good. Is there anything else I can help you with? We do offer a full detailing package."

"Nope." Bennie waved a hand as he exited. He trotted across the great hall, skidding to a stop about halfway across. Two men in suits, all too similar to those worn by the four-man team from the hotel, were at the pedestrian entrance, looking around the assorted crowd.

Bennie dropped to a crouch and made his way across the hall, thankful for the morning rush-hour crowd. Reaching the two women, he said, "We gotta go. Friends just arrived."

Looking at his wristcomm, he flipped a data packet to Nic. "You two make your way there. I'll meet you."

"But I can help you," Nic moaned.

Bennie nodded. "I know, but right now, you gotta protect her."

"I could do that better with a—"

Bennie waved both hands. "Do you think I just have a bunch of beam sabers in my pocket?"

The younger woman looked up at her charge. "Fine. Come on." She looked at Bennie. "Good luck."

He smiled. "I'm a Knight of Plentallus. I make my own luck." He turned and walked out of the small food stall toward the two men near the entrance. Looking around, he ignited his beam saber and screamed, swinging it in a wide arc, careful to not actually hit anyone with the blade. Those closest to him screamed and turned to flee right toward the gangsters. The crowd grew as frightened commuters shoved others ahead of them. In moments, the two pursuers were lost in the sea of panicked people, rushing to the exit directly behind them. He clicked off his saber, grinning to himself.

Bennie turned and dashed toward the access tunnel that led down into the warren of tunnels beneath the spaceport. Ahead, he saw Nic and Lyral duck down the stairs into the tunnels.

Reaching the top of the stairs, he turned to make sure the two men he'd seen were occupied. They were, but as he turned, he spotted another two-man team heading straight for him. Both wore serious expressions, and each had a hand inside his jacket, likely clutching the handle of a pulse pistol.

Bennie knew that if he stayed to fight them, the spaceport would get shut down. He couldn't risk that. So, he turned and darted down the stairs. If he was honest, he was surprised that his stunt with the saber a microtock ago hadn't resulted in an immediate lock down.

The tunnels below the spaceport were full of smaller vendor stalls, mechanical shops, and sitting areas for those waiting for a shuttle. It wasn't safe to have travelers loiter on the main duracrete landing area, so spaceports kept travelers underground until their ride was ready. Several staircases led back up to the main level, exiting onto the duracrete for easy boarding.

He couldn't see Nic or the scientist. That was good. He hoped. Hopefully, they were already at the ship Bennie just bought. He trotted over to the directory mounted on the wall, confirming his location and the tunnel he needed to take to the private field of the shipbroker.

"There!" he heard someone shout.

The trick from before wouldn't work again, not enough people in the tunnel. He looked around and ducked into the nearest storefront, a convenience store.

One level up, Nic and Lyral were wandering between a half dozen ships. "These are pieces of dren," the scientist complained. They had just walked past a ship that might have been mostly rust. Another farther back had been missing one of its atmospheric engines.

Nic nodded. She didn't like agreeing with annoying Data Lady, but in this instance, she couldn't argue. Every ship they passed seemed to be in worse shape than the previous. She looked at her wristcomm, then back up, and pointed. "I think it's just past that rusty one."

"They're all rusty," Lyral complained.

They rounded the nearest rusty vessel and came face to face with something that, while technically not rustier than the rest of the vessels, was in equally bad shape.

"I hope he didn't pay much," Lyral said.

They both stared at the squat, stubby-winged thing sitting on four short landing struts. Nic made a loop around it. Three cargo doors: one on each side, one forward underneath what must be the bridge. Three atmospheric engines that looked really powerful took up the rear of the thing. The little wings seemed to exist so that the sub-light engines had a place to be.

Below in the convenience store, Bennie had wedged himself behind a freezer unit. He had just gotten himself hidden when the two men walked in; splitting up to walk the aisles. He waited, his knees aching from the position he was scrunched into. Finally, a pair of dress-slack-clad legs came into view.

Closing his eyes, he clicked his beam saber on. The magenta blade sprang to life, slicing clean through the left leg of his target. He clicked the blade off as the wounded man's screams forced him to cover his ears. Scrambling out of cover, he looked at the wounded man, now writhing on the ground, a still glowing hole in his pant leg. "I hope that grows back," he said, leaning into a punch that sent stabs of pain up his thin arm but did render his opponent unconscious.

The other man rounded the corner just as Bennie stood up. The Brailack Knight of Plentallus didn't wait. His beam saber activated once more, cutting the shelving next to him, causing the contents to topple into the aisle between him and the other man. He slashed again, taking advantage of the confused expression on the other man's face, sending more foodstuffs raining down. He turned and darted in the opposite direction, a few stray plasma bolts sailing overhead.

Running past the startled store clerk, he shouted, "So sorry!"

Nic and Lyral were sitting on the duracrete against the landing gear of the ship when Bennie came around the front of the neighboring ship. The young Olop girl sprung to her feet. "We were worried about you."

"I wasn't," Lyral said under her breath.

Bennie moved to pat his young apprentice's head, but she batted his hand away. He removed the data card from his pocket, slotting it into his wristcomm. He tapped at the screen for a while before the forward cargo hatch dropped to the ground with a hiss.

Lyral looked up into the darkened interior. "I think you got taken advantage of."

Bennie marched up the ramp. "Then the joke is on them. I used a fake account." He looked around the hold until he spotted the ladder that led to the upper deck.

The data scientist sighed, following him up into the ship. Nic brought up the rear, looking over her shoulder to make sure no one was around. She looked around and found the control, slapping it to trigger the cargo ramp.

With a loud groan, the ramp rose, sealing them inside the dilapidated ship.

From somewhere above, Bennie shouted, "Strap in. I'm not normally the pilot."

PART THREE
FAKE IT 'TIL YOU MAKE IT

CHAPTER 11

BENNIE LOOKED around the small bridge. Calling it a bridge was being kind; the cramped space had a pilot station and one auxiliary station behind it, to the side. After figuring out how to power up the command station, he tapped controls, bringing the reactor online. The secondary console sprang to life, indicators waking up, displays flickering.

The hatch opened. "Well, this isn't any better than the rest of the ship," Nic said. She climbed up into the second seat and started pressing buttons.

"Cut that out!" he snapped. "Where's our guest?"

"In the crew area."

The console showed the reactor was ready for flight. Atmospheric and sub-light thrusters, online. FTL systems, ready to go. Repulsorlifts, online. Easing power into the repulsorlifts, he said, "Crew area?"

He couldn't see her but knew she was frowning. "I mean, that's a pretty generous term. It's a combo lounge-kitchen area. There's a bedroom with bunk beds and a private refresher."

The ship shook and tilted as it left the ground. A light turned on and he pressed it. From below, the sound of the landing gear retracting echoed through the small ship. Something made a loud clunk, followed by a grinding noise, then went silent.

"That sounded good," Nic quipped.

"Shut up," Bennie growled, both hands on the controls. The ship had cleared the top of the spaceport ring wall when the overhead speaker came to life.

"Attention *Bibby's Folly*. We do not have a flight plan for you. Please respond."

"*Bibby's Folly*?" Nic asked.

Bennie waved an angry hand. He looked up. "Spaceport control, this is...*Bibby's Folly*. No flight plan, just testing out my new purchase."

"Copy, *Bibby's*—"

"Thank you, space control." Bennie slapped the comm control, closing the channel.

"Bibby," Nic drawled, chuckling.

Bennie eased the controls back, engaging the atmospheric thrusters. He was used to the loud boom and multiple g-force push that came from the *Ghost*'s own atmospheric engines igniting. *Bibby's Folly*, despite her atmospheric engine's impressive outward appearance, seemed capable of nothing more than an anemic growl. He could hear Wil's laughter in his head.

He had to double check the readouts to be sure the atmospheric engines had, in fact, engaged. *This really is a piece of dren*, he thought. His guilt at essentially robbing the ship broker was dissipating by the moment.

"Should we be shaking like that?" Nic asked.

Bennie's focus returned to the here and now, looking at his console. "Uh..." He scanned the myriad displays. *It can't be this hard to fly a ship. Wil does it, and he's stupid.* He spotted an indicator that was fluttering between yellow and red. He leaned closer to squint at the readout. "Thrust mix imbalance. That doesn't sound good."

"I can't die before I get my laser sword."

"Shut up!" Bennie hissed.

"Seriously, I'm too young. I haven't even had —"

He spun. "Shut it." He turned back to the console, scrutinizing it. "If Wil can do this, I can do this."

"What?"

Ignoring his young apprentice, he reached up and adjusted a setting, watching the fluctuating readout stabilize. The small craft stopped its shaking. He turned and stuck his tongue out at Nic, when the ship shook again, differently than last time. "Dren!" He spun around to see several new flashing warnings.

The *Bibby's Folly* had reached the edge of the atmosphere, which meant that the atmospheric engines had nothing to thrust through and the small ship would be falling back to the planet shortly.

Bennie slapped a few controls, swearing. The tinny whine of the atmospherics shut off. The sub-light engines mounted inside the ship's short wings made no noise when they activated. The only sign was a change in the reactor power level reading and a distinct lack of whine from the rear of the ship.

"Way to go, Captain Grandpa," Nic said. She hopped out of her seat. "I'll go tell Data Lady that we're not going to die...right now."

The crew area was the only other thing on the upper deck with the bridge. Nic hadn't been kidding. The seating and kitchen areas were both a fraction of the size of the *Ghost*'s versions of the same spaces. The bunk room was literally that. A double bunk set against the rear bulkhead with a small desk on the opposite side of the room. Bennie wasn't sure, but he vaguely recalled the crew capacity listed as four, but seeing the sleeping arrangements, he wasn't sure. The single refresher was in the common area.

Bennie found Nic and Lyral in the lounge area, sharing the small love seat. The pair were watching something on a display that looked like it folded down from the ceiling.

Lyral looked up. "Given all the noises this thing makes, we can't already be in FTL. We'd have heard it."

Bennie made a face. "We're about half a tock from FTL. This thing doesn't even have a basic auto flight package, so I can't leave it unattended for long." He looked around. "I have to pee, though." He ducked into the refresher.

Nic looked at Lyral and shrugged.

Before Bennie came out, the ship was rocked by an impact. The lights in the common area flickered. The door to the refresher burst open. "What did you do!?" His gaze settled on Nic.

"Nothing!" she shouted, hopping off the sofa.

Bennie rushed back into the short corridor that ran between the bridge and common area. Nic followed.

Lyral watched the two of them go. "I'll just be here, I guess." She picked up the small remote device for the display screen.

Bennie hopped up into the pilot's chair, scanning the displays to see if he could figure out what was wrong now. The ship shook again, the lights flickering. He looked up through the transparent forward viewscreen. A ship of unknown design rocketed past overhead. "Dren," he hissed.

"Who was that?" Nic asked, scrabbling into the seat at the secondary station.

"Didn't catch their name," Bennie said. He looked up and down at his console. "Do you have shields on your console?"

"What do they look like?" the young girl asked, standing on her seat to get a better view of the console.

"I don't know, a glowy outline of the ship, or the word 'shields.' Figure it out!"

"Don't be so—"

The ship rocked and something, somewhere, made a crackling sound as the lights flickered. A panel overhead exploded, sending sparks down on top of her.

Bennie pushed the flight controls hard over, while grabbing the throttle and pushing it as far forward as it would go. The sub-light engines groaned.

"This thing is a piece of dren," Nic said, still scanning her console. "Oh!" She leaned forward and slapped her hand on the console. "Shields up."

The power readout on the reactor display dropped alarmingly, rose a bit, then wavered before stabilizing.

The overhead speaker crackled. "Turn back to the planet. Now."

"Grolack you, you drennogs!" Nic shouted at the ceiling.

Bennie winced. He found the comm controls and closed the channel. Then he flipped the selector from "auto" to "manual" as he looked over his shoulder. "Are you trying to get us killed? We don't have any weapons."

"Oh, right. Sorry."

Bennie pulled the flight controls in the opposite direction, bringing the *Folly* around toward Multon.

"You're doing what they said?" Nic complained.

"No!" he growled. Outside the forward viewscreen, the planet swung into view but continued past. Before the young Olop could say anything, one of Multon's moons came into view.

"Ohhh," she said.

Outside the viewscreen, hundreds of ships and a half dozen or more orbital habitats were coming into range.

The comm console blinked, but Bennie ignored it. The ship rocked, and the power meter dipped as the shields absorbed several blaster bolts. *Better than exploding,* Bennie thought.

"Are we gonna make it?" Nic asked. "I think this is saying the shields are at half power."

"Half?"

"Don't blame me!"

The *Bibby's Folly* was shaking more often than not. Bennie would never admit it to the rest of the Rogue Enterprises team, but he had a newfound respect for Wil's piloting abilities. Sweat poured down his face. He was gripping the flight controls in one hand, while clutching the throttle in the other. He pushed the not-even-sort-of-agile vessel into wild twists and dives. He had almost collided with no fewer than three other ships, eliciting angry comm requests to fill the comm buffer. While most of his mind was focused on evading their pursuers and not crashing, a small percentage was tallying a running list of improvements to the small ship.

Nic had fallen silent, watching the wild ride through the forward window. The *Folly* was winding its way around a commercial orbital hub.

The moon Preyn kept moving in and out of view through the forward window. As it would pass, she thought it looked pretty, kind of like home.

The hatch swung open with a screech. "This rescue seems to be going well," Lyral said, then nearly fell over as the ship rocked.

Nic looked down at her console, then up again. "Uh, I think

we lost shields." An indicator blinked to life on her console. "Yup, definitely lost shields."

"What?" the two others on the bridge asked in unison.

Before the young woman could reply, something inside the ship exploded. The smell of burned wiring wafted up into the small flight deck.

Preyn moved into view again. Bennie blindly reached out for the communication controls. "Uh, Preyn space control, this is the...*Bibby's Folly*. We're being chased and are definitely going to crash."

The speaker crackled. "Chased by whom?"

"Is that the important thing right now?" Bennie growled. Outside the forward window, the inhabited moon was growing ever larger.

The other ship was using something that didn't seem to alert space control to the fact that they were attacking. Bennie couldn't figure what type of weapon that might be. He had little time or energy to work on the problem at the moment.

"Does this thing have any safety features?" Lyral asked. She had both arms up, bracing herself in the open hatch.

"Did you see a lifeboat when you came aboard?" Bennie asked without looking up from the controls.

"*Bibby's Folly*, you're coming in hot," the space control operator warned. Bennie had forgotten the channel was still open.

"What part of crashing did you not understand, you krebnack?" Bennie said. He slapped the control, closing the connection. "Stupid conversation anyway." This time he did look over his shoulder. "Hold onto something."

The moon ahead of them filled the window. Bennie could make out the cities and towns, and more importantly in the moment, the lights of spaceport ring walls. Large trees filled the spaces in between.

"I think the bad guys are giving up," Nic said. She looked at her console again. "Or, maybe they're just waiting to see if we crash."

"Or where," Lyral offered. She leaned over the young Olop's shoulder to peer at the console. "Wait. I think the local space authority cutters are keeping them busy." On the sensor screen, several new contacts were flitting about between the *Folly* and the attacking craft.

Bennie didn't reply, his eyes glued to the view outside and the distressingly quickly growing spaceport.

The *Bibby's Folly* came in hot, screaming over the mid-sized city next to the spaceport. Bennie had the repulsor lifts at full power and managed to get the clumsy ship turned one hundred and eighty degrees and was using the atmospheric engines as retro thrusters. On paper, it was a great idea to keep them from plowing into the ring wall of the spaceport. In practice, the anemic thrusters were making only the smallest dent in their speed.

The ship was vibrating so fiercely that Nic could barely see the displays on her console. "I think we're going too fast, still."

"You think?" Bennie said. "Hold on!"

He flipped the ship back to flying forward moments before it overshot the spaceport, plowing into some farmland a couple of ploriths beyond. A plume of soil and a crop Bennie didn't recognize shot up into the sky.

The ship came to a rest, creaking.

CHAPTER 12

"MAYBE, NEXT TIME, I FLY." Nic stood up from under her console. A gash ran down her cheek, and dried blood matted her fur. She looked around, spotting Lyral in a crumpled heap under what was left of the pilot's station. She ran over, gingerly poking the Multonae woman.

"Ouch" came from under the heap of blonde hair. A hand moved to wave Nic away. Lyral brushed her hair from her face, revealing her own gash, nearly a twin of Nic's. "You two really are terrible at this." She got to her feet and looked around. "Guess I'm lucky we aren't dead."

"I'm not dead? Then this sucks" came from somewhere on the other side of the pilot's station. There was a meter of open space where the forward window angled down to the deck, presumably meant for storage. Bennie sat up, rubbing his forehead.

Nic moved over next to him. "You okay?"

"Do I look okay?"

"No. You look like dren."

"Well, there you have it." He shooed her away and stood. "We gotta go. Those drennogs that were shooting at us likely were just waiting to see what happened to us. They'll be on their way down."

"What about the authorities?" Lyral asked. She'd gotten her hair into a ponytail using a bit of wire she found somewhere.

"They'll delay them for a bit, but eventually the right people will talk, money will change hands, and those little patrol ships will return to base," Bennie said, patting himself all over and looking around. He grunted and bent down to retrieve his beam saber hilt. He walked around to look at the pilot's station, in particular the communications system—as broken as the rest of the console. "Come on."

To Bennie's surprise, the ship had come through the fight and crash landing more or less in one piece. The forward window on the bridge was spider-webbed by cracks and would probably not hold in atmosphere. Both consoles needed to be repaired or maybe replaced. The common area was a mess, but nothing looked broken. The small windows that lined both sides of the space near the ceiling were uncracked. That was a plus. The mounting brackets for the sofa had sheared off, allowing it to crash against the door to the bunk room.

The cargo hold, engineering, and tiny medical bay also seemed to have survived the crash intact. The port cargo doors were bent in at the seam. The impact crumpled in the forward door and cargo ramp, rendering them inoperable. One of the blessings of a craft with three doors, Bennie surmised.

The *Folly* had come to a rest more or less flat, with a tilt of only a few degrees. Bennie pointed to the small med bay. "Grab what we can carry. We'll get cleaned up once we're on the way." Lyral and Nic nodded and headed off, each sporting an empty backpack. He looked down at his wristcomm and sighed. He tapped an icon.

Gabe's new face appeared. Bennie still couldn't quite get used to the look his new friend had chosen. Version 3 of Gabe was still more humanoid-looking than most droids, but he no longer looked like a mix of Maxim's and Wil's facial features. His body was slimmed down and had moved from a shiny chrome color to a more muted blue-gray color. The disconcerting smile was still there.

"Hello, Bennie."

"Hi, Gabe." Bennie chewed his lip, looking to the med bay. Nic and Lyral were still busy collecting gear. "I could use some help." He quickly outlined the problem. Gabe had an internal comm unit, so the face on the screen was a software rendering of himself, which creeped Bennie out. He had tried to get the droid to just show an audio waveform or even just a logo, but he refused. "I'm sending you details for the ship I just crashed. I'll be out of pocket for at least a few days. The bad guys will be on us in a few tocks at most. There isn't anything aboard this heap, so I'm assuming they'll look it over and move on. Could you reach out and get it into a shop and get it repaired? I'm also attaching the ID credentials of an account that should have enough funds to cover it. You can get the work done under that name as well, just in case."

Virtual Gabe nodded. "I would be happy to help. Are you okay?"

Bennie smiled. "Yeah. You know, this whole Knight of Plentallus thing is turning out to be harder than I thought."

"Indeed."

The two women came out of the med bay, both backpacks full. Bennie looked up, then back to his wristcomm. "I'll call when I can. Thanks, Gabe, I really appreciate it." He tapped the END icon.

"Who was that?" Nic asked, nodding towards his wristcomm.

"None of your business." He turned to the one functional cargo door. When he palmed the control, an angry sounding beep came from the console. He slapped it again. This time the door slid apart, stopping halfway. He turned to the two women, shrugging.

The crash site was nearly two ploriths beyond the spaceport. He was glad they had approached from the direction they had. The opposite side of the port was a city with an industrial area to the side, both stretching for ploriths. Their crash site was some sort of agricultural space, crumpled and burnt stalks surrounded them.

By the time the ragged trio reached the spaceport, the moon was in the shadow of its parent, Multon.

"Who puts spaceports in fields?" Nic complained.

Lyral nodded. "At least we can hire a car here."

Bennie turned toward their crash site. "It's weird that no planetary authorities showed up."

Lyral turned as well. The smoke from the crash had blown away, so spotting the downed *Bibby's Folly* wasn't easy at that distance. "Like you said. The syndicate must have paid them off."

Bennie nodded. "Still, I expected at least a little presence to secure the area, if nothing else." He shrugged and turned to look at her. "What do you know about this moon?" He adjusted his beam saber nervously.

Lyral rubbed at the cut on her face. It glistened with antiseptic ointment. "Preyn was the first colony that my people established when we began to explore our star system." Lyral went on to describe the early years of Multon's space exploration. The discovery that Preyn had a compatible atmosphere had jumpstarted further colonization of the system. Corporations looking to get a foothold off-world led the early colonization efforts. There had been no shortage of corruption back then, and from what she'd learned over the course of her work for the mayor, it was still a bigger issue than most Multonae probably realized. She pointed to the few high rises visible beyond the spaceport's ring wall. "It makes sense that our crash didn't attract much official attention. That town is likely, on some level, tied to the syndicate or one of its affiliates."

Bennie stopped a passing commuter. "Excuse me. Is there a market square nearby?"

The dark-eyed Multonae looked down. "What? Oh, half a plorith that way." He pointed toward the same high rises visible on the other side of the spaceport.

Bennie gestured. "Let's get some new clothes, and," he pointed to Lyral, "you need a wristcomm still." Lyral raised her naked forearm. In all the excitement of escaping Multon, being chased and shot at, and then crashing, she'd forgotten that her arm was bare.

They walked in silence toward the market that had grown up around the west entrance to the spaceport. As the sky darkened further, lights blazed to life atop poles outlining the spaceport and the nearby market, bathing both in daylight levels of brightness. Every time a ship came in for a landing, they looked up to see if it was one of the ships that had attacked them. Not that any of them could be certain of those ships' makes and models.

The market was about what Bennie expected: stalls offering foodstuffs, used starship parts, various other technologies, and even a few that were selling small arms. He tried to look for the telltale signs of the less-than-legal-goods section, but as far as he could see, there wasn't one. He looked at Lyral. "Know your way around a blaster?"

She shook her heard. "I'm a scientist."

"Now you're gonna be an armed scientist," Bennie replied as he turned to continue on.

"Perhaps a small pistol wouldn't be the worst idea," Lyral conceded.

"Can I get a gun?" Nic asked.

"No," Bennie replied without turning.

He smiled and bought a compact pulse pistol. It wouldn't do much of anything against someone with armor on, but it might slow them down enough for Bennie to intervene. Or to run away, depending.

They found the public refreshers in the middle of the market. Bennie took a seat at a small table while the two women went in to clean up. They'd found a stall offering basic spacer attire: jumpsuits, cargo pants, vests, shirts, and the like.

Bennie was scrolling through news feeds to see if the crash had attracted any attention. So far it seemed to have not even been worthy of local gossip.

"You're not from around here," a voice said from behind Bennie.

He turned. "What gave it away?" He looked up to see a middle-aged Multonae woman. She was wearing shorts that were far too short and a crop-top shirt with a faded logo he couldn't make out.

"You see that crash over on the other side of the port?"

"Nope." He turned back around. Guess the crash made the locals-only news.

"I heard some folks say it was a little green guy and two women. One a little furry thing. I hear there may be a reward."

Bennie scowled. "Well, I'm sitting here alone, so..." He waved a hand. "Move along."

A hand dropped onto his shoulder. "I'm wanted in four systems."

"Good for you." Bennie tried to remain calm, despite his

racing heart. Hopefully, the two women would stay in the fresher a bit longer. He casually reached up and put his hand on the much larger one on his shoulder. A quick tightening of his grip followed by a twist, and the woman was on her knees. He turned and whispered, "Perhaps it's you that should be careful—

so many warrants on your head, and all." He was hoping she would take the hint. Looking around, the evening shopping and dining crowd was arriving.

She scowled and wrenched her hand free. "You little—"

Bennie leaned in faster than she could react and bit her arm.

"You bit me!" she growled, getting to her feet.

Bennie hopped from his chair. "Yeah, and you taste like dren. You should bathe more frequently." She reached for him but stumbled. The toxin Bennie's bite released into her bloodstream took effect quickly. Reaching up to capture both of her outstretched hands, he guided her to the seat he just vacated. "Here you go." Maneuvering her took all of his strength.

By the time he had her seated, she was out cold. He looked around to make sure the interaction had attracted no attention. On top of keeping a low profile, it was considered impolite among Brailack to run around biting people. That particular piece of their biology was not something they advertised. He wiped his mouth. "So gross."

A Trollack man walked past, casting a sideways glance at Bennie and the woman. Bennie shrugged. "Drank too much."

"Hey, you," someone growled.

Bennie sighed and turned. A Multonae man was approaching. Judging from his clothes and obvious lack of a recent bath, Bennie assumed he was with the unconscious woman.

"What'd you do to Jilly?" The man was built like Maxim. Muscles seemed to be stacked on top of each other.

Bennie's hand drifted down to his beam saber as he looked

around the open space. His poison glands needed more time to recharge. Biting the big man wasn't an option. Not that it was anywhere near the top of his list. Somehow the approaching man looked even worse tasting than the woman. "She's taking a nap."

"A...what?" By then, the man had closed the distance between them. The conversation had yet to attract attention, but Bennie knew he was on borrowed time. He stepped toward the much larger man, startling him.

"Hey—" Bennie said as he unleashed two quick jabs to the man's groin, doubling him over. When the man's head got close enough, he shot a flat-handed jab into the man's throat. He was glad Multonae were constructed like humans. He wasn't glad he had seen Wil naked more than once, but it was useful information now. He shuddered at the memory.

Two meaty hands tried to encircle Bennie's throat, but another punch to the man's temple dazed him enough for Bennie to slip out of his reach. Spying a nearby Harrith man, he moved behind the big Multonae and shoved him as hard as he could. The Multonae wall of muscle, still trying to breathe and fight off unconsciousness, tumbled right into the Harrith.

Bennie turned toward the public refreshers and met Nic and Lyral as they were exiting. "Let's go this way," he urged.

Behind him, the Harrith man was kicking the much larger Multonae man's midsection.

The cab from the spaceport dropped them in the heart of downtown Oudal. Bennie looked around. "Nicer than anything on Fury." Calling Oudal a town was a bit of a misnomer. It was closer to a mid-sized city, the suburban sprawl reaching almost to the market that abutted the spaceport. The size of the spaceport was likely the reason for the "town" designation. It was a third the size of most spaceports. Bennie hadn't caught the name of it as they careened by overhead on their way to crashing nearby. It likely had "regional" in the name.

"Wait, you're from Fury?" Lyral asked.

Nic's head bobbed. "Yeah. He and the rest of his team live in this super dingy warehouse just outside the spaceport district." Her flat nose crinkled. "It has this smell—"

"That's enough," Bennie interrupted. He pointed to a shop across the street, TechBro. "Let's get you a wristcomm and get settled in for the night." The technology options in the spaceport market were limited, so he'd passed on them.

"He has a team? Where are they? Shouldn't they be here?" Lyral asked.

Bennie made a clucking noise at the two women.

"Can I get parts for a beam saber here?" Nic asked as the trio walked in.

Bennie tilted his head. "Probably. Let's see." He spotted the aisles with "Wristcomms" written over them. "Look for anything that says it has a Drolen Ex operating system. Version 10 or above." Lyral nodded and made her way to the designated aisles. Cleaning up and changing clothes had had a calming effect on her that Bennie was more than happy to experience.

He guided Nic to the section of the store that was miscellaneous electronics. Looking around, he nodded. "It won't be pretty, but I think we can at least get you a solid version 1 saber."

The young Olop girl clapped her hands, hopping from one foot to the next. She had asked out of habit, fully expecting him to swat the idea aside like usual. His agreement caught her by surprise. "Can it have a purple handle? Like my hair?" She ran a hand over the stripe of dyed fur on top of her head. "Oh, and maybe it can have my knife inside it? Or better yet—"

Bennie held his hands up. "Let's focus on just getting you a working unit for now." Her head bobbed up and down as she followed him down the aisle. "I'm not thrilled about it, but honestly, you're more useful armed."

"Thanks?"

Lyral found the pair in the back corner of the store under a hanging banner that read, "Repair Center." They were huddled over a workbench, parts arrayed around the table, price tags neatly piled up in one corner. "There you are." She held up a shrink-wrapped box. "I think I want this one." The wristcomm inside was a newer model with plenty of storage and the latest communication suite and hardware.

Bennie looked up. "Good choice. Once we're settled in for the night, I'll get it hacked and set up."

"Hacked?"

Nic turned. "Look!" In her small hand was a bright purple cylinder with some sort of animals etched into the metal in bright silvery contrast. "Neat, right?" She moved the hilt back and forth, making swooshing noises similar to the sounds that Bennie's weapon made when activated.

Lyral nodded. "Quite impressive."

Bennie held out his hand, offering a smaller containment unit with a pulsing window in the center. A power cell. Nic handed him the hilt, her eyes twinkling.

Bennie deftly unscrewed the base of the hilt, removing the end to allow him to slot the power cell into the hilt with a click. He twisted the power cell to lock it in, then reattached the end piece. When the end unit clicked, the whole device made a noise that startled the young Olop girl. He handed it back to Nic.

Nic accepted the weapon and held it out arms' length. She looked at Bennie, who nodded, and thumbed the activator switch. With a *snap-hiss* she now found familiar, a bright red blade of energy sprang to life. The blade cast an eerie glow across the myriad work benches in the space. She made a few experimental swipes, moving the blade up and down, left and right, once coming close enough to Bennie that he jumped back.

Lyral noticed that the blade on Nic's weapon was shorter than Bennie's by half, more a dagger or short sword than an actual sword. Bennie nodded. "What I've read about the apprentice program is that they grew into their weapons." He shrugged. "Plus, doesn't really make sense for her blade to be taller than her."

Nic thumbed the activation switch and yelped. "It shocked me." The blade flickered, then vanished.

Bennie shrugged. "Version 1. Made from spare parts." He picked up the stack of price tags and tilted his head to the front of the store. "Come on."

CHAPTER 13

AFTER LEAVING THE TECHBRO STORE, the trio found a shabby-looking diner a few blocks away. After a few microtocks of tinkering, Bennie disconnected Lyral's new wristcomm from his. He handed Lyral the device. "Here you go. I erased the built-in identity management and loaded a special program I wrote that lets you manage the identity stuff yourself." He snatched a fried zergling from the bowl in the center of the table. He loved those things.

"I only have the one identity," she said, slipping the device onto her arm. Once in place, small molecular adhesives engaged, bonding to her skin.

He grinned. "Two now. I loaded a default blank profile with a few basics. Use that for any purchases and stuff, until I say otherwise. I also installed some routing algorithms into the communications suite. You can load your profile without it being traced back."

The Multonae woman's eyes went wide. "I had no idea you had these kinds of resources."

Nic hitched a thumb at Bennie. "He's also a criminal code slicer."

Bennie's shoulders bunched. "Reformed." Under his breath, he added, "Mostly." He waved a hand. "I wasn't always a Knight of Plentallus. At any rate, you're back online and should be as untraceable as possible."

She nodded and set about downloading her profile from the local internex node. Nic was busy playing with her beam saber hilt, so Bennie turned away from them and tapped an icon on his wristcomm.

"Hello, Bennie," Gabe's virtual representation said. "I have news regarding your ship."

Suddenly, it felt like a weight had been lifted from his shoulders. "That's great."

Virtual Gabe nodded. "I was able to hire a mechanic from a spaceport two hundred ploriths from your location."

"Two hundred?"

"I am afraid it was the best that I could do. The spaceport you crashed near did not have a mechanic rated for the type of ship you crashed."

Bennie sighed. "How long?"

"Two days."

Bennie made a face. "Okay, that's actually better than I expected." He smiled. "Thanks, Gabe. I really appreciate this."

"I am pleased I could assist you. If you'll excuse me, I am needed in the council chambers." Virtual Gabe dipped his head.

"Don't get yourself elected president."

"I am trying." The small screen went dark.

"Is that Gabe?" Nic asked, craning her neck. "Tell him I said hi!"

Bennie waved his arm. "He's gone. We'll be off this rock in two days."

"Two days?" Lyral echoed. "What are we supposed to do for two days?"

"Staying alive is high on my list," Bennie replied. He told them about his run-in at the spaceport market.

"When did you plan to tell us?" Lyral demanded, foot tapping.

"Now, I guess." Bennie shrugged. "We should find a hotel or something."

"Just when I was beginning to think you two were competent..."

"That's on you," Bennie said, mostly under his breath.

"Look!" Nic pointed to one of the entertainment displays mounted on a pillar on the far side of the restaurant. On the screen, Mayor Dardle was talking.

Bennie flagged the server droid down. "Turn that up."

The droid nodded. The audio feed from the screen piped through the speakers on all three wristcomms. "I cannot apologize to the people of Sentullo enough. It's embarrassing that myself and my campaign were so grossly misled. Lyral Adel is a charlatan who convinced me to run for governor under the pretense of her being able to uncover a wide-ranging criminal syndicate and exposing it. All of which was false. Lies."

"That fat little—" Lyral growled.

Bennie shushed her, his eyes glued to the display. An image of Lyral—from the rally, it looked like—appeared over the mayor's shoulder. Bennie sighed. Her clothes were different. That was a plus.

The mayor continued. "I've suspended my campaign for the time being." He struck a sincere-looking expression. "Now isn't the time."

"Well, grolack," Bennie said. He looked around. So far, no one else in the diner had taken notice of the woman across the booth from Bennie. Then he remembered.

The droid was staring at them.

On the screen, the mayor said, "I've issued an executive warrant for this fraud, this liar. This enemy of the people."

Bennie tapped on his wristcomm, paying the bill. "We gotta go."

"Where are we going?" Lyral asked, trailing behind Bennie. Behind them, the serving droid was following them with its optic sensors. It had said nothing when Bennie paid the bill, or when the trio headed for the door, their meals half eaten.

"My original plan was to find someplace to hole up. But now we've gotta cover two hundred ploriths in two days." He looked around, getting his bearings. He shook his head, unclear where they actually were. "And it's a safe bet your face, for sure —maybe ours—is plastered across every vid screen in this system." With a sigh, he checked the map app on his wristcomm. He pointed. "We're taking a train."

"A...train..." Lyral echoed.

"Neat," Nic said, grinning.

"The upside is that the syndicate bozos looking for us will be looking here." He looked at the data that Gabe had sent. "Not in Nemik. Wherever that is."

"Do you think the droid reported us?" Nic asked.

Bennie turned to look over his shoulder. "You noticed. Nicely done." He smiled, and she bounced from foot to foot as they walked. Maybe the training was working.

"The droid from the diner?" Lyral asked.

Nic nodded. "Yeah, it immediately took notice of us while the newscast was on." She made a face. "You're pretty recognizable." The taller woman blushed, smiling. "Not a compliment," Nic added. The smile fell from Lyral's face. "Anyway, yeah.

The droid was watching us as we left. I saw it move to the window when we crossed the street."

Getting over her initial anger at the small furry adolescent, Lyral said, "That's quite observant."

Nic grinned. "He drilled into me the importance of observing our surroundings. Want to know how many knives were in the bin on the counter at the diner?"

"No."

Nic harrumphed. "Twenty-two." She patted a pocket on her cargo pants, adding, "minus one," under her breath. The knives had really fancy handles, despite the diner being one step above eating from the dumpsters in back.

The transit terminal was nearly a half tock walk from the diner. By the time the trio arrived, it was late in the evening.

Despite the proliferation of easy trans-atmospheric flight, many worlds still chose to employ buses and trains for city-to-city transit. It was much cheaper than air travel and even more cost effective than short-haul shuttles that left the ground, got to orbit, then fell back to the planet.

All of those other options existed if you were willing or able to pay for them, but if you weren't in a hurry, you couldn't beat a mag-lev train between cities.

Bennie had the two women take a seat in the corner of the cavernous reception hall. From outside, the transit depot looked like a good-sized warehouse with a dozen mag-lev rails coming out of the back end. Bennie stepped into line for the ticket counter just as the newscast from earlier repeated across the screens of the reception hall. He grimaced and wished he'd brought a cloak with him. Thankfully, the story was the same as earlier, focused on Lyral and not on Bennie and his new apprentice.

A woman stepped up behind him, saw him making a face at

the distant screens, and said, "Terrible, isn't it? That woman should be ashamed of herself."

Bennie looked up. "What?"

The woman gestured to the screen. "That woman that tricked the mayor down in Sentullo."

"How do you know she tricked him? Maybe she has the data, and the mayor is being leaned on by the syndicate?" He held up a finger. "Maybe...the mayor got in over his head, showing his hand far too early, putting himself and that woman at risk. Maybe that poor woman is now on the run, protected by a handsome Knight of Plentallus and his sidekick, while the mayor does damage control to save his own skin, hanging her out to dry at the same time?"

The woman made a face. "Well, that seems far-fetched."

Bennie waved a hand and turned forward. He was next in line.

Lyral and Nic were sitting side by side in a far corner of the reception hall. Nic pointed. "You're back on the screens."

The other woman looked up from her wristcomm, still getting used to the user interface on this new model. "Oh, lovely."

The reception hall was a maze of seating clusters, with a few convenience stalls scattered around the perimeter between arched access tunnels to the boarding platforms at the rear of the building.

The early days of colonization on Preyn had been a time of rapid expansion. Everyone was scrambling to start up their town or outpost. Getting between settlements had been a necessity almost from the start. The Preyn mag-lev system, it turned out, was quite nice, despite its age. Given how deeply engrained organized crime seemed to be in Multonae society, Bennie had boarded with low expectations. It turned out that being a necessity of life at the outset of the colony kept it crime and corruption free.

Bennie was sound asleep, sprawled out across two seats when his wristcomm vibrated, waking him. Wiping drool from his mouth, he squinted at the small screen. The train was silently gliding along its rail. The view outside was pitch black.

Across from him, Lyral was snoring gently, lying across two seats of her own. Nic was curled into a fur- and overalls-covered ball on the floor between the two sets of seats.

The wristcomm vibrated again. Bennie sat up. He tapped the ACCEPT and whispered, "Wait one."

The public refresher was at the end of the car. He stepped inside, looked around to ensure no one was already there. He raised his arm. "What's up?"

Wil's smiling face looked back at him. "Hey, green dickhead. Max and Gabe said you might've gotten in over your head. I mean, you're short, so that wouldn't be hard."

Wil ran a hand through his light brown hair, turning to look off screen. "No, he's alive."

Bennie scowled. "Hey, Krebnack, did you call for a reason or just to wake me up?"

Wil turned his attention back to Bennie. "We're back on Fury. I thought I'd see if you needed us to bail you out."

Bennie made a face. "Drennog. I got this. I'm not helpless, you know." The door to the refresher opened. Bennie turned. "Get out!"

"These are public freshers," a woman replied.

"I ate Ruknak meal sticks for lunch. You do not want to be in here!"

From the wristcomm, Wil shouted, "He's right. It's foul! Save yourself!"

The door slid closed as the woman on the other side swore up a storm.

Bennie turned his attention back to Wil. "I'm not in over my head. I can do this."

Wil nodded once. "Okay, well, we're taking a transport job to Arcadia, and picking up Gabe, so if you need anything, you know where to find us."

Bennie nodded. "I do. Good luck out there."

Wil tilted his head. "You, too." The screen went black.

Bennie sighed and went back to his seat. According to the information display mounted on the wall between his and Lyral's seats, the train would arrive in Nemik in four more tocks, just after local sunrise. He fished around in the small bag on the ground to find a PADD and opened one of the texts that C7K2 had given him on the Knights of Plentallus apprentice program. He and Nic hadn't had much time to work on her training the last few days. He figured he'd brush up on it for when time was available.

When Nic and Lyral woke, they found a small breakfast feast on a foldout table. Nic looked at Bennie. "This is uncharacteristically nice of you." She reached for a pastry cautiously, worried the meal was a trap.

He smirked. "You know nothing, Jon Snow."

Crunching the pastry loudly, she asked, "Who's Jon Snow?"

Bennie waved a hand. "Next time I go off on my own, I'm taking a copy of Wil's archive." He pointed out the window. "We're half a tock from Nemik. Better eat up and get cleaned up."

Nic snatched one more pastry from the small tray and trotted off toward the public facilities.

Lyral eyed Bennie while munching on her own pastry. "What do you get out of this?"

"A tax write-off."

She made a face. "I mean helping me."

"You haven't seen my invoice."

She shook her head. "I'm serious."

Bennie shrugged. "Nothing. The Knights of Plentallus help when and where needed. It's our creed. Literally, it's written on the wall in the Tower."

She tilted her head. "Aren't you the only one?"

"Currently, but we're accepting applications." He grabbed a little morsel, a pastry wrapped around a bit of seasoned meat. "Might have to grab a few more of these before we get off the train."

The woman sat in silence for a beat, absently chewing her pastry. Finally, she said, "Thank you."

Bennie blinked, wiping his mouth on the back of his hand. "What?"

"You're all I have now. With that fat twirp Dardle selling me out, the only hope I have of clearing my name is getting to the data broker, getting the data, and," she ran her fingers through her hair, tying it back up into a ponytail with the loose bit of wire she had grabbed when they crashed, "I don't know. What do we do after we find the broker?"

Bennie shrugged. "I thought you knew."

CHAPTER 14

THE MAG-LEV TRAIN slid soundlessly into the station. From the look of it, only one other line came or went from the station.

Bennie looked up from his wristcomm. "The spaceport is on the opposite side of town. The message from the repair place said we could pick up the ship tonight."

"So, what do we do until then?" Nic asked.

The train shook once, lowering to the parking rail. Outside the window, station personnel were bustling back and forth, removing luggage from storage units under the train cars.

"Come on," Bennie said.

The three of them stepped off the train. A few hundred, mostly Multonae, were milling around the platform, waiting for luggage or meeting people getting off the train. Bennie led the group into the station.

The mag-lev station was smaller than its sibling in Oudal. There were only two food stalls along the west wall, public refreshers on the opposite wall.

Near the exit was a large display with a map of Nemik. Nic pointed. "There's a park. We could hang out there. Catch a cab to the spaceport."

Lyral looked at the pair. "I could use a breather, Ben-Ari."

He frowned. "We just had a breather on the train."

Nic looked at him, then at the Multonae woman. "We slept. Besides, you have someplace to be? I mean, there won't be any newscasts in the park."

He rubbed his chin. "Good point. Let's go."

Nic turned to Lyral, small hand held up for a high-four. The other woman smiled and planted her fist into the open palm.

Bennie barked a laugh. "You'll get the hang of it. It took me a few tries to get it right."

Lyral lowered her hand. "What did I do wrong?"

Nic chuckled and exited the train station ahead of the other two.

The walk to the park was pleasant. The sun was just becoming visible, having navigated the dance of rising on Multon. Multon and Preyn were moving so that the moon got its sunrise.

The town was still mostly asleep. Few vehicles were on the road, and fewer people were out walking around. No one seemed to notice a Multonae, a Brailack, and an Olop walking through town.

The park was immaculate, several square ploriths of lush lawn and trees. A definite upside of older colonies, mature trees. Bennie spied a few families having breakfast here and there. A running group tromped past on a running trail.

He pointed to a stand of trees that didn't appear to have anyone near it. The women nodded and followed his lead.

Nic dropped down to lean against a large tree trunk, Lyral doing the same. Bennie looked at his young apprentice. "What're you doing?"

"Sitting. What's it look like? Are you having a stroke?" Nic retorted.

Bennie made a face. "I reviewed some of the docs C_7K_2

sent." He swiped on his wristcomm, causing hers to beep at the incoming file. "New forms to practice." He looked around. "Too risky to use your beam saber." He trotted over to a smaller tree and looked it over. One more quick glance around and he snapped his saber to life, sliced off a branch, and had his saber back on his belt. "Here." He offered Nic the branch. It was roughly the same length as her saber, and mostly straight.

Lyral watched the two work through what, to her, seemed like martial arts forms. How her life of quiet morning tea—looking over the latest results from her algorithm's deep dives into databases and archives around the globe—changed to running for her life from gangsters and wearing a scratchy jumper, was beyond her.

She sighed and watched her saviors bicker about something she didn't have enough interest in paying attention to. She closed her eyes.

The trio spent the entire day in the park. Since no one had thought to buy snacks at the train station, they were ecstatic when a hover van pulled alongside the park, selling sandwiches and something called drosh that Lyral assured them was delicious.

The hover cab dropped them off outside the spaceport as the evening was approaching. Multon, large in the sky, was moving to block the sun. Bennie figured they had another tock of daylight at most.

The Nemik spaceport wasn't a multistory ring like most spaceports; instead, it was shaped like a large gear. The outbuildings all had massive hangar doors leading into the central landing area.

Most spaceports had a single central corridor with commercial spaces on either side. Someone could walk the entire circumference of a spaceport like a shopping mall. Often, the customs area was the only break in that pattern, usually serving as the main entry for the spaceport. With its unique gear-shaped design, all the shopping was on the top floor of this port, which provided a fantastic view of the interior and exterior.

Bennie looked at the directory just inside the massive double doors. "There." He pointed to a spot about a third of the way around the perimeter of the port.

"Should we go through customs here or...?" Lyral asked.

Bennie shook his head. "We ain't doin' that. Will leave a trail."

Lyral was about to ask for clarification, but then decided against it, shrugging instead. "Lead the way." There was a bank of lifts on both sides of the open reception area, allowing access to the shopping level.

"This is one of the weirdest spaceports I've ever been to," Bennie said as they passed a staircase that led down to whatever engineering firm was in the tooth of the gear below them. They had passed a half dozen similar doors.

They found the door they were looking for and descended back to the ground level. Motto and Associates Shipwrights had an impressive sounding name. The reality did not match the marketing, as far as Bennie was concerned. The stairwell exited into the small lobby. Opening the door, they came face to face with a gaggle of diminutive repair droids. Bennie wasn't familiar with their design: saucer-shaped heads with a single bulbous optical sensor. Two of the small units turned, their optical sensors spinning, moving various lenses into and out of position. They jabbered to each other in a dialect Bennie couldn't parse.

Bennie approached the pair. "We're here to see the owner. Polly."

Two more droids joined the first two, and the pack of droids chirped to each other before turning as one, bowing, and exiting through the door that led to the workshop.

"That was weird," Lyral said. Nic bobbed her head in agreement.

Just when Bennie was beginning the think the droids had failed to notify their employer, the door slid open to admit a petite woman of middle years. Her leathery skin, browned by too much time in the sun, was stretched over a wiry frame.

"Hi," she said. "If you're here to buy the Star Rambler 3400, I need to wait two more days for the owner to no-show."

"I am the owner," Bennie said, frowning. She was already looking for buyers? Didn't Gabe already pay for the repairs?

The woman looked down at Bennie. "Well, aren't you just the cutest little thing?" Her gaze moved over to Nic, and she cooed, "Well, forget lizard guy, you're my favorite now!" She pushed Bennie to the side to kneel next to Nic, petting her head. Nic swatted at her, doing little to dissuade the petting.

"I'm not a lizard, you wrinkly old—" Bennie grumbled. He waved his arms to attract the shop owner's attention. "Guessing the ship is done, if you were already putting out feelers for buyers."

"What? Oh that. That's nothing, don't you worry. Your ship was perfectly safe with me. And yes, it's as repaired as it's gonna get." She gestured for the party to follow her out into the work area.

The Motto and Associates space was larger than Bennie expected. Stopping just below the shopping level of the ring wall, racks of parts and even a few partial ships lined the rear and far walls. The space was wide enough to house at least two ships the size of *Bibby's Folly*. Polly Motto was doing well for herself, it seemed.

"Oh, wow," Nic said, taking in the cavernous space.

The *Folly* was not just repaired but improved. There was a small blaster turret on the top of the ship, accessed through the common area, Bennie assumed. The stubby wings that housed the sub-light engines now sported pods at the ends, presumably for missiles, though they were currently empty. The damaged cargo doors were like new, and the forward windscreen was replaced.

Polly said, "See, good as mostly new."

Bennie nodded. "This will work."

Entering the cargo hold, the trio followed the shipwright aft as she showed them the improvements she and her droids had made to the small med bay. After looking through the engineering space, they headed for the access ladder that led to the upper deck. When they reached the ladder, Bennie stopped short. It wasn't a ladder anymore, at least not solely. There was a small platform attached to the side rails.

Polly stepped onto the platform. "Ladders. Accessibility nightmares." She waved as the platform rose. Bennie and the women followed her up one at a time, leaving the beeping and bopping droids in the hold to entertain themselves.

The tour of the refurbished *Folly* ended on the bridge. Bennie beamed when he saw that the seats at both stations had adjustments for smaller operators. The large transparent hull panel at the front had been replaced and looked a bit more modern. Bennie noticed data projectors along the four edges.

"So, what do you think?" She held both arms out to take in the bridge and the ship as a whole.

"Good work," Bennie offered, tapping a few controls on the

main console. The ship booted up and ran through a diagnostic that displayed as an overlay on the forward window. Everything seemed to be online and working.

He turned. "Really good work."

She grinned. "Not cheap work, either." She rubbed her fingers together.

Lyral leaned into the hatchway. "The bunk room is even clean. New sheets."

Back down in the cargo hold, Bennie turned to the ship repairwoman. "One last thing. We need to leave from here. Not through customs."

The diminutive, weathered woman rubbed her chin theatrically. "Ten thousand. Each."

Bennie barked a laugh. "Two, for all of us."

"Two, per."

"One, per."

"Deal." The woman leaned down and offered her arm. Bennie reached up and grasped her forearm as she grasped his.

Two tocks later, after ordering and waiting for delivery of foodstuffs and other supplies, the *Bibby's Folly*, now operating under the transponder of *Rocky Nontee* was loaded and ready for takeoff.

"What's that mean? Rocky Nontee?" Lyral asked as the port and starboard cargo doors slid closed. Nic, standing next to her, waved at the small repair droids gathered outside. They waved back.

Bennie shrugged. "It's from a show my friend Wil really likes. It was the ship that the heroes flew in." The other woman shrugged. Bennie headed for the access lift to the upper deck. "I'm going to get us underway. Get situated."

As the small platform rose, Bennie smiled to himself. He had a ship, and it didn't completely suck. Now he just had to not crash it again. He would never admit it, but he now understood how Wil felt about the *Ghost*.

Polly Motto had been true to her word. The *Rocky Nontee* glided out of the repair bay into the spaceport landing area, cleared for departure under the ship's new name.

A few rough twists, turns, and bumps later, the *Rocky Nontee*, a nondescript Star Rambler 3400, was leaving the atmosphere of Preyn. Bennie tapped the intercom. "We're clear of the atmosphere. FTL in half a tock."

He leaned back, watching the stars through the sloped transparent section of hull. It was weird to be aboard a ship with windows. Not just the huge one at the front of the small bridge, but the *Nontee* had a few narrow windows that ran the length of the common deck. Wil's ship, the *Ghost,* didn't have a single window anywhere on it. He guessed that was par for the course with warships. Until now, he hadn't given it much thought. He kinda enjoyed having windows. Especially ones that doubled as a display. He had configured the heads-up display to show power levels, shields, navigation details and other vital pieces of information on the transparent surface in the hopes it would make flying the ship easier.

Walking into the common area, he spied Nic lying on the sofa holding a PADD before her. "Where's Lyral?"

"Data Lady is in the fresher." Nic didn't look from the tablet device.

"What're you doing?"

"Reading."

Bennie looked at his wristcomm, tapped a few icons. "No, you're not. You're playing a game."

"You hacked into my PADD?"

"Technically, it's my PADD." He shrugged. "Let's work on your forms."

Nic was on the deck trotting toward Bennie before the

PADD landed on the sofa. "Won't it be dangerous to use our sabers in the ship?"

They rode the small lift platform to the cargo deck. Even having stocked up on some supplies, the hold was mostly empty. Bennie gestured to the middle of the space. "Yeah, we're definitely not using beam sabers. At least you aren't." He pointed to something leaning against the bulkhead near the med bay. A mostly straight, thin piece of metal tubing.

Nic looked at it. "Where did you get that?" She picked it up, swinging it in slow arcs. It had good weight to it, compared to the branch from the park.

"Found it in a waste pile at Polly's. Figured it would work well enough. Better than a tree branch." He pointed at the floor. "Get going."

Nic nodded, affecting as serious an expression as she could. Slowly at first, then with more speed and confidence, she worked through the training forms that Bennie had shown her.

The *Rocky Nontee* dropped from FTL near the outer orbit of the Apennul system. Bennie was pretty pleased with himself. The ship didn't even rattle once, and it hadn't exploded.

"*Rocky Nontee*, welcome to Apennul system. Please state your destination."

Bennie looked over his shoulder. "Hey! Where am I going?"

Lyral appeared in the hatchway. "I don't know."

Bennie's jaw fell open. "What do you mean, you don't know?"

"I thought we'd make contact once we were here."

Bennie opened his mouth to say something, stopped, then said, "Well, we're here." He turned back to his console.

"Apennul space control, we're inbound to Tro Ella. I don't know where yet."

"*Rocky Nontee,* maintain current course and speed. You'll need to file a landing permit, so figure it out before you get here."

"Uh, yeah, okay." He turned back to Lyral. "Okay, how do we get ahold of your data guy?"

She moved to the auxiliary console, eyeing the myriad displays and controls. "Ah." She sat down and began typing. Bennie was about to ask what was taking so long when she said, "Okay, he's in the capital, Vablim. He agreed to meet me there and give me the access codes for the data center."

Bennie called in the flight plan and filed the landing permit. They received clearance to land in Vablim Spaceport 2.

Tro Ella was an industrialized world. The Trollack were longstanding Galactic Commonwealth members. Like most planets in the galaxy, it boasted what many considered to be the galactic standard atmosphere and physical makeup: scattered mountain ranges, a good-sized ocean, crop-bearing plains. Most of the landmass was marshland and shallow lakes. Almost one hundred percent of the population lived in the marshlands.

Despite the type of land available, the Trollack had built hundreds of massive cities. Vast sprawling forests of metal and glass dotted the landscape, built on thick pilings driven deep into the marshes.

As they neared the planet, space traffic increased. Thousands of ships of all sizes were coming and going. Tro Ella had a single airless moon. The Trollack never colonized it, so they covered it in shipping and storage facilities. It served as a way station for inter- and intra-system commerce. The low gravity made it an excellent place to stage goods. Signs and advertisements were visible from hundreds of ploriths away, luring freight haulers and others to the various storage facilities and other cargo-related service providers.

Bennie was ogling the fields of storage modules when his console started making a noise he hadn't heard before. By the time he found the blinking indicator and glanced back up through the wide transparent window, an enormous bulk freighter was lumbering into his flight path, surrounded by blinking red brackets.

"Dren!" he hissed, pushing the flight controls to take the *Rocky Nontee* into a dive that immediately put him on a collision course with what looked like an intra-system mass transit shuttle. "Grolack!" He pulled the controls over while grasping frantically for the throttle.

"*Rocky Nontee,* do you require flight assistance? You're... flying a bit erratically," the overhead speaker said.

Bennie looked around, cursing that shipwright for reactivating the auto accept on the communications suite. He flipped it back off, then opened the channel. "No, I'm okay. Sorry about that. Everything is fine here. How are you?" He grimaced, remembering that movie Wil made him watch that had an exchange like the one he'd just had.

"Okay, but try to not collide with anyone else, or we'll have to force the issue."

"Understood." He slapped the control, closing the channel.

Nic appeared in the hatchway. "Are we under attack?"

Bennie repeated the question in a nasal whine, then looked over his shoulder. "No."

The young girl approached the auxiliary station and pressed a control on the seat. With the faintest hydraulic hiss, it lowered to a more comfortable height for her. Once seated, the chair rose back into position.

The two sat in more or less companionable silence for a bit until Nic said, "So..."

Bennie didn't turn. "So…"

Before Nic could say more, the heads-up display information on the forward window came to life. Bennie hoped he stifled the yip he felt come out when it did.

The *Rocky Nontee* was next in the queue to enter the atmosphere.

"Vablim Spaceport 2, here we come," Bennie said to no one in particular before tightening his flight harness.

CHAPTER 15

THE *ROCKY NONTEE* sailed through the upper atmosphere. During the transit, when the two women were asleep, Bennie had been sneaking to the bridge to run flight simulations. When the indicator on his console blinked to life, he deftly cut over from sub-light engines to atmospheric. The ship made the slightest stutter but otherwise continued along.

"Well done, Old-Timer," Nic quipped from her station.

"Don't make me take your beam saber away."

"You wouldn't."

"Try me."

"You're mean."

"Yes. Hold on." He angled the ship around, bringing into view what Nic assumed was Vablim. The city was easily as big as any she'd seen elsewhere. The outer suburbs spanned several ploriths in all directions, broken only by the three spaceports that surrounded the city core equidistantly. The overall design resembled a cluster of floating plants, massive ploriths-wide circles, connected by large roads and bridges.

From that distance, it was hard to see that most of the city and surrounding suburbs were sitting on massive pilings overtop the marshland. In many places where a road might be expected, the buildings parted with ramps and stairs down to the wetland below. Many Trollack still preferred to get around by swimming through the murky shallows that their cities were built atop.

"Does everything just float on the swamp?" Nic asked.

Bennie shrugged. "I've only been here once. If I recall, they drive thick pilings into the swamp until they hit bedrock. They like the marshes so wanted to keep them accessible. Each circle is held up by a few dozen pilings."

"Isn't it dark?" She hugged herself, thinking of dank swamps cut off from sunlight.

"You know? I don't know. I didn't go anywhere near them. Too gross."

Lyral came in, bracing herself in the hatchway. "This thing needs more seating."

"Or fewer guests," Bennie quipped.

Lyral clucked. "I've never been to Tro Ella. I thought it'd be more...I don't know, swampy."

"It's pretty swampy," Nic said.

Through the transparent forward window, they could see the spaceport growing as they neared.

As much as he had gotten the hang of flying the lumbering *Rocky Nontee*, landing was a different matter. The blocky ship tilted and dipped as he tried to guide it toward the illuminated landing area that the ship was assigned.

"You're going to miss it," Lyral said.

"No, I'm not, shut up," Bennie growled.

A display on his console showed a camera view from under the bridge. When he saw the boundary of their landing pad appear while they were still several plor above the duracrete, he killed the repulsor lifts. The ship fell to the ground with a bone-jarring clank.

To his surprise, the icons for all four landing gear flashed yellow, then settled to green.

Bennie turned in his seat. "See." The ship rocked, causing him to clutch the edge of the seat to keep from falling. One light on the landing gear panel flashed red. While everyone watched, the indicator blinked yellow, then settled back to green.

The port cargo doors opened, and Nic and Lyral both took a step back. Bennie looked at them, grinning.

Nic put a hand to her small nose. "It's sew gwoss."

"What did you think swamps smelled like?" He motioned for them to follow. "Come on. There's probably gonna be a line at customs."

There was indeed a line at customs. While the trio was waiting their turn, Lyral looked down at Nic, who was playing a game on a tablet. "So, what's your story?"

The young Olop looked up. "What do you mean?"

The scientist shrugged. "Well, from what I understand from Ben-Ari, he's trying to put together this Knights organization. Hence the getup and the laser sword." She pointed from Bennie to Nic. "But you. He doesn't seem to like you. You just got your first laser sword the other day."

In front of them, Bennie said, "She showed up on my doorstep, like some dingy little street urchin."

Nic made a rude gesture at his back. "Cranky Grandpa doesn't like anyone." Bennie made a noise. Nic continued, "I really didn't have anywhere else to go. Gram died—"

Bennie spun around. "You said she signed the permission slip you made up."

Nic frowned. "I was embarrassed that I didn't have any other place to go. I wanted you to take me in because you wanted to. If you knew I was an orphan you would have taken me in out of pity."

"I didn't want to take you in," Bennie replied. "My friends

made me. I don't care if you're an orphan." The Trollack woman in front of him stepped forward. He followed.

Nic made a noise like a cough, looking back to Lyral. "Anyway. Mom and Dad died a cycle ago on Olopnal and left me with Gram. Then she died." She pointed at the Brailack in front of them. "He was the only other person I knew, so I looked him up. I knew he was a Knight of Plentallus because he saved Gram and me from pirates."

Lyral raised an eyebrow at that. "Really?" She found it hard to believe the acerbic Brailack was the "save women and children from pirates" type.

Bennie didn't turn around but said, "My friend and I had a job to get to. The pirates were a delay. It wasn't personal."

That sounded more like the Ben-Ari that Lyral had gotten to know over the last few days.

Tro Ella customs, thankfully, wasn't very hard to get through. Most GC member worlds had pretty open borders to beings from other member worlds.

The trio exited the spaceport into the pedestrian traffic, making its way to the transit hub and waiting taxis and buses just beyond the port.

Lyral cleared her throat. "We're going to go shopping."

"Sorry, what?" Bennie asked.

The taller woman leaned down. "I think she might need someone to talk to. That isn't you. You know, get away from all this for a bit."

Bennie's mouth fell open. "You're 'all this.' All this is because of you."

She waved away his complaint and glanced at the young girl. "We'll catch up with you." She looked at her wristcomm.

"Here's everything I have on the data broker we hired and where he wants to meet up. There's plenty of time."

Bennie chewed his lip. "I could use some time without my furry hanger-on," he agreed.

"Delicately put." The Multonae woman guided Nic toward the bus that advertised a stop at a shopping district.

Bennie watched them go, then turned toward the line of waiting hover cabs. Reaching one, he hopped in, telling the droid control system, "Til Tik Tik Park." The vehicle beeped an acknowledgement and pulled out of the line before it sped off.

Sitting in the back of the vehicle, Bennie watched the landscape roll by. The platform that the spaceport was on receded, giving way to marshland. The cab didn't need to use the bridge that connected the spaceport platform to the nearest city platform. Tall purple-hued reeds reaching almost two meters tall swayed with the breeze. Winged reptilian creatures leaped into the sky to glide between the reeds. Occasionally, a large furry thing would leap into the air to snag a winged snack. Bennie was a little surprised that nature was so close to the city, but then again, the city sat on stilts above the marshes. Nature was everywhere. He wondered if any of the older original cities existed anymore.

This was the first time in...longer than he could remember... that he'd been free of his would-be apprentice. Or his friends back on Fury, for that matter. He hated to admit it, but he was growing kind of fond of the furry little annoyance.

He wasn't sure it was the best idea to help her build a beam saber. According to the histories he had read, the order did not give apprentices beam sabers for several cycles. Given the situation, he figured it was the safest play, one more armed person to help protect the data scientist. He hoped she didn't cut off her arm.

His wristcomm beeped. It was C7K2. He rolled his eyes.

Was that felgercarb droid psychic? He tapped the icon, accepting the call. "What's up?"

"Greetings, Sir Knight. A great many things are considered up. Depending on relative position, planetary suns are up. Inbound ships are—" Unlike Gabe, C7 was sitting in the Tower's communication room, looking at a camera.

Bennie clucked. "It means, what do you need?"

The droid tilted its head. "Ah. I am glad you are not dead. How is your training mission going?"

"Oh, you know."

The droid made a clicking noise. "Ah, that badly?"

Bennie nodded. "I haven't had as much time as I'd hoped to actually, you know, train her. We kinda got ourselves into the middle of some criminal stuff."

"Criminal stuff," the droid repeated, the doubt clear in its tone. Bennie nodded. "Do you require any assistance?"

Bennie looked out the window. The cab had moved back over built-up city platforms, leaving the marsh behind. It was gliding along a roadway. He sighed. "No. I think we're good. We're on Tro Ella and should be done soon." He brightened. "Upside of all this: it'll make an excellent adventure for us to advertise. No killing of innocents or destruction of property... Well, only a little."

"'Not much killing or destruction.' I am not sure that has the message you are hoping for."

"Fine. Whatever." The cab beeped. "I gotta go." He closed the comm.

Til Tik Tik Park was not what Bennie expected, but in hindsight, he should have. The several ploriths-wide park was an archipelago of islands surrounded by low-lying swampland. Ornate wood carved bridges connected each island to at least one other. The entire park was a maze of interconnected islands and ramps down into the marsh.

The purple reeds he had seen before were everywhere here, surrounding each island in a veritable wall of purple.

According to the data Lyral had given him, the broker wanted to meet on Island 42. He made a slow circuit through the park, stopping at several islands before arriving at 42. He found a bench and took a seat.

The bus rose from the ground and left the transit terminal. The auto drive system announced the first stop, then fell silent.

Nic looked up at the Multonae woman next to her. "You're not trying to abduct me, right?" She fingered the hilt of her small beam saber.

Lyral laughed. "No. I just thought maybe you'd like some time away from Ben-Ari. To, you know, talk. Just us girls, as it were."

"About what?"

"About whatever you feel like." The other woman shrugged. "This has been quite the adventure, and none of us have really had much chance to calm down, process what's happening."

"Fun, right?" Nic beamed, her fur rippling as her small ears twitched.

Lyral looked out the window. The hover bus was currently gliding over a marshland of purple reeds and small, damp-looking islands. "Fun isn't how I'd put it. What was it like? With your grandmother? She raised you on Olopnal?"

Nic's head bopped as she looked out the window. "Yeah... Mom and Dad and I lived in Dae. They were structural engineers. They had an assignment off-world, so they left me with Gram. I never saw them again." She made an ugly snuffle sound as she wiped a hand across her nose.

Lyral nodded once. "I'm sorry."

The small girl's shoulders hunched. "It's okay. It's fine."

Lyral smiled. "I lost my parents. Later in life than you did, but they were in a shuttle that crashed. Everyone aboard died."

The small girl looked up at her, resting a hand on her knee. "I'm sorry."

Lyral grunted a laugh, looking at Nic's small hand. "Thanks. You know, I've not met many Olop before. I had heard your people tended to be...blunt."

Nic nodded. "Yeah, Olopnal has a fast rotational period. My people are industrious, getting as much done as anyone, in a day that's thirty percent shorter than most planets'days." She shrugged. "No time for small talk or, well, most common social niceties. Some folks don't like it." She grinned. "We're an acquired taste."

Lyral grinned.

The bus arrived at a three-story neon-lit shopping center.

"Wow," Nic said.

The building had glow tubing outlining its entire exterior, giving it a soft blue gleam, even in the daylight. Holo-signs filled the sky above the shopping center, advertising all manner of goods and services.

The pair meandered in companionable silence for a while. They looked at clothing stores, gift stores, a store that sold only sauces for foods, all of which made the both women's eyes water.

Sitting at a cafe table after buying a few pieces of clothing, Nic said, "Did you ever..." She looked down at her drink, a syrupy sweet thing with bits of small floating sugar balls bobbing around. "...Get picked on?"

Lyral stopped sipping her own drink, setting it down. "Yes." She waited until Nic looked up, making eye contact. "I was always smart, sometimes smarter than my classmates. It often made me different, which made me a target. Kids, at least

Multonae ones, don't take kindly to being different." She took a breath. "You?"

Nic's gaze fell back to her drink. She nodded. "I'm small."

Lyral cocked her head. "I mean, Olop aren't as tall as other—"

"No. Me. I'm short for an Olop. The kids teased me."

Lyral inhaled. "Ah."

"My parents said to ignore them." Lyral remained silent. "Easy for them to say. They were perfectly average Olops." She reached up to touch the streak of dyed fur on her head. "They didn't stand out or cause any disturbances."

Lyral looked around, realizing that maybe, just maybe, she had bitten off more than she planned.

Nic inhaled. "Well, whatever. Gram taught me to fight and not give a grolack." The other woman's eyes went wide at the expletive. "Now I'm a Knight of Plentallus, with my own laser sword."

Lyral could see the pride swelling in the young girl. "It means a lot to you, being a Knight like Ben-Ari? Being able to take care of yourself?"

Nic nodded.

They resumed their slow progression from shop to shop.

Lyral's wristcomm beeped. Looking at it, she sighed. "I guess we should get going."

Nic was bobbing from foot to foot, both hands clutching shopping bags. "Okay."

"A park, at night," Bennie complained.

"Technically, it's barely dusk," Lyral corrected, pointing at the sky and the sun still visible on the horizon.

"Whatever." He turned to Nic. "I want you to watch our backs."

Nic's grin might have broken her face. She clapped as she bounced up and down.

Bennie patted the air between them. "Calm down. I just need extra eyes." He pointed to an island near their destination, not directly connected by a bridge, but only one island away. "That tree—get up and keep an eye out."

Grinning, she nodded and trotted off over the bridge that would get her to the island Bennie pointed to.

He looked at Lyral. "You good?"

She nodded. "Of course. I can do this."

Bennie squinted. "Was that for me, or you?"

"Yes." She nodded and strode toward Island 42.

Bennie smiled and followed her. That late in the afternoon, the park wasn't very busy and the island they were meeting the broker on was empty. The pair sat down on a bench, looking out at several other islands and marshland beyond.

Bennie was kicking his feet, since they didn't reach the ground. "So...how'd it go with Nic?"

Lyral looked down at her erstwhile protector. "Oh, it went fine. She's a lovely girl. If you gave her a chance."

"I'm not trying to date her," Bennie replied.

"Don't be gross," she scolded, then said, "You're all she has. I don't know if you grasp that."

Bennie shifted. "I didn't sign up for fostering. I'm not a parent or a teacher."

"Well, that much is obvious." She turned. "She's young. Impressionable. She's conflicted about the death that seems to suddenly be all around her."

Bennie groaned. "Okay, well, we can work on reducing the killing."

The taller woman chuckled. "A few days ago, that statement

would have concerned me. Now, the fact that it doesn't, bothers me." She shrugged. "Well, figure it out. She's committed to," she gestured to his beam saber hilt, "whatever it is you're all about. It's all she wants. A chance to show you, and I think a lot of others, that she can do it. That she's tough."

Bennie opened his mouth, closed it, opened it again, then shook his head. He caught sight of a shadowy figure on the next island over. The figure was clearly a Trollack, based on its size and unique shuffle-walk that they all did. "Look."

"Is that him?" Lyral asked.

Bennie turned. "How the wurrin would I know?"

She shrugged. "Well, fair." She squinted into the waning daylight, then looked at Bennie and shrugged again.

The mysterious figure crossed the bridge and approached the pair. It was hard for Bennie to keep a straight face. The Trollack man before them was in an oversized trench coat with a scarf wrapped around his thick neck. The back of the coat was twitching. No doubt the man's stubby fishlike tail was wagging frantically. His bulbous eyes were moving this way and that, independent of each other. "The weather has been pleasant lately."

Lyral sighed and mumbled, "I forgot about this part." She ran a hand through her hair. "Uh, yes...it's been lovely. I just wish we got more rain?"

The stocky being shifted from foot to foot, sighing. "Whatever. That's fine." He focused both eyes forward before shifting his gaze to both sides.

"What's your problem?" Bennie asked.

Lyral ignored him, focusing on the man before them. "You have what I need?"

The Trollack man shifted again. One of his eyes seemed intent on not meeting Lyral's gaze. "Well..."

Lyral frowned. "Well, what?"

"It's going to cost you."

"Cost us?" Bennie said.

"We have already paid you," Lyral said. "Mayor Dardle on Multon paid your invoice for this cycle. You know full well it was for a full cycle of data processing support and storage. A cycle that hasn't ended yet."

The data broker rubbed the back of his scaly purple neck, transparent eyelids blinking rapidly. "Right, right. If you want the data, though, you have to pay more than he paid to keep it from you."

"He who?" Bennie leaned forward. "You spoke to Mayor Fat Ass? When?" He looked around. The sun was kissing the horizon now, and shadows were stretching out toward them.

The data broker's eyes twitched in every direction. "I have to go."

Bennie leaped from the bench, snatching the man's arm. "Oh, no you don't." The other man immediately began flapping his free arm while making a wet gurgling noise.

Lyral was on her feet. "What are you doing?"

Bennie glanced over. "This stubby-tailed grolack sold us out. The mayor and his syndicate friends got to him. A team is probably on the way." He looked at the Trollack. "Yeah?" The other man's head bobbed. Bennie nodded and grasped the flailing arm by the wristcomm. A few deft twists and touches caused the device to release and slide from the broker's arm.

Pushing the Trollack man back, Bennie looked at the device. "What we need is on this."

"No, it isn't!" protested the data broker from the ground where he fell.

Bennie made a rude noise. "I know your type. This thing is encrypted and full to capacity with your keys and storage locations." The other man's purple scales shifted to a deep maroon.

"Yeah..." Bennie turned, slipping the purloined device over his other forearm, locking it in place.

Lyral kicked at the fallen man. "You little squeeblit. Why would you work for the syndicate?"

"Money," the other man croaked, getting to his feet and scrambling toward the bridge. He waddled over the bridge out of site.

"You have friends coming," Nic said over Bennie's and Lyral's wristcomms.

CHAPTER 16

BENNIE HISSED. "HOW MANY?"

"Mmmm...six, I think?" Nic replied from her perch in a tree on the nearby island.

"You think?"

"Yes—wait. Two more. Okay, eight. Definitely eight," the young apprentice said.

Bennie looked at Lyral. "Come on!" He motioned toward the bridge. Island 42 had only one bridge accessing it, but the next island had three bridges.

Halfway across the bridge, Bennie heard the first shouts. He shoved Lyral forward, telling her to head for Nic, as he grabbed his beam saber. He stopped just short of the end of the bridge.

He closed his eyes, straining to hear as much as he could. He concentrated, applying what he heard to the mental map he had created earlier in the day and added to as they walked through the park to the meeting.

He darted to the end of the bridge and crept to the bridge that led to Island 39. He crouched next to the bridge, listening. Two pairs of footsteps thundered over the bridge. "They should be over there," a voice said.

When the footsteps reached the end of the bridge, Bennie ignited his beam saber, bathing the area beneath the bridge in an eerie purple glow. He sliced through the bridge, its railing, and a pair of legs with ease. The luckier of the two gangsters jumped backward a split second ahead of Bennie's blade, landing close to the bridge's high point.

When the loose end of the bridge crashed into the swamp, Bennie vaulted over the railing, his saber hilt pointed at the startled man. The startled gangster raised his pistol a fraction of a millitock slower than Bennie could press the activation lever, firing a single purple bolt. It caught the man in the shoulder, spinning him.

Bennie ran past the fallen man, firing one more shot into him, eliciting a groan. He continued on toward the other voices.

He looked at his wristcomm. "Nic, you okay?" No answer.

Nic watched Lyral and Bennie split up. Lyral was crossing to Nic's island from one bridge while two men were approaching from another. The bad guys hadn't seen Lyral yet, but they would soon enough. The pulse pistols in their hands made their intent pretty clear.

In that moment, Nic decided. She leapt from the tree. Olop were arboreal, though usually the distances jumped were a plor or two. They rarely dove onto things from four plor up. Midflight, she realized she should have spent a millitock or two doing some math. She was rapidly approaching the ground, likely to land just short of where the two men would be.

One goon spotted Lyral, tapping his friend's arm. They increased their pace, pistols up at the ready. Their quickened rate closed the gap between where they were and where Nic was about to land. The sound of Nic's beam saber activating would have alerted her targets, but since it failed to activate when she flicked the activation switch, surprise was on her side.

One of the men looked up a moment before she landed. His

horrified shriek was cut short and replaced by screams of the
agony type, as she landed on his shoulders and immediately bit
and clawed at him, using her malfunctioning beam saber hilt as
a bludgeon to bash his head.

The other man turned, a look of horror crossing his face.
The repeated bashing on her opponent's head seemed to have
knocked something into alignment inside her beam saber hilt.
The man raised his pistol just as Nic's beam saber sprang to life
in her hand. She didn't hesitate, swinging the weapon in a wide
arc that separated the other man from his gun arm at the elbow.

Nic closed her eyes and swung her crimson blade down into
the man beneath her. He made a wet gurgling noise, then
collapsed under her.

"You little flobin!" the wounded man shouted, reaching for
his pistol with his remaining hand. Before he could reach the
weapon, a thud and a crack echoed through the park. The man
fell to the ground. Lyral, standing over him, dropped a soggy-
looking—now broken in two—

log.

"Thanks," Nic huffed. She flipped the switch on her beam
saber. The blade flickered, then disengaged. She shrugged.
"Version 1."

"We should go," the taller woman urged. She spotted the
faint glow of a purple laser sword two islands over. Several pulse
blasts lanced out into the early evening gloom.

Nic led them across a bridge toward an island she had seen
from her tree. She had killed those pirates back in their base
when she'd first met Bennie, but that was more instinct. This
time, she'd attacked. Was she no better than those Knights she'd
seen in the archives? She was acting to protect Data Lady. That
felt like a good thing.

Bennie dropped into a roll as a pair of Multonae came at him. His last two victims were squirming on the ground behind him. Well, one was. He thought the other might be dead. The two in front of him saw their comrades fall and were ready. Pulse blasts shredded the wood of the bridge that Bennie ducked behind.

"Dren, dren, dren!" he hissed, darting out from behind the remains of the bridge. With a loud crack, the near section came free of its base and slid into the swamp. Short of a leap he didn't think he could make, that route was now closed.

"The obstacle is the way." He whispered to himself a mantra that the Knights of Plentallus used when facing difficulty. In the blaze of weapons' fire and darkness all around, the two men had lost track of him. He inched his way backward into the marsh. The slick muck oozed into his shoes with a *splurch* noise.

The two men spread out to search the small island. He sank deeper until only the top of his head was above the water, all but invisible in the darkness and reeds.

"Where is that little green krebnack?" the nearer of the two asked.

His friend shook his head. "Maybe we got him? He fell into the swamp?"

Bennie moved as slowly as he could around the island toward the sole remaining bridge. By his count, there should be only a few more.

"I'm not going in there to look," the first said.

"No need. We're here for the woman and the data. The greenie and the fuzzball aren't important." He waved toward the only other bridge on the island. "Come on."

They reached the bridge and started across. As the pair reached the apex of the bridge, a dark, slimy form crawled over the railing to land in front of them with a *splurt*. Before either man could raise their pistols, a purple energy blade sprang to life. Bennie slashed with practiced ease. Glowing gun barrels hit the bridge, followed by hands, then bodies.

Nic and Lyral could see the edge of the park, three islands away. They stopped dead in their tracks. Another pair of armed men were standing at the bridge that connected to the raised city level platform.

"I thought you said there were eight?" Lyral whispered.

"They didn't check in with me," Nic replied. The pair crouched in a clump of scrub at edge of the island, next to the bridge they'd just stepped off.

The Multonae woman looked down at her small friend. "Now what?"

Nic shrugged. "There's no way I can sneak up there."

Lyral stood. "I guess we have to bring them to you. Don't let me die, Little Knight." She waved. "Excuse me, are you two looking for me?" She didn't wait for the reply, turning to head back over the bridge she and Nic had just crossed.

The two men hustled down the bridge onto the island, pointing and shouting. One raised his arm, saying something into his wristcomm.

Nic crouched deeper into the shadows, her dark-colored apprentice garb blending with the blackness.

The two men rushed by, not even sparing a glance in her direction. She jumped out onto the gravel path. "Hey, you kreb-nacks. Stop!"

Both men skidded to a stop. The nearest, a heavyset man with pale skin, cocked his head. "Kid, what're you doing here?"

The other man elbowed the first. "Hey, I think that's the kid that was with the Brailack on Multon."

The other shrugged. "I dunno. She looks a bit young? Do you know what Olop look like when they're children?" He had blonde hair like Lyral, even in a ponytail like hers.

His partner shrugged. "Beats me."

The big man stepped forward. "Hey, little girl, where's your green friend?" He leaned down to reach for her.

"I'm not a kid." She bared her teeth and held out her beam saber hilt.

"What's this?" He reached for the metal cylinder.

"Mine!" She moved her hand away.

He snatched her arm in his. "Listen, you little dren..." he hissed, squeezing her arm.

"The scientist is getting away!" the other man said. "Get rid of her and let's go." He didn't wait for his friend, turning toward the bridge Lyral had taken.

The blonde-haired man reached for Nic's other hand, the one with her beam saber clutched in it. Without thinking, she moved her finger to the activation switch. For a second, nothing happened. Her eyes went wide. The man smirked and closed his much larger hand around hers.

Shaking her, he lifted her up off her feet, bringing her face close enough to his to smell his breath. It wasn't good. "You picked the wrong team, kid. I'll make his quick," he growled.

The beam of focused crimson energy lanced out, piercing his head. It would have surprised them both, but the big man was already dead. Nic yelped as she fell to the ground, the man's body falling atop her. She opened her eyes after hitting the ground to stare into her attacker's lifeless eyes, a cauterized hole where his nose had been a millitock ago. She struggled to free herself from the now very dead weight crushing her.

His friend on the bridge turned and released a distinctly non-intergalactic-gangster-sounding scream. He raised his pistol and opened fire indiscriminately, bolts striking the bridge railings and the body of his friend equally. The moment the weapons fire eased up, Nic rolled off the bridge into the swamp.

Pulse blasts tracked her, striking the bridge, splintering it into flaming debris before following her to the swamp, the water sizzling as bolts sought the submerged Olop girl. The man scanned the area frantically, firing a few more shots into the murky water.

After a moment, he gave up and turned to resume his pursuit of the scientist; she was the goal. Her and, if possible, whatever data she had access to. Where there had been an empty bridge before, there was now a grime-covered Brailack.

"Who sent you?" Bennie asked.

The other man's pistol only made it halfway around before a magenta energy blade sliced through the man's arm, severing it at the elbow. The gangster screamed, his free hand moving to clutch the burned stump of his other arm.

Over the man's sobs, Bennie said, "I can keep asking, but you're going to run out of things for me to cut off."

Lyral came up behind him, and Nic appeared behind the wounded gangster.

"You can't run from the Bol Naar syndicate. They'll send more teams." He looked past Bennie to Lyral. "You're on borrowed time, flobin—" Whatever other insults he had planned died in his throat as a beam of solid purple energy slid through his chest.

The body fell to the ground, faint wisps of smoke trailing from matching holes in the front and back.

Getting back to the *Rocky Nontee* proved easier than Bennie had feared. The men that had been at the edge of the park had the access codes to their rented hover van, codes Bennie easily lifted from the wristcomm of the dead man on the bridge.

Lyral drove them to the spaceport, while Bennie and Nic did their best to clean swamp gunk off themselves. It was a mostly losing battle, but it helped, a little.

Bennie was sitting cross-legged on the van's floor, the data broker's purloined wristcomm on his lap, connected to his own by a handful of colorful wires.

Nic leaned over to peer at the stolen wristcomm's screen. "You get in?"

Bennie looked up, smirking. "Of course, I did. That bubble-eye is no match for my slicing skills."

"That's a bit racist, you know," the young girl scolded.

Bennie bit back a reply, then nodded. "You're right." He looked at the wristcomm in his lap. "Anyway, I'm in and copying everything he's got. It's only a matter of time before he gets to a terminal he trusts and moves or deletes everything."

From the driver's seat of the vehicle, Lyral turned. "You found my data?"

"What? No." He shook his head. "The security on this," he held up the wristcomm, "is dren, but his opsec is pretty solid. From what I can tell, skimming the data, he's offloaded all storage and processing to orbital complexes over Tro Ella. What I'm getting is the map. Once I get it all and can parse it, we should be able to identify which orbital structure he stored your research on."

Lyral turned to face forward. "Still just *closer*." She sighed.

Nic looked up. "We'll get there. Don't worry." She grinned, baring her small, sharp teeth.

Bennie disconnected the cables connecting his wristcomm to the other one. Standing, he reached for the window and chucked the stolen unit into the street.

The trio drove in silence for a while, collecting their thoughts on the last day's adventure. Bennie was absently scrolling through the data he had loaded onto his wristcomm. Prior to seeing the recordings in the Tower, he hadn't thought a lot about killing. All his life, killing had been a part of survival.

Now he was reflecting on the trail of bodies they had left in the park. Those men were evil, to be sure, but was that enough? Weren't they just doing their jobs, after all?

Nic had moved to the back of the hover van, hugging her knees. Killing those men in the park had been as much instinct and muscle memory from her training with Bennie as anything else. Lyral had been defenseless and if she hadn't acted, the woman would be dead now. She had her beam saber in hand, turning the device over and over, careful to keep the emitter end pointed away from her, given its hair trigger and seemingly random activation problems.

"Hey, uh...Knights? I think we're being followed," Lyral reported. The spaceport ring wall was visible up ahead, a few ploriths distant. Ships were visible coming and going. In the rearview display, a van very similar to theirs was following them two vehicles back.

Bennie came forward to peer between the two forward seats and look at the rearview display. Nic stood to peer through the rear window. She shouted, "They're Multonae."

"Turn here," Bennie said. Lyral followed his direction, even though the turn took them away from the spaceport. On the small display on the center console, the other van made the same turn, now directly behind them.

"Not good," Nic said.

"How many goons work for this grolacking syndicate?" Bennie growled.

"Thousands, at least," Lyral offered.

Bennie looked at her. "It was rhetorical." She shrugged. "Turn back toward the port." She nodded.

Bennie moved to the rear of the van, joining Nic. "We gotta buy ourselves some time."

She was still peering through the window. They crossed an intersection, the van behind following them. She noticed that the intersection had the standard traffic control systems installed on arms that spanned each street.

She turned to Bennie. "Traffic." He turned to look at her, question plain on his face. She grinned. "Hack the traffic management system."

Bennie clapped his hands together. "You might earn your keep after all!"

"Can you do that?" Lyral asked from the front.

Bennie dropped to the van's floor, already swiping screens on his wristcomm. "I was a code slicer long before I met that drunk old space wizard that got me into this." He gestured to his grime-covered outfit. "This is gonna be tricky. When I say to do something, do it. Got it?"

The researcher nodded, hands gripping the van's manual controls.

Bennie was glad that this little adventure was taking place on a Tier 1 Commonwealth world. The infrastructure was advanced and standardized, and to Bennie's pleasure, store bought.

After accessing the city's local network, it was no trouble breaking into the secure nodes where municipal systems lived. Finding the traffic management system, he found the video feeds and located their van and their new friends.

"Turn right," Bennie shouted. He leaned as the van made a hasty turn, its gravpads groaning. The other van turned as well.

Nic, watching from the rear window, said, "That didn't work."

"I know that," he growled. "Speed up, then turn left!" The van tilted again. On his wristcomm screen, he watched them cut off a delivery van, swooping in front of it.

"Yes!" Nic hissed, pumping a fist.

Bennie scanned ahead on the map. "Get ready to make a right, and speed up. There's a big cluster of vehicles merging from an alleyway."

"Okay." Lyral quickly released the controls one hand at a time to wipe them on her trousers.

"Go!"

The van lurched and tilted. The sound of one of the gravlift modules scraping the street reverberated into the vehicle.

They continued the slow speed cat-and-mouse game until Bennie declared them clear. The hover van hadn't fully come to a stop before they were scrambling from the side door, running for the departures terminal entry.

They were through customs by the time Lyral spotted a cluster of well-dressed Multonae men enter the hall. The men apparently did not care that they stood out amid the half-as-tall, mostly Trollack crowd.

"They won't cause a scene, yet. Let's hurry," Bennie whispered, urging the two women ahead of him toward the larger arched exit.

The *Rocky Nontee* was where they had parked her, and according to the onboard systems, had not been tampered with or even approached since they landed. Bennie would take every minor miracle he could.

The port side cargo doors parted, and a small ramp slid out and clanged to the duracrete. Bennie looked toward the exit of the customs area. Dozens of beings funneled out every minute, heading off toward various commercial shuttles and personal craft.

Just as he was turning around, he spotted a group of tall, dark-clad figures emerge onto the duracrete. "Hurry up!" He shoved the two women up the ramp and trotted to the small combination lift and ladder. He scurried up the ladder, calling over his shoulder, "Get strapped in!"

CHAPTER 17

BENNIE WAS SLAPPING controls before his seat even finished fitting into place. He slapped the communications controls. "*Rocky Nontee* requesting emergency departure clearance."

"*Rocky Nontee,* what's the emergency?" the spaceport control operator asked.

"It's uh...Well, I mean we..." He rubbed his forehead. "It's private?"

From the hatchway, Nic shouted, "Medical emergency!" She climbed into what had become her seat on the bridge. "Weird Olop thing."

Bennie gave her a thumbs up. "Spaceport control. We've got an Olop on board with something wrong with her. We're taking her home."

"What's wrong with her?"

"Explosive diarrhea!" Nic said, loud enough to be heard.

"Uh. Permission granted, *Rocky Nontee.* Sending your departure vector, now," the controller said before closing the channel.

The reactor was already nearly ready for flight. The nav system was pulling down current tracking data and flight paths.

The nav console came to life with a plot out of the spaceport control zone and into orbit.

Bennie reached over and made sure the comm system was still set to not automatically accept comm requests. Looking over his shoulder, he said, "Buckle up."

He pushed the repulsorlift power lever forward. Overlaid on the main window, power levels for the lift system increased. The boxy, stubby-winged ship shot straight up into the air, throwing dust and loose bits of trash in every direction.

"Oops," he whispered, easing the power lever down a bit.

The moment the ship rose above the ring wall, he pushed the atmospheric thrust controls forward, easing the ship into outbound traffic.

In defiance of the repairs and upgrades the ship had undergone, her atmospheric thrusters, despite their size, were nowhere near capable of the same thrust as those on Wil's Ankarran Raptor, the *Ghost*. Bennie hoped they wouldn't be trying to outrun anyone in an atmosphere anytime soon.

The *Nontee* made it out of the atmosphere without trouble. Space traffic around Tro Ella was as thick as when they had arrived, hundreds of ships moving into and out of orbit. The planet was ringed by massive orbital complexes; some were residential for those wealthy enough to take advantage, others were made up of commercial units, and a few were entirely devoted to industries deemed too polluting and dangerous to leave on the planet.

Bennie looked over his shoulder. "I need you to take over."

"Take over what?"

"The controls, dummy, what else?" He pressed the control to turn and lower his seat.

"What? I don't know how to fly a starship!" Nic hopped out of her seat.

"Neither do I," Bennie said, pushing her out of the way.

"You'll be fine. I need to dive into this data and figure where we're going." Over his shoulder, he added, "Just don't crash into anything."

Nic climbed into the seat and rode it back into position and looked over the controls frantically. Lights were blinking, and there was a sensor return display with blinking dots. There were several levers with glowing indicators. "I have a bad feeling about this." She looked up through the forward window and the data overlaid upon it.

Bennie connected his wristcomm to the ship's computer and was using the auxiliary station's displays to parse through the data he'd taken off of the data broker.

He had to admit, the Trollack man's system of keeping track of things was impressive.

"Um. I think the bad guys found us."

"Uh huh..." Bennie was focused on the display before him; maps of data structures whizzed by amid notes and clumps of metadata.

In the common area, Lyral was sitting on the sofa, thumbing through screens on her wristcomm. She flicked something on the screen, and the holo screen in the middle of the lounge area came to life.

A recorded news clip began playing, showing another interview with Mayor Dardle. In this one, the earnest interviewer was pushing the mayor on his sudden about-face regarding organized crime. He claimed he had put his name forward for the governorship because Lyral Adel had assured him she could help him rid the system of one of the biggest criminal organizations around. It then turned out that she worked for said organizations, intending to undermine the government from within.

The interviewer pressed him on the timing, coming just a day after his big rally. The sweaty man ran a thick hand over his head. He sidestepped the question, mostly by repeating how devious Lyral Adel was.

She swiped on her wristcomm screen, stopping the playback and disengaging the holo screen.

The ship made a maneuver severe enough that she felt it through the artificial gravity and inertial damping systems. "That's probably not good."

"Uh, there's a light blinking over here," Nic said. She had the flight controls and throttle in death grips.

"Just one, that's good. You're doing fine." Bennie didn't look over but waved a hand.

The hatch slid open and Lyral walked in. "What's going on?" The ship shuddered, forcing her to clutch the sides of the hatchway.

The view out the front of the bridge swung wildly. A massive commercial orbital station came into view, then just as quickly passed by the other side of the window. "You can fly a ship?" Lyral asked.

"No, not really," the Olop girl replied, not taking her eyes off the displays on her console. She risked a brief look over her shoulder at Bennie. "The light that was blinking?"

"Yeah." He was still intently focused on the display before him.

"Still blinking."

"We're not on fire, so it's not important."

Lyral moved to stand behind Nic. "I don't think that's how it works." She looked at the console. "Is that ship following us?" She pointed to an icon on the sensor display.

"I think so. I'm trying to lose them, but it's so crowded," the young pilot complained, pointing to the myriad of other dots on the sensor display.

"Got it!" Bennie shouted, causing the two women to jump. Nic nearly rammed the *Nontee* into a pleasure barge.

He joined them at the main console, holding a PADD. Looking up at Lyral, he grinned. "Found your data." The much taller woman grinned. Maybe this nightmare was almost over.

Bennie stretched up for the console but could only reach the lower controls. He grunted and handed the PADD to Nic. "Scan for this orbital."

"Uh, how do I do that?" Nic asked. Before anyone could answer, she pulled the flight controls back toward her. The *Rocky Nontee* veered into the flight path of a large freighter, then swung wide over the top of the massive hauler to dive behind another ship. She cut their thrust to match the other ship's speed.

Bennie leaned back. "Nice trick." He poked her in the side. "Now get out before you really do crash us into something."

Nic hopped from the seat to allow Bennie to take over. He checked the sensors. "Gods, how many goons can one criminal organization employ? Looks like we've got three ships trying to keep eyes on us. Nic's maneuver seems to have shaken them for a moment." He input the details for the orbital they were looking for. When the sensor board pinged, highlighting a single commercial district orbital facility, he fed power to the sub-light engines. The *Rocky Nontee* drifted away from the freighter they were hiding next to.

Lyral watched in silence until she asked, "So, what's the plan?"

Bennie's shoulders hunched. "The best I can come up with is that we land at the orbital and you two get off. I'll take the *Rocky* back out and see if I can't keep them busy."

Nic raised an arm, sniffing. "I should clean up."

Bennie and Lyral nodded their agreement. The Multonae woman said, "That's not a very good plan. What if the broker told them which orbital? What if they don't follow you?"

Bennie turned. "If you have a better plan, I'm here for it. As far as the broker telling them, based on his data security, I doubt he kept those details in his head. But either way, we'll know soon." He pointed out the forward window. A spherical space station was looming directly ahead. Several dozen ships of various sizes were coming and going. Large cargo haulers were attached to external docking arms. Smaller ships like theirs were pulling into the large central landing bay that formed an equator around the station.

Nic appeared in the hatch, free of swamp grime in a new apprentice tunic and trousers. "That's it, huh?"

Bennie nodded. "Lyral will fill you in. Get down to the cargo hold. We'll have to move fast."

Nic followed the Multonae woman out of the bridge and town into the cargo hold. From the overhead speaker, Bennie said, "Starboard doors. I'll land, open, and lift off."

"What's he talking about?" Nic asked, fidgeting with her beam saber hilt. She had cleaned it, but otherwise hadn't had time to figure out what was causing the intermittent malfunctions.

Lyral explained the plan, finishing as the *Rocky Nontee* touched down with a louder-than-normal clang. The cargo doors slid apart. "Go, go, go," Bennie said from the ceiling.

Lyral and Nic exchanged a look and ran down the ramp. The moment they cleared the ramp, the boxy ship was lifting off, ramp rising and cargo doors sliding closed. In a matter of millitocks, the *Rocky Nontee* was passing through the atmospheric shield on the far side of the landing bay.

Nic and Lyral made their way to the center of the landing bay. The bay was the widest part of the station, at least two kilometers across. In the center was a massive pillar that connected the two hemispheres of the orbital complex.

The entire bay was chaos: ships coming in, unloading, and departing as quickly as they could. Dock workers of all races, but predominately Trollack, were moving with purpose all over the place.

The *Rocky Nontee* departed, passing through the static atmosphere barrier that surrounded the entire bay. Bennie had sent everything he had been able to find, to Nic's wristcomm. Looking at it as they reached the central pillar, she said, "We need to go up." The other woman nodded, pressing the call button for the bank of lifts they were nearest.

The central pillar housed flight control and cargo operations for the station. Several banks of lifts made up the pillar's ground floor, with the offices and control center stretching out to form a wider circle above.

Nic was rocking on her heels waiting for the lift, when she turned to see six Multonae men in black suits exiting a shuttle.

She swore and pushed her much taller companion around the side of the central pillar toward a different bank of lifts. She slapped the button and said, "Guess they didn't fully buy Bennie's plan." The other woman's eyebrows shot up. Nic nodded. "Six of 'em. They really are endless, aren't they?"

The lift arrived, and they boarded. Lyral exhaled. "What do we do?"

Nic shrugged. "We know where to go. We get there first."

"That's all?"

The younger woman shrugged again. "I can make up a bunch of other steps if that'll make you feel better." Her ears twitched nervously.

Lyral made a face.

The lift stopped and two Trollack entered: a man and a woman, both in dock worker jumpsuits. The woman turned to Nic and Lyral. "I like your outfit," she said to Nic.

The fur around Nic's cheeks flattened as she bobbed her head in thanks. She stammered out a nervous thank you, reminding Lyral that her life was in the hands of an adolescent.

The doors parted shortly after, and the two Trollack left. Lyral and Nic rode in silence until the lift stopped again.

"She liked my outfit," Nic said aloud, but mostly to herself. She was rocking on her heels.

Each level of the commercial orbital was nearly identical to the one above and below, except for its diameter shrinking or growing, depending on location. Stepping off the lift, the two women took in their surroundings. The central pillar had a wide-open ring around it, with several wide aisles angling outward like spokes on a wheel.

"Which way?" Lyral pressed.

Nic was looking at her wristcomm. "This way, I think."

"You think?"

The look Nic gave her ended the conversation.

There were people everywhere, which was good. It gave them cover. Each deck was home to anywhere from dozens to hundreds of businesses: anything from clothiers, entertainment establishments of all types, restaurants, and data centers, to name a few. Their focus was on the latter, and according to the public network, there were three on this level. Bennie's data packet didn't include the name of the data center, just a numeric code that, as far as Nic and Lyral could determine, didn't match up to the station's internal addressing system.

"If we survive this, I could eat," Lyral said as they walked past a Fluivv Arro that looked like it was just finishing the dinner rush.

Nic nodded. "I was hungry before we left Tro Ella." Next to

the restaurant was a toy store, then a men's clothing store specializing in Trollack fashion. After that, a data center facility.

Nic looked around. The ceiling on this deck, presumably on every deck, had a holographic projection of sky, complete with stars and a nondescript moon, that hid pipes and conduits.

The data center before them, Data Town, was closed for the day. "This it?"

Nic hunched her shoulders and looked at her wristcomm. The data Bennie sent was clear on which deck, but after that, the numerical code he had included made little sense to her. It wasn't any type of coordinate system. It wasn't the address. She stared at the numbers on her wristcomm screen.

"Wait!" Nic jumped, clapping her hands. "I've got it."

Bennie wiped sweat from his forehead. His plan had sort of worked. Two of the three syndicate ships were still chasing him. One had broken off and landed in the commercial orbital's landing bay, though. The women would have to take care of that on their own.

The comm system beeped again. He wasn't sure if it was space control calling to yell at him about his winding path through traffic and several orbital landing bays, or if it was the syndicate goons trying to urge him to surrender. Neither was a conversation he was eager to have, so he ignored the beeping.

According to the sensor board, his friends were getting more aggressive. Both ships were much closer to him than was safe or allowed by space control regulations. So far, they had held off on firing weapons.

He juked the controls, slowing the ship rapidly. It forced the ship nearest his rear quarter into a maneuver that almost sent it on an collision course with a private yacht nearby.

"Okay, this isn't as easy as I thought," he said aloud. Using the confusion he'd just caused, he angled the *Rocky Nontee* toward a factory station. It wasn't in the same orbit as the commercial and residential orbitals. In fact, it and a few similar facilities occupied the last orbital track before open space.

He checked his sensor display. The two ships were still back there. One was still on top of him; the other, the one that had almost collided with the yacht, was a hundred or so ploriths back.

Bennie wiped his head again and pulled the throttle back to the stop position. The two pursuing ships caught up immediately.

Bennie tapped a few controls and hopped out of his seat. He looked at the ceiling. "Wish me luck."

Both syndicate ships were civilian class cutters: smaller than the *Rocky Nontee*, similarly armed, and in a straight-out race, twice as fast.

Both cargo hatches on the *Nontee* had a personnel hatch set in the larger sliding cargo doors for ship-to-ship connections. While Bennie stood in the middle of the cargo hold, syndicate cutters were pulling alongside, extending docking tunnels—thin flexible chutes capable of holding an atmosphere, allowing crew to move between ships easily without environment suits.

He sent a command via his wristcomm; the lights went out.

The starboard personnel hatch swung in first. The scant light from a floodlight on the cutter was the only illumination. "What the—?" the first man through said.

Bennie moved aft, to ensure he was in the darkest part of the hold, and waited until five men had entered it. Each had a pistol in one hand. One flicked on a portable light unit. That was Bennie's signal.

He clicked on his beam saber, the sound enough to startle the intruders. The *Rocky Nontee*'s hold wasn't very long, but

Bennie pumped his legs as hard as he could to build up speed. He dropped into a slide, passing between two men. He slashed one, taking out his leg below the knee. The other was less lucky. Bennie was already passing them, so he slashed a wide arc behind him, catching the man up through the groin and across his back.

That was when the screaming started. Plasma bolts were flying in every direction, lighting up the darkened hold, scorching the hull.

After his slide, Bennie clicked his saber off. He scurried to the side as energy bolts attempted to follow his path, leaving carbon scores on the forward bulkhead.

He paused long enough to listen to the chaos in the hold. One intruder was calling for help from the docked cutter. Another was trying to call the second ship and get it to dock as quickly as possible. One was screaming gibberish, probably the newly minted one-legged man. Two others were moving around, having missed that Bennie had continued forward. No one seemed overly concerned about the dead man or newly single-legged man, as far as he could hear.

He crept up to the nearest man. Twisting the control ring on his beam saber, he stopped just short of the man's back, raised his weapon, and pressed the activation plate. Purple light bathed the hold momentarily, the bolt striking the bulkhead. The gangster must have heard him—he darted to the side a moment before Bennie fired. Turning, the much larger man swung his free hand, balled into a fist, catching Bennie on the side of the head. He was seeing stars before he hit the ground.

"He's over here!" the gangster shouted. He fired several times, striking empty deck. Bennie had rolled to the side the moment he landed.

Bennie rubbed his head, wincing. He got to his feet, pulse blasts still lighting up the room. He darted a few steps closer to the man, in between shots. Finally close enough, he said, "That hurt!" and fired another bright purple bolt, this time into the man's chest, sending him flying across the hold.

Before anyone could react, Bennie darted toward the other man calling in for help. The man had a pistol in one hand, firing wildly as he backed away from the source of bright purple light, and had his wristcomm up to his face, screaming into it.

Switching his saber back to normal, Bennie activated it just as he passed the man, cutting the wristcomm and the arm inside it in two just below the wrist. The man screamed briefly until Bennie's blade came back up in an arc that brought it through the man's midsection. He clicked the saber off before the body hit the deck.

CHAPTER 18

"WHAT IS IT?" Lyral asked.

Nic was furiously working on her wristcomm. "It's not this one. There should be a data center, two streets over and at the end, near the outer hull." She headed off.

"What did you figure out?" Lyral repeated.

Nic didn't look up. "It wasn't coordinates. It was a cypher. The numbers matched up to a name, StorTek." She held up her wristcomm. "And StorTek, is..." She looked around. "...Right over there." She pointed down the road where it met a cross street.

The pair rushed down the wide street-like walkway, crossing an intersecting walkway that went around the level in a wide circle halfway along its axis. They followed that for two intersections until finally they were standing in front of yet another entirely nondescript building.

Like the other data storage facility, StorTek was closed. "Can you pick the lock?" Lyral asked, looking around to ensure no one was nearby.

Nic kneeled next to the door. "Maybe, but this will be

faster." She held out her beam saber, tapped the activation switch. Nothing happened. "Grolacking thing." She slapped the device against her open palm twice. A third strike caused it to activate. She walked past the doors of the facility to a section of wall. Before Lyral could ask, Nic said, "There are, for sure, sensors on the doors. But the walls..." She shrugged and pushed the tip of her red blade into the wall.

It was slow going. Whatever the building was made of was not overly giving to a cohesive beam of super charged plasma. A few tense microtocks later and she was kicking in a roughly circular piece of wall into the building. She looked up. "Careful, the edge. Hot." She ducked inside. The edge of the circle was still glowing orange.

The room that Nic had cut into was someone's office. There was a desk, with a display mounted to it on an articulated arm. A few pictures and documents of some type hung on the wall, along with a pennant for a sports team she didn't recognize the name of. The door led to a short hallway. One door opened to the lobby, the other into the bulk of StorTek's real estate. Dozens, maybe hundreds, of racks longer than the *Rocky Nontee* filled the single cavernous space.

In each rack, lights and displays blinked and flickered. As far as Nic could see, the only labels were a sign over each rack naming it, and she thought she spied hand-applied labels spaced along the top of the racks, likely client or project names. She hoped.

"Now where?" Lyral asked.

Nic looked at her wristcomm. "Let's see. There has to be something here." She thumbed through the data. "What's Balderguphlim?"

Lyral blinked several times. "That's...that's the project name! The mayor's stupid pet finkle. I hated it when he brought it to the lab." She spun to look at the rows of racks. "It'll take forever to find the label for that." She looked toward the door to the hallway and lobby beyond. "And we don't have long." As if waiting for a signal, a sound came from the other side of the door. Voices.

Lyral grabbed the back of Nic's tunic and hauled her down the nearest aisle. To make the search harder, each rack had two faces, so each aisle had two sets of processing cores to look at.

Nic swatted at the other woman's hand. "I think I get it. The next bit of data in Bennie's transmission—I think it's a coordinate system. Row, then number of processor clusters down the row to yours."

From the front of the room, the voices became more distinct, one asking, "Did he say which set of cores the data was in?"

"Lemme look. At the end he was jabbering so quick, I think he told us whatever he could, hoping it would make us spare his life." Laughter followed. Then, "He was wrong." More laughter.

"Why those..." Nic growled. "They killed that man."

Lyral nodded and whispered. "Don't forget, he tried to extort us for more money, and sold us out to the syndicate."

"That doesn't mean he shoulda died," the younger woman protested.

"You're right, but there's nothing we could do." She made a point of gesturing to the Olop girl's wristcomm. "You said you thought you knew where we needed to go?"

Nic shook her head. "Yeah. Six over, twenty-seven up." She looked around. "Are we in the fourth or fifth row?"

The other woman straightened and looked around. She shrugged. "I don't know. I didn't count."

Nic closed her eyes. Bennie had drilled this into her over and over. Observe your surroundings. Catalog what you see. You never know what will be useful later. She opened her eyes. "We're in the fourth row."

The last two men of the first boarding party were shouting at each other, occasionally firing blindly, lighting up the hold.

Bennie was creeping along the port side wall when he heard and felt the second ship attaching to the *Rocky Nontee*. Time was running out.

The two men had moved back-to-back and were creeping toward the open hatch to their ship. Bennie said, "You should've found better work." The moment he finished speaking, he leaped to the side, just in time to avoid a few scattered plasma blasts that tried to home in on his voice.

"What the wurrin is that thing?" one asked.

"The boss said it was a Brailack, but I've never seen one like this."

From closer this time, Bennie said, "Racist much?" He dove into a roll that brought him next to the men. The sound of their frenzied fire drowned out his movements. He stood and activated his beam saber. The purple blade appeared, skewering both men, ending their excited shouting.

As the bodies fell, the port side personnel hatch swung in. "Gilder? Troka? Status report?"

Bennie crept closer to the hatch. The first man through, still calling the names of his colleagues, lost his gun hand before being kicked in the crotch and head butted.

From behind, two men with pulse rifles opened fire. Bennie pushed the dazed man up as a shield, then darted back into the darkened hold. He watched three men cautiously make their way in, easing their dead friend to the deck next to the hatch. Hand lights played around the space, finding the dead and dying of the first boarding party.

Bennie snuck toward the hatch to the first cutter and made

his way across the docking tube, as shouts filled the *Nontee*'s cargo hold.

The cutter was empty. The syndicate thugs, it seemed, thought it unlikely that their prey would make it aboard the ship freely. He looked over the cockpit, a simplified design, not that dissimilar to the *Nontee*'s basic design. Two stations, side by side, with a small station and jump seat in back.

He could hear the men aboard his ship knocking things over and making an even bigger mess of the hold. He wasted no more time, connecting his wristcomm to the pilot's station. Overriding the safeties for the reactor took less time than hacking the auto flight systems. By the time he was back in the docking tube, peering into the still darkened cargo hold of the *Rocky Nontee*, the cutter's autopilot was preparing to retract the docking tube.

When he crossed back into the *Nontee,* the hold was empty. The syndicate goons must be up on the common deck. He closed and sealed the personnel hatch and headed for the access ladder. Behind him, the clank of the disconnecting docking tube echoed.

From above, he heard the shouting of the men searching for him and the two women who weren't aboard the ship. Given the ship's small size, they'd figure it out quickly now that they had access to the common area. The small freighter simply didn't have many places to hide. With a final soft clank and a beep from the hatch, the docking tube on the starboard side fully disengaged. The cutter would move off on its own until it exploded. He wasn't completely certain of his math, but was pretty sure the other ship's explosion wouldn't harm the *Nontee.*

He moved across the hold to the port personnel hatch and second cutter. He crossed through the docking tube into a ship nearly identical to the first, except for one key factor. There was a woman sitting in the secondary seat on the small bridge.

She was looking at her console, watching the other cutter

move off. She didn't hear Bennie's approach. "Troka? Swoll? Someone from Team Alpha, report? Did you bag the target? Why are you breaking off? Where are you krebnacks going?"

Bennie thought Troka, whichever one he was, must have been in charge of this little operation. His name kept coming up.

She reached for the comm panel, likely to switch to the team channel for her ship. He had to act. Killing her wasn't something he was comfortable with. She wasn't attacking him, and while her choice of employment was repulsive, he kept seeing those archive recordings Nic had found: Knights doing questionable things, and worse, in the name of doing good. He didn't want to be that kind of Knight of Plentallus.

He crept up behind her; she was focused on her consoles. Beam sabers were useful in many ways, not least of which was as a blunt object. One solid whack to the back of her head and she was slumped over in her seat.

He didn't have the strength to move the Multonae woman, so sending the ship off to explode wasn't an option. If he sent the ship off on its own, he'd be committing to eliminating the boarding team. He shrugged. He was okay with that. They'd boarded his ship with the intent to kill. They'd made their choice. Still, that was a lot more death.

He connected his wristcomm to the ship's computer and got the programming uploaded. While programming the ship, an idea occurred to him. He added a routine to the communications suite before disconnecting. Smiling, he headed back to the boarding tube connected to the *Rocky Nontee*.

He was just crossing into the *Nontee*'s cargo hold when the ship shuddered, the other cutter exploding. He looked at the timer on his wristcomm and saw that it had hit zero.

From every wristcomm on the ship came the recording he'd made on the bridge of the second cutter, timed loosely to when the first was supposed to explode. "Hi, losers. You're hearing this because I just set your only remaining ride out of here to automatically decouple in three microtocks. You've seen what I can do. The choice is yours. Stay here and I kill you, or get your asses to the cutter." A pause. "Just over two microtocks, now."

From the common deck, he heard lots of shouting and pushing. He went aft and crouched near the entrance to the med bay. He glanced inside and made a face. The small med center was in shambles. "Drennogs," he whispered.

First one, then all four, remaining gangsters slid down the access ladder and darted toward the open personnel hatch. When he was certain there weren't any stragglers, he ran over and slammed the hatch shut.

Nic and Lyral crouch-ran to the nearest end of the aisle. They could hear the syndicate men moving around somewhere in the data center but couldn't tell where. Nic got down on all fours and leaned out past the end of the aisle. Each row was made up of three segments. They were in the first, and if all the rows were more or less uniform, the data they wanted was in the second, two rows away. She didn't see anyone in the walkway that ran lengthwise. She stood and motioned for her companion to follow.

The pair ran toward the row that held their target and came face to face with a suited man looking at one of the processing cores. He turned in time to make a strangled sounding yip before a blade of bright red energy pierced him. She turned the device off as he made a final gurgle before slumping to the ground.

Nic grimaced. "It worked this time." She shook her head. "You know what I like most about beam sabers versus my knife?"

Lyral stared at her, then at the dead man at her feet, but said nothing.

"I don't get as much blood on my clothes." Lyral opened her mouth, but Nic didn't wait for a reply, turning to look at the processors the dead man had been looking at. "Here." Nic pointed to a unit near the top of the rack, out of her reach.

Lyral moved next to her. "I see it. This core looks like it has two removable drives. Should I take both?"

"Do you want to do this again tomorrow?"

The taller woman frowned. "I see why you like Ben-Ari." She reached up and pulled both drives from the processing core. Activity lights flickered, then went out, replaced by two solid red indicators. "Got 'em."

"Great. Hand them over," a voice said.

Nic and Lyral turned to face three men, all Multonae, all much bigger than them.

One of the men, bald with a cybernetic eye, raised his arm. Into his wristcomm, he said, "We got the scientist, and some kid."

Nic took a step forward. "Some kid? I'm an apprentice Knight of Plentallus."

The man lowered his arm. "I don't know what that is." She opened her mouth to answer, and he cut her off. "Or care." He pointed to Lyral. "We're here for her and the data." He looked at the storage drives. "That's it?"

Lyral nodded.

He held out his hand. "Give it."

Nic stepped in front of the other woman. "If we don't?"

One of the other men, skin a darker shade than Nic's fur, stepped around his colleague, pistol held loosely at his side. "We kill ya."

"Rude," the young Olop replied. Her hand drifted to the hilt of her beam saber. Lyral's hand fell to her shoulder.

The other woman held out her other hand, the two storage modules balanced on her palm. "Here."

As the man reached for the offered drives, Nic shrugged off Lyral's hand and leapt into the air. She landed on the man's upper body, her small fists raining blows on his face. The third man, who had until then been standing behind the bald one, moved and swatted the girl off of his friend.

Nic hit the bank of processing cores and fell to the ground. Lyral kneeled next to the girl, still clutching the storage drives. "Are you okay?"

The girl looked up and wiped her mouth with the back of her hand. It came away wet with blood. She nodded.

"Get up. Both of you," the bald man ordered. He gestured to the darker-skinned man. "Get 'em up." He reached out and took the data storage units from Lyral.

Bennie brought the *Rocky Nontee* in to land next to a ship that looked like the other two he just finished dealing with. As far as the ship's sensors could tell, the cutter before him was empty. He guided the bulky *Nontee* in to settle next to the other ship, almost completely blocking the smaller craft from view from the center of the bay.

The landing bay was as busy as it had been when he dropped Nic and Lyral off, with dock workers and shuttle crews moving this way and that. No one paid him any attention as he left the ship and headed for the central column that connected the two hemispheres of the massive commercial orbital. He was almost to the section with the lifts when a pair of doors slid open to reveal three large Multonae men, one Multonae woman, and an Olop teen.

He stumbled and fell backward, his feet tangling themselves

up. He barely rolled behind a crate of repair parts before the group walked past. The Multonae men weren't holding weapons, but the outlines of pulse pistols were visible under their suit jackets.

One of the men was holding Nic's beam saber, examining it. Another, next to Lyral, had in his hand what had to be the data storage units.

Bennie crouched and made his way between crates back toward the *Nontee* and the waiting syndicate cutter. He had to move fast if he was going to save the women.

As the group rounded a pile of crates containing fruit bound for Harrith, Nic gasped. Lyral slowed, first looking at her small companion, then in the direction they were walking, her own breath catching.

"What?" the leader of the syndicate men demanded. "What's wrong with you two?" He turned back toward where they had parked the cutter, noticing the ship next to it. "Isn't that the junker you were in?"

One of the other men leaned forward. "It is. What happened to the other teams?"

In one fluid motion, Nic twisted, dropping into a crouch to shrug out of the dark-skinned man's grasp, and with two steps leapt onto the bald man's shoulders, her small knife clutched in one hand.

The other two men shouted their surprise, drawing their pistols.

Lyral spun and jumped on the man next to her, pulling him to the ground in a tangled heap amid shouted expletives. The data storage drives clattered to the ground. The man Nic escaped from fumbled for his weapon.

Before the bald-headed man could process what was happening, a small blade was plunging into his shoulder and neck repeatedly. He tried to shout, then scream. It all came out a gurgle. He fell to the ground, his small Olop attacker still clinging to his chest.

Nic spun on the man she escaped. The man behind her was clutching his neck wounds, gurgling. She bared her teeth. "Go away." The other man did not hesitate. He turned back to the center of the massive landing bay and sprinted away. He shouted to his remaining colleague, who was still flailing on the ground with Lyral.

The man struggling with Lyral pushed her away and reached for the pistol in his shoulder holster. Coming up empty, he looked around. His pulse pistol was out of reach. He looked at his colleague, now well away from the scene of the brawl, then at the blood covered Olop girl brandishing her knife. He got to his feet and was gone.

Bennie appeared from around the *Rocky Nontee* and stopped. His mouth fell open as he took in the scene. Finally, he said, "I was going to save you."

Nic picked up her beam saber hilt, clipping it to her belt. "We didn't need it." She ran a hand across her face to wipe away some of the blood stuck to her fur. It didn't really help.

Bennie joined them, helping Lyral to her feet and fetching the two data storage units. "These them?" The data scientist nodded. "Then let's get the wurrin out of here and figure out how to clear your name."

"And take these grolacking drennogs down," Nic added.

Bennie walked aboard the syndicate cutter and looked around. It was the same model as the other two. He wondered if the syndicate bought these things in bulk, maybe from the same place they got their goons. The computer wasn't as much help as Bennie had hoped for.

"Anything?" Lyral asked, leaning over his shoulder.

He shook his head. They had hoped that the cutter would be tied into the syndicate network. To their collective chagrin, the cutter was running the basic operating system it came off the assembly line with. Zero customization or personalization. Luckily for Bennie, also no updates to the security software.

"They didn't even name it," Bennie complained. He slapped a three-fingered hand on the console. "Let's blow this poop cycle vendor." Nic looked up at Lyral. The other woman shrugged. Since meeting Bennie and his friends, Nic had gotten used to what Bennie referred to as Earthisms. Something the brown-haired Multonae-looking guy said a lot, she guessed.

Bennie stood. "Okay, let's get out of here. Those two goons will eventually be back. Once they feel brave enough."

When the *Rocky Nontee*'s cargo doors slid open, Lyral screamed.

Bennie made a face. "Oh, sorry. I shoulda warned you."

She spun on him. "You think?"

Nic peered inside. "Felgercarb, that's a lot of blood." She took a step into the hold. "Is that an arm?"

"Just ignore it," Bennie said, heading for the access ladder.

"Ignore the severed arm?" Lyral said, shaking her head.

The *Nontee* left the orbital without fanfare. There was no sign of any other syndicate ships loitering nearby. Now that Bennie was certain they only used the one type of ship, he fed its signature into the *Nontee*'s computer.

The three of them were on the small flight deck watching the stars through the forward window.

Nic rocked on her heels. "So, uh, now what?"

Lyral held up one of the data storage units. "We have to turn these over to someone."

"The Peacekeepers?" Nic offered. Bennie clucked. "What's

wrong with the Peacekeepers? Maxim and Zephyr used to be PKs."

"Used to be." Bennie wagged a finger. "What's *not* wrong? Most of them are corrupt, and there aren't many left after the war with Janus and his nightmare brigade." He rolled his hand at the wrist. "Yada yada."

"Ya da ya da?" Lyral asked, emphasizing the wrong syllables.

Frowning, Nic asked, "Then who?"

Bennie rubbed his head. Suddenly, this felt incredibly familiar. "Everyone. We tell everyone."

A tock later, the *Rocky Nontee* was at FTL. Bennie came down the access ladder into the cargo hold. Lyral and Nic had bagged and piled the bodies in a corner. The med bay had body bags in its inventory, or it did. They'd used them all. Bennie grabbed a scrub pad. "Surprised the med bay had enough body bags."

Lyral blanched and looked away. Nic frowned. "Well, it didn't. We had to get creative to fit everyone in what we had."

"Creative?" Bennie asked. He held up a hand before his apprentice could answer. "You know what? I don't want to know."

Lyral pushed a bucket of water toward him. "Good call. So, where are we going?"

"Nexum," Bennie replied.

Nic's head jerked back as she gasped. "Really? To the Tower?"

Bennie nodded. "If you have a better idea, I'm all ears."

Lyral leaned to the side, head tilted. "You don't have external ears."

"It's an expression."

"Not one I've heard. Certainly not a Brailack one."

Bennie exhaled. "Never mind. We need to regroup. The

syndicate found us here because Mayor Big Ass knew about your setup. They won't know to go to Nexum."

"You hope," Lyral said.

Bennie shrugged. "Not a lot of options." He looked around. "We can drop out of FTL, drop those," he pointed to the pile of body bags, "and get to work on those drives."

PART FOUR
LIKE OLD TIMES

CHAPTER 19

BENNIE LOOKED up from his wristcomm. "These are encrypted." The three of them were in the common area aboard the *Rocky Nontee*. The two women were on the sofa watching something they'd found on the ship's computer. The last time Bennie looked up, it was a Ruknak melodrama, thankfully with subtitles.

Lyral looked over at the makeshift workbench Bennie had set up on the dining table. Arrayed before him were the two data storage modules, each connected to his wristcomm by wires. "Can you decrypt them?" she asked.

He tilted his head. "Yeah, I just thought I'd share that these," he gestured to the devices on the table, "were encrypted. So you'd know and all." He made a face. "No, I can't decrypt them. Not with this." He waved his arm, the wires connected to his wristcomm swaying. "The *Nontee*'s computer somehow has less processing power than my wristcomm!"

Nic sighed louder than was strictly necessary and paused the program. "Can the olds please be quiet? I don't want to miss anything. Flurm is about to discover who his partner is cheating on him with."

Bennie made a rude gesture before turning back to Lyral. "That wobble-eyed hacker you hired was good. Not *me* good, but damn close. My wristcomm doesn't have the processing power to brute force this."

Nic sighed again, turning her attention from the show. "So, what? The Tower has the processing power, right?"

Bennie disconnected his wristcomm from the data storage units. "I'm worried that Nexum, the Tower, are too obvious."

Lyral ran both hands through her hair, first undoing the loosened ponytail, then pulling it together tighter. "We're so close. What about your office? You have an office, right? A base, you said?"

Nic made a face, her small nose wrinkling. "Their building is pretty gross. A rundown dren heap."

"It's not gross, it's vintage," Bennie retorted.

"It was a slave brokerage."

Bennie pointed a finger at her. "Not for a long time."

Lyral made a face and sighed, loudly.

Bennie waved a hand and said, "I think both are out. For the same reason, too obvious."

Lyral stood and moved to the small kitchenette and retrieved a bottle of water. "I suppose that makes sense. They know who you are, where you're from. That leaves us what for options?" She took a sip of water, then snapped her fingers. "My lab."

Bennie shook his head. "No way. Too dangerous."

Nic clucked. "Speaking of obvious."

Lyral moved to sit next to Nic. "Hear me out." Bennie made a *go on* motion. She took another drink, then said, "My lab has plenty of processing power. It should be more than enough to brute force through that encryption. It's also the last place they'd think to look for us."

Bennie squinted. "If you were outsourcing the processing, why's your lab got such beefy equipment?"

She shrugged. "When Mayor Dardle hired me, we initially set up a workspace where I could crunch the numbers myself, locally." She took a deep breath. "When I saw where the data was leading, I got nervous. That was when I hired the broker on Tro Ella." She grinned. "The mayor was too lazy to move the equipment out of my lab. We already paid for it."

Bennie rubbed his chin. *It could work*, he thought. The syndicate was for sure still hunting for them and knew who he was by now. That meant Nexum and Fury were likely being watched or would be.

Maybe going to Multon, surely the last place the syndicate's upper management would expect them to be, wasn't so crazy of an idea. He rubbed his hands together. "Okay. Let's do it." He stood up.

Changing course to Multon wouldn't add much time to their travels. He would need to hack the ship's transponder, though. By now, the *Rocky Nontee* was on every watch list the syndicate had access to.

He dropped into the pilot's seat and waited for it to raise and rotate, bringing him into position before the flight console. He pulled the FTL control back, returning the ship to local space. They were in deep space. The sensor board showed zero contacts. A couple of taps later, he was pushing the FTL controls up, driving the ship to faster than light speeds.

After changing course, the three of them turned in, the mad scramble of the last few days finally catching up to them.

"We're out of food," Nic said as Bennie stepped out of the sole refresher on the ship.

He shrugged. "Eat less."

"I dunno how Brailacks work, Gramps, but Olop need calories."

Bennie sighed. "Fine. I'll find a commerce station along our route. We'll need a new transponder first. Come help me."

She clapped her hands and followed him. "Ooh, sounds fun."

Lyral was still in the small crew bunk aft of the lounge. The beds were uncomfortable, and Nic snored, but she was getting used to it. It felt like a lifetime ago that the mayor of Sentullo had approached her with a special project. Something of particular civic importance.

She had been so proud. The first few months had been fantastic. The data sets the mayor provided had been massive, bigger than any she had worked with before, from such a wide variety of sources.

Not a day went by that she wasn't updating or tweaking her algorithms to accommodate the data sets and what they were exposing.

Sighing, she rose from the bed and went to the refresher.

Across the hall in the small bridge, Bennie had the auxiliary console opened up. He was lying on his back looking up into the console's inner workings. "Hand me the wide band diagnostic reader." He reached out and wiggled his fingers. Nic slapped a tool into his hand.

"No, no, no. This is a narrow band memory writer." The green hand and the tool in it shot back out from under the console.

"Sorry." She swapped the device in his hand for another. "So, you think this will work?"

A cluck came from under the console. "This isn't the first transponder I've hacked. This one isn't even in the top ten, difficulty-wise."

Nic scowled. "No. I mean going back to Multon."

Bennie slid out from under the console. He had wire insulation adhesive on his forehead. He shrugged. "Beats me."

"Inspiring."

"You have forms to practice, don't you? Go find inspiration in those." He raised one eyebrow ridge. He gestured to what passed for a toolkit aboard the *Nontee*. "Hand me the multiplexer." She did.

Lyral appeared in the hatchway. "Did you know we don't have much food left?"

Nic turned to Bennie, eyebrow raised.

He leaned back under the console. "Why are you still here? Go work on your forms! Take the scientist!"

The two women said several rude things on their way out of the bridge. When he heard the hatch close, Bennie closed his eyes, exhaling. "I thought it was hard to deal with Wil..." He returned to his task.

He reached down and felt around for the programmable module he had jury-rigged from what parts he had on hand. Slotting it into place, he waited for it to initialize. The blinking green light confirmed that it was online and ready.

Looking at his wristcomm, he saw it had connected to the unit. "This is more Wil's thing..." He tapped his chin. "Varth Dader? No, he was evil." He made a raspy breathing noise. "Boob Felt. That'll do." He tapped in a few commands on his wristcomm. "Done."

After putting the console back together, he scrolled through the navigation computer until he found a commerce station only a few tocks off their course. He wasn't familiar with it, but it had an okay Zelp rating.

He tapped the intercom. "Hold on. Dropping from FTL for a microtock." He pulled the FTL control back, dropping the ship back into local space. After adjusting their course, he eased the ship back into FTL.

Down in the cargo hold, Lyral was leaning against the bulkhead watching Nic go through a series of motions that Lyral didn't understand.

Nic moved from one form to the next, her focus on defensive postures. She looked over to Lyral. "Can you really decrypt the data? When we get to your lab, I mean?"

Lyral shrugged. "Probably. I hope."

"Well, you're dead if you can't, so…" She spun in a circle, arms moving through the fifth form. The other woman gave a pained expression.

Bennie turned in his chair. "Okay, in and out. Fast as we can. We're still on the run and don't know how far the syndicate's reach is."

Nic and Lyral nodded before exiting the bridge. Bennie turned back and consulted his console, ensuring the connection to the station was secure. He put the ship into standby and hopped off his seat, not waiting for it to lower to the ground.

The trade station was a plorith square flattened to be at most ten decks tall. Docking arms of various lengths covered all four sides, like spines of a massive metal sea urchin. The station's management and space control facilities were in a large spire extending up from the center of the flat top of the station, where a handful of bulk freighters was parked.

By the time Bennie made it to the cargo hold and the open personnel hatch, the two women were long gone. The station was in deep space, so there was no customs area outside the docking arm. Instead, he exited into a wide corridor that likely ran the entire perimeter of the massive square on each deck with docking arms.

Nic and Lyral were already deep inside the station, walking through one of the aisles in the shopping district, a large bag balanced between them. The younger of the two grabbed a bundle of flavorless protein cubes. Looking up, she said, "Just in case."

"Good call," Lyral agreed.

Bennie found the tech sector shops on the uppermost deck of the station below the command and control facilities. The shops were subpar compared to even the markets on Fury that were near the Rogue Enterprises office. He found a vendor with spare parts and walked inside.

Nic put a hand on Lyral's arm. "I think we're being followed." The other woman moved to look over her shoulder. "Don't look," Nic hissed.

The pair turned into a stall selling vegetables from several GC worlds. Lyral glanced over her shoulder, but no one stood out. "Who?" she whispered, then added, "Should we call Ben-Ari?"

Nic made a face. "The red-haired woman with the scar. And, are you crazy? He'll never let us live it down."

She picked up a melon the size of her fist. It was blue with pink speckles. "Then what do you suggest?"

Nic grinned, showing her teeth. "We take care of this ourselves." She slipped a handful of small berries into a pocket and left the stall. Lyral stared after her a moment, then followed, dropping the melon back onto the display.

The pair meandered from stall to stall, making their way to the end of the aisle and the far bulkhead of the station. By then, Lyral had managed to get a look at their shadow. She was definitely doing her best to keep a low profile, but after a dozen stalls, she was still there. The Multonae woman couldn't recall seeing the other woman before and had a hard time believing that the syndicate's reach was this powerful.

Nic guided her friend around the end of the aisle. The moment she was certain they were out of their shadow's line of sight, she reached into her pocket and withdrew the berries, scattering them across the deck.

"Go," she whispered, pushing Lyral toward a gap between the backs of two stalls.

They had just moved into the shadows when the red-haired woman came around the corner, stepping on the berries. She cursed, raising her boot to examine the mess. Nic wasted no time, rushing out of hiding to knock the woman over. Straddling her opponent's torso, she leaned down. "Who are you?" She had her beam saber hilt in one hand, aimed at the other woman's shoulder. "Why are you following us?"

Before the woman could answer, the beam saber ignited, crimson blade blazing through the woman's shoulder and the deck beneath her.

Nic jerked as the woman screamed. The saber shut down as quickly as it had turned on. "Oh, gods. Sorry," Nic stammered. "It wasn't supposed to do that."

Lyral helped Nic up, careful to avoid the business end of the younger woman's weapon.

"You stabbed me with a...a...I don't know what that is, but it hurt!" the red-haired woman said. She rolled over, revealing a still glowing hole in the deck.

Nic reached over and patted the other woman's shoulder. "Well, you shouldn't have been following us."

Lyral rolled her eyes. "You'll live. Why were you following us?"

The woman winced. "The Bol Naar syndicate put out a bulletin." She moved to raise her wristcomm, but screamed, the ruined shoulder protesting. "It was you two and a cranky looking Brailack. I figured I'd follow you until they arrived."

"You already called them?" Lyral asked. The other woman nodded, teeth clenched. Lyral looked at Nic. "Time to go."

Nic nodded, then leaned in. "You'll survive. Forget you saw us." The other woman's head bobbed. "We know where to find you." She grabbed Lyral's hand, and the two stalked off.

"Bit dramatic, no?" the taller of the two asked.

Nic looked up, grinning.

CHAPTER 20

AFTER GETTING the *Rocky Nontee* back on course for Multon, Bennie met the women in the lounge. "Come on, Tiny. Let's figure out what's wrong with your beam saber."

He hadn't asked why the two women were in such a hurry to depart, and they had volunteered nothing as far as a reason went.

Nic sprung from the sofa. "Really?"

Bennie nodded. "Can't have you killing yourself or burning a hole through the hull." He motioned her to the hatch.

Lyral, in the kitchenette area, murmured, "Or stabbing someone accidentally."

Bennie glanced at her but said nothing as he ushered his charge toward the hatchway and the small lift beyond.

Down in engineering, Bennie had arrayed the parts he purchased at the station, along with various other bits and pieces on the workbench. In the middle of the work area sat Nic's beam saber.

Bennie looked down at her. "Any idea what you did wrong?"

"How do you know I did something wrong?" she retorted, not looking at him. She was gently disassembling the device.

"Well, I didn't build it. And if I did, it'd work." He stuck his tongue out.

She growled. "It has to be the activator switch." He nodded and held out a hand toward the workbench. She looked around, grabbing a piece of technology off the bench. A few twists and gentle pulls, and her saber hilt came apart. She spread the constituent pieces out in the general shape and pattern that they fit together.

She picked up a piece, turning it over in her hand. She turned to Bennie. "Look, this is crimped." The small piece of technology was a physical switch with several wires tucked inside. One was indeed pinched, a small section of insulation missing. The malfunctions were likely caused by it brushing against the hilt's body randomly.

He smiled. "You're right." He hadn't realized until then how proud he was of his apprentice. She took to building a saber faster than he had, not that he'd ever tell her that.

She unclipped the faulty activation circuit, fashioning a new one from parts on the workbench.

Lyral appeared in the hatch. "Such an intricate piece of technology. Is that something your order has always carried?"

Bennie looked up and nodded. "Normally, a Knight builds their beam saber under less chaotic circumstances, with better parts, but," he shrugged, "we do what we can."

Bennie had built his first saber in the Tower, in the lab that Knights of Plentallus for hundreds, probably thousands, of cycles had used to build their sabers. He was a little embarrassed that twice Nic had been forced to build hers from spare parts.

He said, "The beam saber is as much a badge of office as it is a weapon. In the old days, just seeing a Knight walking into a place, you knew justice was at hand."

Nic finished screwing her hilt back together. She looked at Bennie. He nodded and took a few steps back and motioned for her to keep the business end away from him and the reactor. Lyral leaned back out the hatch, her hand on the control panel, ready to close it should the new device explode. Just in case.

Nic frowned at both of the adults, then thumbed the activation control. With a *snap-hiss*, her red energy blade sprang to life.

She let out a breath she hadn't realized she was holding. She looked at Bennie, who was releasing his own breath. He nodded to her, his chest puffed out more than normal.

Bennie's wristcomm beeped, breaking the silence. He looked down and sighed. He tapped the ACCEPT icon. "What?"

"Don't *what* me. What're you doing out there? Why are there, like, two dozen dressed up Multonae lurking around the building?" Wil demanded.

Bennie grimaced. "Guess that answers that." When he saw Wil's expression, he said, "We're on our way back to Multon. We've got data that can bring down the entire Bol Naar syndicate, but it's encrypted. This bucket doesn't have the power."

"And you figured Fury was off limits. Correctly," Wil added. Bennie nodded. Wil inhaled. "Well, what can we do to help?"

The *Rocky Nontee* dropped from FTL further out in the system than required by space control. It gave Bennie a chance to get the lay of the land from a safe distance. Before that, Bennie had reset their transponder again, this time naming the ship the

Sprock. He was pretty sure that was one of the names Wil liked to use.

All three of them were on the bridge, staring out the front window, watching data scroll by as the sensors returned new data. Multon was still too distant to be anything other than a slightly brighter pinpoint of light amid all the stars. Bennie looked over his shoulder. "We'll be in space control comms range in a tock." He checked the long-range sensors. "Lotta ships in orbit. Too far out to tell who or what."

A tock later, the overhead speaker said, "Inbound freighter *Sprock*, you're cleared through. Transmitting approach details."

Nic looked over. "That was easy."

Bennie shrugged. "I hacked the space control system. As far as that space control operator knows, we're hauling sensitive materials from a Multonae colony."

Lyral, standing next to Nic, clucked. "Do you just lie and steal your way through life?"

Bennie rolled his eyes. "Mostly." He pointed out the window. "Should I just broadcast our true ID and why we're here? I'm sure there are a dozen or two of those syndicate cutters loitering about in orbit. Would make their jobs easier."

The ships he was pointing at were almost impossible to see with the naked eye, barely blinking lights zipping around between them and the planet. It was a certainty that many of those little lights were cookie cutter syndicate cutters patrolling for them.

Lyral made a noise but otherwise did not reply. Bennie smirked, then said, "We'll land outside Sentullo just to be safe." He consulted his console, now that they were close enough for space control to feed landing options to them. He looked at Lyral. "How's Varlo Hem?"

She raised her hand, palm up, and wiggled it. "It's fine."

"Ringing endorsement," Bennie said as he transmitted their destination and adjusted course.

"There are certainly worse places on Multon," she replied.

As the *Nontee* approached the planet, passing the dozens of orbital stations, bulk freighters, and more, the trio alternated between watching out the forward window and looking at the sensor display. None of the cutters Bennie had tagged gave any indication that they saw through the transponder change. Plenty of barely held together crap heaps hauled cargo in and out of the system. The *Rocky Nontee* blended right in.

The moment the ship hit atmosphere, plasma streamers began to form against its shields, and the trio released a collective breath.

The ship shuddered as it made its way through the atmosphere. In the distance, the downtown core of Sentullo became visible.

"Hey, look, the park where the rally was," Nic said, pointing.

Lyral groaned. "The place my life came to an end."

Bennie waved a hand. "Don't be so melodramatic." The ship tilted, nearly sending all three of them crashing against the bulkhead. "Oops." He adjusted their course, Sentullo sliding out of view through the forward window.

The VarloDrome spaceport was pretty much like every other spaceport Bennie had seen on Tier 1 and 2 GC worlds. A five-or-so-story ring wall a few kilometers in diameter. A control tower reaching another five stories into the sky sitting atop the wall facing north. The wall itself was full of mechanical bays, ship brokerages, import and export businesses, and customs. The upper floors were offices and spaceport-related businesses.

The ship settled on its landing gear with a groan. Nic looked up from her console. "You're getting good at that."

Bennie frowned, remembering the years of mocking he had

been dishing out on Wil for his inexpert landings. Turned out it wasn't as easy as Bennie thought it looked. Not that he'd ever admit that to Wil.

As his seat rotated and lowered, he swiped on his wrist-comm, sending new identities to the two women. "Here you go. These should install right over your regular ident. Don't worry, your real you will be in a protected partition."

Nic nodded looking over her new identity. Her face fell, and she glared at Bennie. "A homeless runaway taken in by a brothel before finding the God Flubnut?" She looked at Lyral for support.

The other woman shrugged. "He made me a research scientist."

"You already were a research scientist!"

Lyral held up a hand. "Actually, I'm a data scientist."

It never ceased to amaze Bennie that no matter what planet, no matter what city, capital, or backwater, spaceports were always crowded and busy. More so for those with customs areas. They had arrived mid-morning local time, and it was past lunchtime by the time they got outside. As a precaution against the syndicate putting a watch out for laser swords, he rigged up a carrying case that made his and Nic's hilts look like parts of a sleep aid machine.

Varlo Hem wasn't a backwater by any stretch. As the trio exited the customs screening area onto the wide promenade fronting the port, they could see the glittering downtown district a few ploriths distant.

"I'm hungry," Nic complained.

Bennie ignored her.

"I could eat," Lyral offered.

Bennie grimaced. "Fine." He looked around. As in almost all spaceports, there was an open-air market snuggled up against the ring wall stretching almost a third of the circumference. He pointed. "We'll grab something to eat there." He headed for the market. Behind him, the two women bumped their fists.

Like most spaceport markets, this one had food stalls near the center in a kind of courtyard, with tables scattered about.

The three of them sat down, having grabbed food from different vendors. Around a mouthful of seasoned jerlack— according to Wil, space beef—Bennie said, "Okay, since we're sitting here, tell me about your lab."

Lyral finished chewing and said, "It should be empty. I had three assistants, but I'm guessing the mayor reassigned or fired them."

Nic took a bit of something on a stick. Mid-chew, she said, "Or they're dead."

Bennie tilted his head. "Dark, but not out of the realm of possibilities." He looked to Lyral, making a *go on* motion.

She took another bite, thinking of what else to say. "The building itself is pretty plain. It's in an industrial park on the outskirts of Sentullo. Literally dozens of identical buildings, most of them labs and manufacturing facilities—oh, and a couple of vehicle restoration shops."

"Security?" Bennie asked. "Fences, guards, patrols? Anything like that?"

Lyral shook her head. "No, nothing. Each building has an alarm system and such, but beyond that, no."

Bennie nodded slowly, taking another bite of his meal. "Okay, that's good, at least." He looked at the two women. "Ready?"

"I need to pee," Nic announced.

He pointed to the set of once portable refreshers. Over the

cycles, someone had built a platform around them, including a hand washing station.

Lyral watched the youngest member of their group walk away, then turned to Bennie. "So, what's your plan?"

He thought for a moment, then said, "If what you say is true, I think we just walk in."

"It was true last week," she offered.

He bobbed his head. "Do you know that model of processing cores you had?"

She shook her head. "I know they were top of the line when I started the project. Mayor Dardle complained, a lot, about the cost."

He rubbed his chin. "Okay, that's promising. Still, though, at a guess, we're looking at a few tocks, at least, to brute force this encryption." He patted the satchel containing the two data storage modules. He had slung it over a shoulder.

She looked at the table. "I hope we have that long."

He grinned. "Well, don't jinx it."

Nic returned. "Ready."

"Did you wash your hands?" Bennie asked. Nic's rude gesture was all the answer he got.

The bus that went where they needed to be was not a popular route. After a half dozen stops, it was just the three of them.

Watching the city core slide by outside, Bennie turned to Lyral. "You said outskirts. Are we even in the same voting district?"

She made a noise but said nothing.

CHAPTER 21

"SO MUCH FOR the last place they expected us to be," Nic said, peering through a gap in the shrubs the three of them were crouched behind.

Bennie nodded. "These drennogs aren't as dumb as I'd hoped." He looked at his companions. "That's bad news for us."

Across the street from their hiding bush was the building that Lyral's lab occupied. It was a bland two-story building with few windows and almost two dozen not-even-kind-of-discreet well-dressed gangsters milling around the front and rear of the building.

Lyral leaned back. "What now?"

"I wonder how much they get paid?" Nic said to no one in particular. Her two companions eyed her a moment.

Bennie motioned them back around the corner of the building behind them, taking them fully out of sight of the syndicate goons patrolling the lab.

Leaning against the wall, Bennie sighed. "Maybe the sewers?" He knew how much most beings hated sewers and thanked evolution that Brailacks had adapted the ability to close off their sense of smell.

Nic wrinkled her nose. "It'll get all in my fur. I'll stink for weeks."

"You stink now," Bennie quipped. He yelped, quietly, when she reached over and pinched him. "You're not supposed to pinch your mentor. It's in the rule book." Under his breath he added, "Probably."

Lyral shook her head. "I'm not certain, but I don't think that'll work. This entire development is only ten cycles old, give or take. The plumbing will be new. The sewer will be accessible under the street, but the branch to the buildings will be too small to get through."

"Dren," Bennie hissed.

"Literally," Nic added. She snapped her fingers. "What about cutting our way in? Like Lyral and I did on the commerce orbital over Tro Ella." Bennie looked at her blankly so she added, "We figured the front doors would be alarmed, so we cut our way into the building through the wall, into an office next to the lobby."

"Good thinking," he complimented, then said, "We'd need a spot that they wouldn't notice." They had seen several of the syndicate men and women crossing from one side of the building to the other so assumed that they were watching the back as well.

"The roof?" Lyral offered.

"All this time we've been together and you never mentioned you could fly. Can all of you do it? I might respect Rhys Duch more if that's the case." Bennie leaned in to examine the woman opposite him.

She adjusted her braid, pushing it off her shoulder. "No, we cannot fly, you krebnack." She pointed up.

A mobile advertising sign was drifting by overhead on repulsorlifts. It was advertising a casino the next district over. The floating platform was oval shaped, the advertisement itself a hologram projected under the device. It was drifting away from their target, toward the next block of buildings.

Bennie stood. "Let's go!" He darted off in the direction the floating advertisement was heading. Over his shoulder he said, "If we can get aboard, I can reprogram it and we drift right over the bad guys."

Lyral made a face. "Can you fly?"

Bennie didn't answer. They reached a building in the path of the mobile advertising platform. The hum of its repulsorlifts was barely audible.

The building Bennie chose was the former home of Bo Tan Pharma. It wasn't clear if they'd moved or gone out of business. Bennie didn't actually care.

The service ladder was in back, the last segment from the ground held out of reach by a lock. He activated his beam saber and handed it to Lyral. The small DNA scanner he had added to this latest version only came into play when the saber was activated, so handing it to her once engaged was relatively safe. "You're tall—be useful."

She took the weapon and gave him a dirty look before slashing the blade sideways to cut through the lock. The metal ladder to rattled to the ground. She handed him back his weapon.

"Come on, come on! It's almost here," Bennie shouted from the rooftop, looking down at the two women still coming up the ladder.

He looked toward the advertising platform making its ponderous way toward them. He raised his wristcomm, hoping...There. There it was: a wireless network meant for technicians to take control of the platform for maintenance.

A few quick taps and his password-cracking app had broken through. Obviously, the people in charge of these advertising platforms couldn't fathom someone trying to take one over. A small flight control program appeared on his wristcomm screen. Great, more flying.

Lyral and Nic watched as the large platform drifted closer and closer to the building, lowering as it did.

"Uh..." Lyral said.

The platform continued to descend.

Bennie was tapping and swiping on the digital flight controls as the platform came lower and lower. Sensing their closeness to an object, the holo projectors shut off.

"Bennie?" Nic said, taking a step back.

The platform was really low now.

Its repulsorlifts flared, their gentle drone rising in pitch. The craft came to a stop, barely a plor from Bennie's head. He turned. "I wasn't worried."

"Pretty sweaty for someone who wasn't worried," Nic replied, joining him under the hovering advertising platform. "So, we steer this thing back the way it came, over Lyral's lab?" Bennie nodded. "Neat."

Bennie found the command to extend the small service ladder. "All aboard."

There wasn't much in the way of creature comforts aboard the platform. It was a flat deck with a small cluster of equipment, enclosed in a weatherproof cover, occupying the center. There were no seats, safety rails, or anything else on the platform to hold on to. They must carry maintenance out in a more controlled environment.

The two women chose to lay flat on the deck, while Bennie sat next to the module in the center attempting to wrestle the ungainly mechanism under control.

The vehicle rose into the air, the holo projectors coming online.

Bennie had hoped for manual controls of some sort, but found none, so was still steering the vehicle with the virtual controls on his wristcomm.

"This seemed like a better idea on the ground," Lyral complained when the platform shifted to the side before dropping nearly a plor, leaving her stomach somewhere above them.

"You want to take a turn at the helm?" Bennie asked, holding his arm up, the virtual controls visible on his wristcomm screen.

Lyral shook her head.

"Can I try?" Nic asked.

"No," the two adults said as one.

Bennie turned his attention back to trying to guide the advertising platform back to the lab building. Overriding the auto navigation system had been easy, but it kept trying to re-engage and bring the craft back onto its original flight path, so he had to keep overriding that system.

To anyone looking, the advertising platform looked drunk. It was changing altitude, swerving this way and that, and occasionally a shout or scream would come from it—all while an animated character hovered below, enticing viewers to a casino nearby.

Nic crawled to the edge to peer over the edge. She looked back. "I think we're almost there. I see the goons."

Bennie wiped his forehead. "Good. We're going to have to jump. Trying to land this thing will attract attention."

"Jump? Are you crazy? We're four plor up if a plorum," Lyral said, inching over next to Nic to get a look.

"I can extend the service ladder," Bennie offered, even though he knew it was only a plor or two long at best, and he wasn't going to be able to lower the craft much beyond where he currently had it.

Nic pushed Lyral's head back when she saw one of the men below look up. He pointed to the platform and said something to the man nearest him. The two chatted about the amenities of the casino and potential for extramarital fun. Nic made a face as the two men passed underneath. She looked at Lyral and Bennie. "We're over the roof."

Bennie issued a command to slow down, then deployed the service ladder. "Time to go."

Lyral gestured for Nic to go first. "Why me?" the younger woman asked.

"You're young, your bones are soft, and you're furry. If I fall, I want to land on you," Lyral said, her expression flat. Nic made a rude gesture, so Lyral went first. Hanging from the last rung of the ladder, she closed her eyes and let go.

She hit the rooftop hard, her legs buckling underneath her. She did her best to not scream out or make any more noise than her impact had.

Nic hit the ground in much the same way but tucked into a roll at the end to soften the landing.

Bennie landed, tucked, rolled, and sprang to his feet. Looking at his companions, he wiggled an eyebrow ridge. The advertising platform's programming reset again, and the platform shuddered and adjusted its course.

After a few minutes of collecting themselves, Bennie looked at Lyral. "Do you remember the layout of the second floor well enough to know where we should cut in?"

She nodded and gestured to a corner of the building near the rear wall.

While Bennie and the ladies were on the advertising platform, an Ankarran Raptor, model 89, better known as the *Ghost*, was coming for a landing.

Zephyr looked up from her station, her jet-black hair pulled back into the tight ponytail she preferred. "His ship is down there, alright."

Maxim looks at one of the screens on his tactical console. "That's an ugly ship."

Wil stifled a laugh and nodded. "You have his locator?"

Zephyr nodded, and a sub window opened on the main display at the front of the bridge, showing a map with a pulsing green dot. "Looks like an industrial park a few ploriths from here."

Maxim looked up from his station. "I'll go down and pack some toys." He stood and left the small bridge, heading for the armory on the deck below.

Wil reached up and ruffled his brown hair before grasping the flight controls with one hand while preparing to switch between the sub-light engines and the powerful atmospheric thrusters. The ship rocked a few times, buffeted by wind and plasma streamers.

A light on his console told him when it was the optimal time to make the cut over, and with practiced ease, he pulled back the throttle control for the sub-light engines. He pushed the atmospheric thruster throttle forward in the same motion. The telltale boom that echoed through the ship, accompanied by a sudden pressing into the back of their seats, confirmed the activation of the atmospheric engines.

Like the *Rocky Nontee*, the *Ghost* wasn't aerodynamic enough for atmospheric flight. Her wings weren't shaped appropriately to generate any lift, and the FTL engines in the nacelles at the ends were an awkward weight.

The upside of the design was that the engine nacelle

mounted repulsor lifts that allowed the ship to stay aloft in an atmosphere. They were powerful enough to provide a cushion for the ship from several kilometers in altitude. It never ceased to amaze Wil how well balanced the whole system was. He could power up the repulsor lifts, and the ship would rise straight up off the ground, balanced on the twin energy buffers perfectly.

Minutes later, the *Ghost* set down with a creak and groan as her full weight settled on her landing gear, a pair of birdlike legs on which the ship balanced.

Cynthia, Wil's new wife—which was going to take some time getting used to for both of them—stood. "I heard back from Duch. He said good luck, but he's not getting involved in Bol Naar syndicate business."

Wil shook his head. "Bennie, what've gotten yourself into? Go train your new sidekick, that's it. Not stir up a hornet's nest of organized crime." He sighed. "Let's go bail him out."

Wil put the ship's systems into standby mode, locking the bridge stations down.

The three of them met Maxim outside the bridge as he was coming up the stairs from the armory on the deck below. The big Palorian man had two duffel bags slung over his shoulders. They looked heavy. Wil did not offer to take one. Zephyr extended an arm to her partner, taking one of the bags.

Maxim had a long brown duster slung over one of the bags. Wil snatched it, slipping it on. He looked at Zephyr, then Cynthia. "Better get dressed for fun." They nodded and went down the stairs. He looked at Maxim. "Let's go rent a car."

CHAPTER 22

"OKAY, I'M IMPRESSED," Bennie said as the trio walked between processing cores taller than Lyral. "These are BryoDynamics Lexar Fours." He ran a hand along one of the devices, admiring the blinking lights and soft vibration of the cooling system.

Lyral shrugged. "I don't know what that means, but I told you they were high end."

Bennie waved a dismissive hand. "This won't take as long as I feared." He turned. "Your workspace has a direct link?"

Lyral nodded and led them down a hallway.

As they walked, Nic asked, "So, what's on the first floor?"

Lyral didn't turn but said, "The canteen, refreshers, a small gymnasium, and locker rooms. Most of the rear is warehouse."

"What's all that stuff for?" Nic wondered.

"I had a staff, a few junior researchers and interns. The mayor thought he had to compete with local startups for talent." A door slid open. "Here we are."

Lyral's workspace was impressive, Bennie had to admit. Massive displays were mounted to three of the four walls.

Smaller processing cores lined the other wall, while workstations lined another.

He remembered seeing a large communications array on the roof. "So, all this did local crunching before you uploaded to your fish-faced data guy?"

Lyral nodded. "Right. We'd collect and collate the data from sources across the Multon system, do some initial analysis and collation, tagging metadata, yurlo-yurlo, then upload to his data center. That's where the real crunching came into play." She sighed. "Like I said, the original plan was to do all the analysis here, but when patterns started to emerge and it became clear just how deep the syndicate's reach was, Mayor Dardle lost his nerve."

Nic clucked. "Not enough to pull the plug completely."

Lyral inclined her head. "Just so. He saw the results of my research as his ticket to stardom, political stardom."

Bennie's wristcomm beeped. He looked at it, accepting the call. Wil's face appeared. "Hey, Kermit, we're planetside in a rental hover van. What's the situation over there?"

Bennie handed Lyral the satchel. As she moved to her workspace, placing the drives on her desk, he said, "We're inside the lab, just getting started. The processors are top-notch. I might have Gabe help me borrow a few on our way out. It shouldn't take more than a tock or two to decrypt."

"Then what?" Maxim shouted from somewhere in the vehicle with Wil. Wil flinched.

"I think we can repurpose the comm array on the roof. Tap into the local internex and flood it with data. Be impossible to ignore or stamp out."

"Like old times," Wil said.

What felt like tens of cycles ago, a wayward human had accidentally put together a team that stumbled onto a conspiracy that would have seen several independent star systems joining the Galactic Commonwealth under duress. Bennie, Wil, the Palorian couple, and Gabe had nearly died doing the right thing, transmitting the data in the middle of an actual war zone. Bennie still told the story, at least the version with him as the primary hero, whenever anyone asked.

They'd all been together ever since and added Cynthia to the family a few cycles later. He still thought Wil wasn't good enough for her, but what could you do?

"Hey!" Wil shouted, breaking Bennie from his reverie.

"Oh, yeah, old times," he agreed.

"Okay, well, don't get killed before we get there," Wil said before closing the channel.

Bennie looked around. "Okay, I'm going back up to the roof. See if I can get that comm array rewired into the local internex." He pointed at Nic. "Help her."

"I don't need any help."

Lyral didn't look up from connecting the data storage units to her workstation and loading the brute force decryption Bennie had sent to her wristcomm.

Bennie shrugged. "Okay, go downstairs, see if you can scope out what the goons are doing. Don't let them see you."

"Duh, Grandpa." Nic waved a dismissive hand as she walked out of the lab. "They won't see me!" she shouted.

Bennie rubbed his face. "Call if you need anything," he said. Lyral nodded.

"Don't let them see you," Nic said in a not very good imitation of Bennie's voice, as she descended the stairs, fiddling with her beam saber. Leaving the stairwell, she rounded a corner and collided with two men in suits. She screamed. They screamed. She swung her arm in a wide arc, her thumb reflexively flicking the activation switch of her beam saber.

The nearest man fell, his head bouncing to the ground a split second before his body. The heat of the blade cauterized the arteries and veins, thankfully, keeping gore from squirting everywhere.

Nic screamed again, her beam saber flicking off. The other man screamed again. He turned from his fallen friend to the furry little girl. "You cut his head off!"

"I know! I'm so sorry! Oh, my gods!" She waved her arms frantically as she jumped up and down.

After the initial shock wore off, the syndicate man's wits returned. He raised his pistol, aiming for Nic's chest. He fired a split millitock too late, her training kicking in and allowing her to dodge the blast, barely. She tucked into a roll before springing back to her feet. Plasma bolts followed her path.

She leapt sideways to the other wall of the hallway, activating her beam saber. She swung it in a tight arc in front of the man, forcing him to take a step back—which led him to kick his friend's head, eliciting a yelp as he stumbled. Nic didn't waste her opportunity, slashing diagonally across his chest. The pistol clattered to the ground. A glowing line traced across his chest. His suit jacket and the shirt underneath were smoking. The second corpse collapsed on top of the first.

She stared at the two bodies, numb. She'd killed them. Sure, they were bad guys, she knew that. These certainly weren't the first two people to die at her hand. She kneeled down to look at the second man, his lifeless eyes staring ahead. She reached out and closed his eyes.

Standing, she clipped her saber to the belt hook and hugged herself for a moment. Inhaling, she shook her head and looked around. No one else was around, and she couldn't hear anyone. Why were those two in the building? As far as they had been able to tell, the goons had been content to wait outside. She looked at the doors near her. Oh. The door opposite her was the refresher. She looked down at the men. "Sorry, guys."

She crept down the hall, passing the door to the warehouse space on one side and the locker rooms on the other. Up ahead, a hallway branched off. She leaned around to get a look. The lobby was not overly large. A pair of sofas lined the walls, leading from the transparisteel double doors to the reception desk. Someone had placed a terminal on top of the desk, turning it to face guests. Next to the terminal, three well-dressed women were studying something on the screen.

One woman said, "See, the stairwell door was opened."

Another nodded. "Maybe Fjorb or Deez couldn't find the refresher?" Nods all around. She said, "We should check this floor to be sure. Just in case." More nods.

Nic swore to herself and crept back the way she came. Scowling, she tapped the earpiece jammed into her ear. "I, uh, think they know we're here."

"What? How?" Bennie demanded.

Reaching the stairwell door, Nic nudged the severed head to the side of the walkway next to the bodies. "I...uh...Is that important?"

"Quite."

She slipped into the stairwell, closing the door behind her.

"What did you do?" Bennie demanded.

"Nothing. Well...Look, it doesn't matter, but they're going to be checking the floor soon."

Bennie swore. "Can you secure the door to the stairs?"

"Yeah. I think so."

"Do it. Lyral, can you disable the lift?"

From her desk, the data scientist said, "I'll try, but I don't know."

"Do your best."

Nic reignited her beam saber. She first jabbed the blade into the lock, ensuring it was a fused molten mess. She gingerly tapped the hinges with the tip of her blade, just enough to melt them into slag. Slag that would no longer permit the door to open. Nodding at her handiwork, she clicked off her weapon and headed upstairs.

Lyral was tapping her fingers on the workbench, watching Bennie's program work. True to his boasts, it was an impressive program; the monitoring software for the processing cores in the other room showed that every unit was running at maximum capacity. She'd never seen them working that hard before, even when they had been crunching the data locally. The room sensors were already registering increases in the ambient temperature.

She pulled up a new interface window. She was no code slicer, but she'd see what she could do.

Up on the roof, Bennie was pacing a slow circle around the communications array. He was equal parts annoyed and impressed. The array was modern and quite advanced, capable of throughput that put his gear on the roof of Rogue Enterprises to shame. Being able to have an open channel that spanned, what, thirteen light years? Impressive. He wondered if he could load it into the *Nontee* when this was done.

He reached into the internal space and flinched back as an arc of electricity jumped from a loose connection to his arm, stinging him. "Grolack," he hissed, brushing at his singed arm. He reached back in, careful to avoid the loose wire. The hardest part of what he was trying to do was change the broadcast parameters. Knowing that the syndicate knew they were there meant he didn't have time to waste figuring it out.

He glanced down at his wristcomm and noticed that it said NO SIGNAL. *Great*, he thought. The syndicate was jamming local internex connections. He glanced around to see if he could see a jammer tower, but wherever it was, he couldn't see it.

Nic joined Lyral. "How's it going? Were you able to kill the lift?" the small Knight of Plentallus asked.

The other woman shrugged. "It's not like there's a progress bar or anything." She gestured to the screen nearest her seat. Lines of code were flashing by too fast to read. Every once in a while, the scroll would stop and a line of code would flash before the scroll resumed.

She gestured to a small window floating over that. "I was able to push a maintenance request through submission and approval, since they apparently set my account up as building manager." She shrugged again. "That probably won't hold them long, though." She held up her wristcomm. "They set up jammers." Her wristcomm screen had a flashing NO SIGNAL message in the corner.

Nic grunted. "I'll go see if I can mess anything up." She turned and left.

Bennie consulted his wristcomm screen. "Yes!" He pumped a fist in the air. The diagnostic was returning full signal acquisition. When they cracked the data storage units, the upload would be fast.

He began entering details for local and GC media companies and journalists, as well as governmental agencies across the sector. He made sure to add the mayor's office to the list.

Nic hopped into a seat next to Lyral. "Think this will work?" She nodded to the screens before both of them, still scrolling data faster than either could read.

"Done with the lift?" Lyral asked.

The younger woman grinned.

Lyral inclined her head, smiling. "I hope so. Ben-Ari is quite capable. You said that the two of you single-handedly defeated a pirate squad, on their home turf, even. Plus, a band of mercenaries aboard that cruise ship?"

Nic shrugged. "Yeah." She looked at the computer displays. "That was, like, only a few people. There doesn't seem to be any end to these syndicate goons." After a pause, she added, "The cruise ship stuff was just him and his friends. I was stuck with a Xelurian scientist. He wouldn't shut up about whatever it was he was going to be working on if he made it off the ship."

Lyral put a hand on the Olop's shoulder. Nic closed her eyes. "What if I'm just a mindless killer now?" she snuffled.

"Uh, what?"

The smaller woman looked up; her bearlike ears twitched, then lay flat. "The Knights were cruel killers, at least sometimes. It seems like so long as the purpose is noble, killing is okay."

Lyral shook her head. "I don't think killing is ever okay. I do think, more so now than ever before in my life, that it's often needed." Reaching out to Nic's chair, she spun it so that Nic faced her. "But no. You're not a mindless killer. Know how I know?" The girl shook her head. "Because you're crying." Nic reached up and rubbed her eyes. The fur around her cheeks was wet and matted.

A loud bang from somewhere nearby interrupted the conversation.

Nic was on her feet immediately, beam saber in hand, crimson blade humming.

Bennie came in rubbing his forehead. "Who stacked all that crap in the hallway?"

"Oh, sorry." Nic's saber snapped off, and she clipped it to her belt. "I thought that would slow them down if they made it up here."

Bennie looked around. "Slowed me down. How's it coming?"

Lyral gestured to the screen. "It's going, but I couldn't say if it'll be one more microtock, or two more tocks."

Bennie motioned Nic out of his way. Tapping commands into the console, he said, "See if you can see what they're up to out front."

"Who?" Lyral asked.

Bennie shrugged. It was true there was no progress meter on his application, but checking the logs revealed the process was just about half done. His software was attacking the data on two fronts: a brute force attempt at entering a decryption key, and another brute force attempt at decrypting individual blocks of text, looking for patterns it could exploit to speed the process along. Every bit it found made finding the next that much easier.

Unfortunately, it took as long as it took. There was no way to predict when the next breakthrough would come, so guessing at progress was impossible.

He looked at his wristcomm. Still being jammed. He had thought about trying to rig up a broadband connection to the array up on the roof but worried the longer he was up there, the more likely he'd be noticed. If that array was destroyed, that was it. Game over. He hoped that Wil and the others were close. As much as he hated to admit it, even to himself, this felt like more than he could manage.

"They're coming," Nic said, entering the lab.

"Who?"

"The Nudon and his thirteen helpers. Who do you think, Gramps? The well-dressed murderers. They're trying to break down the door to the stairs."

Wil stopped the rental van two streets from where Bennie's locator was pinging on the map before it went dark. The vehicle lowered to the ground as the gravlifts powered down. "At least it's not a sewer." He looked over his shoulder. "Gear up."

Everyone was in a mix of light armor and street clothes. Since their crime boss, sort-of-friend Rhys Duch refused to get involved, they had to pass through customs like anyone else. Personal weapons were allowed on most worlds, thankfully. Heavy armor and combat gear, less so. To Maxim's chagrin, grenades fell into the frowned-upon category. Pistols it was.

Wil looked to Gabe. The droid was standing next to Zephyr. "Anything?"

Gabe had recently changed his physical appearance, again. An ability unique to him. Early in his time with the crew of the *Ghost*, they had encountered a sapient warship from thousands of light years beyond the Galactic Commonwealth's border. Gabe had covered the team's retreat when the gargantuan ship's systems had attacked, but had, at least temporarily, died.

The massive ship's own sapient intelligence, intrigued by Gabe, extracted his core programming from the frame that was his body.

Gabe had been able to turn the tables on the ship's system, using its own fabrication system to build a body he found in its database. That body, it turned out, was full of all kinds of tricks he had been discovering over the last few years, the latest of which was the ability to entirely reconfigure the body to a new design.

Gabe's eyes flickered blue. "There is a dead spot in the local internex where Bennie's beacon was last heard from. However, we are too far for my sensors to pick up life signs."

"Closer, we go," Maxim said, sliding a pulse pistol from his holster.

As the five of them made their way toward the building that Bennie and the two women were planning to defend, Wil looked at his friends, and now, his wife. He had gone from stranded in an experimental space pod to having a team of people he loved liked family and a spaceship that let him travel the galaxy.

Life was weird.

Maxim, in the lead, held up a fist. Everyone stopped. Gabe joined him, then over the shared mesh communication network that their wristcomms created, said, "There are eleven men and women gathered around the front of the building. I believe there are five more around the sides and back of the building." He leaned back to look again. "Two industrial vans. I believe one is temporary lodging. There are eight more life signs within it. Sleeping, I think. The other has only two people inside."

"Command center," Maxim said. Gabe nodded his agreement.

Zephyr slid both pulse pistols out of their holsters on her thighs. "So, what's the plan?"

Wil smiles. "I play friendly neighborhood Multonae."

When Wil first encountered a Multonae person, he thought he had found another human lost in the Galactic Commonwealth, until he learned that, in fact, there was an entire society of beings that looked exactly like humans. Five fingers and toes, two eyes, one nose. Even their internal arrangement was almost identical to humans'. Wil had looked them up on what he called space Wikipedia. Multonae had larger lungs and two spleens, or spleen-like organs. Wil had gotten distracted when reading the medical jargon about the organs.

The more he learned about Multonae culture, the gladder he was that they weren't some precursors to humanity or something.

He strode out around the corner, duster flapping in the breeze. "Hi there!" He waved.

Gabe looked at the others. "If he can get twenty steps closer to the building, I believe that will allow Bennie's wristcomm's mesh system to connect to us."

"He'll get dead in ten steps," Cynthia said. Maxim and Zephyr nodded.

Everyone leaned out from the building to watch whatever Wil had planned, unfold.

CHAPTER 23

BENNIE AND NIC left Lyral's lab, closing the door behind them. They heard the sound of locks clicking into place.

Nic looked up. "Those won't hold for long." She pointed at the door.

Bennie nodded. "Yeah, if they get to this door, and we haven't uploaded everything, well, we'd better be dead."

"Okay, that's dark."

He shrugged and pointed to the stairwell. "How well do you think your breaking of things down there will hold?"

"I fused the locks and the hinges, but the door itself is pretty flimsy." She wiped both palms on her dark trousers.

Bennie opened the door to the stairwell. "I guess that'll be our first stand."

They made their way down the stairs, slashing light fixtures as they went, plunging the space into near complete darkness.

They reached the first-floor door, and Bennie kneeled down to inspect Nic's work. "Nice." He stood. "Your precision is much better." The door banged; they could hear shouting on the other side.

She blushed, the fur around her face rippled. Rocking on her heels, she said, "Thanks."

A loud crash rang out against the door, visibly rattling it.

Bennie motioned for Nic to move back up the stairs a few steps. He whispered, "Don't accidentally cut my head off." He grinned and turned to face the door.

Nic's stomach did a somersault. She hadn't told Bennie about her meeting with the two gangsters, and their bodies were on the other side of the door, so the odds of him ever seeing her handiwork were slim. Still, the innocent comment froze her in her tracks. The look on the first man's face the moment before he died haunted her.

The door shook again, the fused hinges buckling. The door tilted on its remaining hinge. Bennie had positioned himself to the side of the door on the small landing and the stairs that continued down to the basement.

Light flooded in from the hallway, blocked by the crush of bodies trying to get into the stairwell.

"They have to be up there. This door wasn't blocked when we checked the building earlier," someone said.

"How'd they get in? We've had the front and back doors under watch," another voice, a woman's, retorted.

Several more voices chimed in with opinions on the topic.

Before the conversation could continue any further, Bennie shouted, firing two beam saber bolts into the nearest shadowy figure. Through the smoke of the weapon's fire, the figure fell to the ground.

The gangsters outside began shouting and screaming. Bennie joined in, flipping his saber to blade mode, sending the blade humming through someone's arm and a portion of the doorjamb.

Two women that might give Maxim a run for his money on muscle mass ripped the door from its final hinge, tossing it back into the hallway. Bennie scrambled to avoid a kick that might have sent him through the wall.

Nic flicked her saber on and leaped from the upper stairs onto the nearest woman's shoulders. Holding her saber high, she leaned down and bit the woman's face before spinning her blade and plunging it straight down through the shoulder joint.

The scream was deafening as the burly woman crashed to the ground, her good hand cradling her ruined arm. Nic's attack hadn't severed the limb but had vaporized bone and muscle tissue.

Nic tumbled back and clambered back up the steps, joining Bennie on the midpoint landing between the two floors where the staircase doubled back. Plasma bolts rang through the enclosed space, scorching the stairs, the wall, and everything else.

Bennie pushed Nic. "Go, go! We can't hold this!" He flipped his saber back to what he called long range mode and fired a volley of energy bolts. He heard a few screams and shouts. The smell of burnt flesh filled the stairwell.

His wristcomm crackled. "Bennie?" He looked down as he climbed stairs, nearly tripping. The screen showed he had a mesh network connection. "Gabe? Thank gods of reproduction!"

"Ew," Nic said, pulling open the door. They were officially out of fallback positions. She slammed the door closed, examining it. "Hinges are on the inside." She pointed at the door.

Bennie looked up from his wristcomm, meeting his apprentice's gaze. He shrugged. She rolled her eyes and trotted off.

From his wristcomm, Gabe said, "We are outside. Wil is causing a distraction to allow himself to get close enough to —" The signal dropped.

Bennie looked at the door again. Guessing where the hinges should be, he jabbed his beam saber into the seam between doorjamb and door, mimicking Nic's move from below. He hoped.

Behind him, Nic returned pushing random things she'd found throughout the floor into makeshift barricades.

"I work the next street over and saw all this." Wil made a sweeping gesture toward the assembled men and women. "Was wondering what was up? This a sting or something? Someone important about to show up?" He leaned in conspiratorially. "They not pay their rent?"

"What?" demanded a burly man. He was stepping out from behind one of the large vans across the street from the building with Bennie inside it.

"Yeah, I guess you lot don't look very much like local security. Or building management," Wil replied, still taking slow steps closer to the building.

A woman moved toward him from closer to the building. "Stop. Moving." She pulled aside her blazer to reveal a pulse pistol in a shoulder holster.

Wil took another step, then stopped. "Oh, sorry. So, you are local security?"

The man from the van planted a hand on Wil's shoulder. "I think it's time for you to go."

"Hey! I think I know that guy," someone shouted from near the building. "Yeah, that's the guy that was in the news all those cycles back." The blonde-haired gangster came over to Wil and leaned in close. He looked at the others. "Yeah, this is definitely him. Filbur or Bill?" He rubbed his bearded chin. "Calabas?"

"Filbur?" Wil stammered.

"Yeah, I thought so."

"Calder, you dummy. Wil Calder," Wil blurted.

From their hiding place around the corner, the rest of the team released a collective sigh.

The blonde-haired man stepped back. "I knew it!" He pointed at Wil. "This guy was the one that—"

Before anyone could say anything further, a shout from inside said, "The stairwell doors are blocked or something. We found Fjorb and Deez, dead. The Stellinio girls are on it!"

The big man, still grasping Wil's shoulder, looked at Wil, then the man who identified Wil. "They've got to be in there. This is it. No survivors! Destroy every piece of equipment up there! Kill all three of them!" The blonde-haired man turned and ran into the lobby. The man in charge turned to Wil. "Don't you roll with a Brailack?"

Wil did his best to shrug with one shoulder immobilized. "Dude, Brailack are everywhere. Did you know they come in blue? Very rare."

"They say yours carries a laser sword, like the one the Brailack we've been trailing has been using."

Wil again shrugged. "I mean, who doesn't have a laser sword these days?" The man squeezed his shoulder, eliciting a strangled sounding noise. "Okay, I might know him."

From inside the building, several people started shouting and screaming. He could hear the sound of weapons fire.

Wil tilted his head. "Okay, probably my Brailack. Do they also say that I travel with a pair of kick ass ex-Peacekeepers and a droid?" He let his legs go limp, pulling the big man, still clutching his shoulder, with him toward the ground.

From across the street, the bark of pulse pistols came a split second after bolts of super charged plasma burned through several of the well-dressed men and women outside the building.

Wil rolled out from under the man in charge, kicking him twice in the midsection, while both were on the ground. The head honcho tried to grab for him, but Wil scurried on his elbows, out of reach.

The shouting and weapons' fire inside the building had died down, but outside, it was chaos.

Maxim, Cynthia, Zephyr, and Gabe were crossing the street, weapons blazing. Cynthia turned to Gabe. "Can you reach Little Green?"

The droid tilted his head. "I will try." His optic sensors were bright red, combat mode. In his previous body, his hands would shift and merge into his forearms, freeing blasters, and a large bore cannon would unfold from his back. His new configuration had blasters that shifted and rose from his forearms, leaving his hands free. Less powerful than the previous version, but more versatile.

Wil was trying to get to cover, wrestling with a woman with a shaved head except for a topknot tied into a long ponytail.

Gabe fired two rapid shots into the woman's side, sending her flying from Wil. "I had Bennie, but Wil moved out of range."

The others joined as Wil said, "How is that my fault?"

A crouched Bennie leaned out from behind a planter and fired two quick blasts from his beam saber. While it was more than effective as a makeshift blaster, it lacked the aiming capabilities of a pulse pistol. The other drawback was that the energy that made up a beam saber's blade required the hilt to form the blade with an electromagnetic confinement field. In blaster mode, the bolt of energy dissipated after far too short a distance.

Nic was crouched behind what looked like a food re-energizer tipped on its end. Her beam saber was clutched in her hand. "I need a gun!" she shouted over the din of weapons' fire.

A plasma bolt struck the cooking unit, burning a hole in its casing, sending sparks everywhere. She growled and looked over the top of the unit. "You missed!" She ducked as another bolt of super charged plasma struck her barricade, driving her lower under cover.

Bennie popped up and fired. He heard a scream as he ducked back down.

"Bennie? Kermit!" his wristcomm barked. He tapped a control switching his earpiece to the Rogue Enterprises mesh comm network. "Wil? You guys here?"

"Yeah, we're outside. Stay alive," Wil said.

Bennie looked back at Nic. "Move back. I'll cover you!" She didn't argue. He leaned out and blasted the ceiling, driving sparks down on the half dozen armed men and women just down the hall.

Nic dropped into a roll and got behind a chair that she had turned on its end. Plasma bolts struck the chair, burnt stuffing flying everywhere.

Bennie looked over his shoulder. The door to Lyral's lab was only plor or two away. He looked at Nic and nodded his head toward the door. She shook her head. He nodded. She shook. He stood and fired into the food re-energizer, making it explode. One of the men that was creeping closer to them fell to the ground, his suit coat on fire.

Bennie looked back to Nic. "Go."

"I'm not leaving you."

He screwed up his face. "Of course, you aren't, dummy. I'll be right behind you." He shook his head. "I'm not dying here." He made a motion, ushering her toward the lab door.

He leaned out to fire when a plasma bolt struck the edge of the filing cabinet he was behind, sending molten metal and sparks into his face. Screaming, he clutched his face with his free hand.

Nic darted next to him, pushing him back. She grabbed his beam saber and squeezed off a few shots. While the gangsters took cover, she pushed Bennie toward the door.

Turning to fire again, she banged on the door. "It's us!" She ducked as several bolts of plasma struck the door and the wall beyond.

The door opened and Bennie fell in. Nic kicked his feet in to clear the threshold, then ducked in, closing the door behind her. The locking bolts slid back into place, securing the door.

"Is he okay?" Lyral asked.

Nic moved to shove a file cabinet in front of the door. "Do I look like a doctor?"

Lyral bent down, pulling Bennie to his feet and guiding him to a chair near her work station.

"How's it coming?" he croaked.

She looked up at the screen. "We're close."

Outside the building, Wil and the team were at the doors to the lobby. The surviving syndicate operatives were falling back deeper into the building.

Wil looked at Gabe. "Mind going up and over? They might need help before we can get to them."

Gabe nodded and stepped back outside. His calves shifted and whirred. The hum of repulsorlifts flared to life, and the tall matte gray droid shot up out of view.

CHAPTER 24

GABE LANDED on the roof of the building. He immediately noticed the comm array and the open panel with loose wiring visible. He moved to look over the array, confirming his assumption that Bennie had reconfigured the device to a new purpose. He did not understand why the brilliant Brailack hacker could not tidy up his work space after a project. Shrugging, he looked around.

The only other structure on the roof was the outbuilding over the roof access stairs.

He reached the door and entered. The access tunnel was dark, the lighting slashed with what could only have been a beam saber.

Over the shared channel he said, "Bennie, I am coming in from the roof."

Bennie didn't reply.

The door to Lyral's lab was banging loudly. The sound of bodies and bolts of energy striking it did not let up.

Lyral looked at Bennie; he was conscious but still dazed. Bits of melted filing cabinet were still stuck to the side of his head, and a large dark green bruise was forming.

She looked at the screen. The brute force attack was working. As best she could tell, the program had cracked nearly ninety percent of the encrypted data. The temperature readout for the processor room was flashing red. She was fairly certain the processors would be useless after this, assuming they even kept working until the end. At least one appeared to have overheated and died already.

Down in the lobby, Maxim and Zephyr had taken up stations on opposite sides of the door to the stairs. Syndicate resistance had been fading as more of them fell or made their way to the second floor to break into the lab. Both of their light armor chest plates sported new scorch marks.

Cynthia was crouched next to a man with a smoldering hole in his chest. She plucked an earpiece from his ear and did her best to fit it into her not-quite-shaped-like-his ear. It wasn't a great fit, so she kept the tip of her finger against it, holding it in place. "They're all upstairs," she reported.

Maxim and Zephyr nodded and stormed into the stairwell, Cynthia and Wil on their heels.

"Was that a headless body back there?" Cynthia asked as they rounded the midflight landing on the staircase.

Wil shook his head. "I'm pretending I didn't see it."

"Bennie is getting a little gruesome," the feline-featured woman whispered as they moved.

Over the shared channel, Gabe said, "I am at the stairwell door."

Maxim reached the second floor and peered out into the hallway. Over his shoulder, he whispered, "They're gathered outside the lab."

Cynthia said, "Gabe, we're at the other staircase door."

"I have you on sensors."

"Pincer?"

"I concur," Gabe replied, adding, "I will go high."

She looked at Maxim, nodded once.

The big Palorian holstered one of his pistols and stepped into the hall in a crouch. He opened fire the moment he cleared the door. Zephyr followed, moving in beside him, also crouching. Their fire caught the gangsters at the same time as Gabe's blaster bolts struck from the other side.

Maxim glanced down the darkened hallway and could have sworn he saw Gabe standing on the ceiling. The smoke and lack of functioning lights might have been playing tricks.

A moment later, Cynthia stepped out. "You could have left one or two for us."

Maxim turned, grinning. "Sorry."

From the other end of the hallway, Gabe said, "You are in luck, Cynthia. I am detecting the arrival of a new van downstairs. Twelve more beings are about to enter the lobby." He was indeed standing on the ceiling.

Wil looked at the droid. "Uh..." He pointed to the ceiling.

Gabe released whatever he was using to grip the ceiling, expertly spinning in midair to land on his feet.

Cynthia cocked an eyebrow. "Interesting approach." The droid inclined his head. She turned back to the staircase, her tail twitching back and forth.

Wil said, "You three get in there and help Green Bean. We'll hold this bunch off." He leaned in to give Cynthia a kiss on the cheek, then checked the power cells on both of his pistols. "I really wish we had bigger guns." She winked, and the two of them stepped into the staircase, firing down the stairs.

"Took you long enough," Bennie drawled when his three friends entered the lab. It had taken Lyral and Nic a few microtocks to pull away the makeshift barricade, a task made easier with a beam saber and the knowledge that they probably would not need the barrier again.

"Good to see you, too," Maxim said. When he got close enough to see Bennie clearly, he added, "You look like dren."

Bennie nodded. "That's good. I feel like dren."

Zephyr looked at the displays on the wall. "So, what is all this? What's the end game?"

Lyral answered, "We're endeavoring to brute force our way through the encryption on these data units. I've spent that last while building a substantial data set documenting the depth and breadth of the Bol Naar syndicate's involvement in Multon government affairs." She smiled. "I'm Lyral Adel, by the way." She offered her arm.

Zephyr smiled, clasping the woman's forearm as the Multonae woman squeezed hers. "Nice to meet you. I'm Zephyr, that's Maxim, and tall-dark-and-not-chatty is Gabe."

"We're Rogue Enterprises." Maxim grinned. "I really do like that sound of that."

Zephyr laughed. "Easier than explaining that we don't have a name." She looked at Nic. "Good to see you, Little One."

Nic's facial fur rippled in a blush. "Glad you all could come. I didn't want to die with Grandpa Grumpy." She was doing her best to put on a brave face, but Zephyr could see the shock behind the young woman's eyes.

The terminal behind Lyral beeped. She turned. "It's...it's done," Lyral said, walking to the terminal.

Bennie spun his chair. "I was beginning to worry."

"What? With the rest of your team here?" Maxim said, leaning out the door to look at the hallway. He could hear the weapons fire from the stairwell he and the others had come up earlier. "Better hurry."

Bennie started tapping on his wristcomm, occasionally swiping information at the terminal. He was having a hard time focusing. Finally, he slid his wristcomm off and handed it to Lyral. "It's all there."

She took the device and looked over the screen. He had set up a handful of routines that would broadcast various segments of the data to different addresses.

Smart. The data was enormous. His approach ensured that the entire thing got out, just to different organizations.

Once the first batch went through, his routine would reshuffle the data and transmit again, the idea being that if it was left alone, every contact on the list would eventually get the entire thing.

If anything happened to the transmission, the header file explained who else received data and what part. She nodded as she got to work finishing the connections needed to start the transfer. While she had been waiting, she compiled a timeline of events from her perspective, starting at the mayor's hiring of her and ending with his giving her up to the Bol Naar. A few quick taps and she appended her file to the data packets, ensuring that hers went to every recipient.

She glanced over at the monitoring software for the processing core room. Not a moment too soon: another unit had already failed, and two more were on the brink.

She looked around the room, finger hovering over an icon.

Nic looked at her. "What're you waiting for? Dramatic music?"

Lyral tapped the icon.

"Did it happen? Did you break it?" Nic pushed Lyral's arm aside to look at the screen. She turned to Bennie.

The Multonae woman glared. "I have three advanced degrees, one in information systems. I'm more than qualified to press a button."

Nic rocked back on her heels. "Just checking."

Gabe looked at the ceiling, his optic sensors taking on a blue tint. "The rooftop array is transmitting."

Wil and Cynthia entered, backing into the room. "Do they just clone these goons? There's so many."

Bennie said, "That's what I want to know."

Lyral sighed. "Welcome to Multon."

Plasma bolts slammed into the doorjamb, sending Wil and Cynthia scrambling into the room. Four pairs of pistols, a pair of arm-mounted blasters, and a beam saber shot up, aimed at the door.

From outside the door, someone said, "I'm coming in. Don't shoot." The voice belonged to a well-dressed man in his later years, gray hair cut high and tight, almost military-like. "Hello."

"Hi," Wil replied. He looked the other man up and down. "You are?"

The other man ignored Wil. "You all," he looked around the room, his gaze settling on Bennie, Lyral, and Nic. "Well, you three in particular have been a pain in my ass." He looked at the rest of the team. "I don't know you, but you're obviously involved." He sighed. "This ends now."

Bennie made a rude gesture.

The man Wil met earlier—the one with the strong grip— came in behind the first man, his arms crossed, glaring.

Gabe stepped forward. "You are correct. This is over. However, your assumption of how this will end is incorrect."

The crime boss tilted his head. "What kind of droid are you?" He held up a hand. "I don't actually care. My organization runs this planet. Well, most of it, anyway. Enough to make sure killing you all doesn't even make the gossip columns. Our influence runs deep." He looked at Lyral. "Well, I guess you know that. Mayor Dardle was quite chatty about what you've been up to. He's come to realize the error of his ways. In a few years he can run for office again, with our blessings."

Before anyone could reply, a bespoke-suited woman with flaming red hair that contrasted with her dark skin brilliantly, stepped into the doorway. "I think we have a problem." She had a pulse rifle held across her chest in a very military bearing.

The boss man scowled, not looking over his shoulder. "What is it?"

She coughed once. "Our contacts in Sentullo civil security just called. Every unit is mobilizing, coming here. Same with several nearby jurisdictions. Planetary security seems to be on the way, too." She held her breath.

"What? Why? We didn't call them in." The man demanded, "Call them off."

His lieutenant shrugged. "We don't know." She looked around. "Our people aren't with them."

Wil raised his hand. "I think this is where you scream some expletives and storm out."

Cynthia nodded, her tail swishing languidly behind her. "He's not wrong. This is when it happens, usually."

"More often than not," Zephyr offered.

The glare that the other man turned on Wil caused him to take a step back. "Maybe I'll kill you first," the man finally replied. The red-haired woman adjusted her rifle, taking aim on the Rogue Enterprises team. The man Wil met before produced a pistol from a holster under his jacket.

Cynthia cocked her head. "I think we both know that won't work out well. You'll definitely be dead. All of us have you in our sights. Your empire will still crumble. Where's the win?" She smiled. "I can already hear sirens." Her left ear twitched.

"Boss?" The other man put a meaty hand on his employer's shoulder.

The man looked at the Rogue Enterprises team, swore, and spun on his heel.

Wil grinned. "It's always a cuss word and stomping off."

"Just once I'd love one of these baddies to say, 'Curses! If it wasn't for you meddling kids...' Just once," Wil said, looking around the lab space. "This place is a dump."

Lyral rubbed her forehead, mumbling something about seeing where Ben-Ari gets it.

By the time the local security services arrived, the few remaining Bol Naar syndicate goons and their boss had vacated the area. On their way out, they ensured their vehicles were burning heaps, and the bodies of their friends bore no idents or wristcomms.

By the time was the sun was setting, hundreds of security people were milling around from a myriad of services. The Rogue Enterprises team, along with Lyral Adel, stood off to the side while the building was secured.

A commander from the planetary security service came over, the two data cores cradled in his palm. He looked the group over, his gaze settling on Lyral. "Looks like we all owe you a bit of thanks. And an apology." She blushed, reaching up to smooth her ponytail. The man continued, "I won't lie, their reach is deep." He gestured to the people all over the complex. "When the data began to arrive, those of us waiting for the right time saw that this was it. When eight out of ten officers are corrupt, or at least not your ally, you learn to wait for the right moment." He bowed. "Thank you for providing that moment."

Lyral smiled. "You're quite welcome. I hope this is a turning point for all Multonae."

"I share that sentiment." He smiled. "We're already rounding their plants up. We'll have the big players by tomorrow. The Bol Naar syndicate is on the ropes. We'll finish what you started." He turned and merged back into the mass of security people.

Wil turned to the data scientist. "Well done."

Zephyr put a hand on Lyral's shoulder. "Dismantling an entire syndicate single-handedly— that's up there with our big wins."

Before she could reply, Bennie said, "What am I? Chopped jerlack?" He shuddered. "Also, I could use some medical attention."

Wil looked down. "Oh, shit." The Brailack hacker and Knight of Plentallus was several shades of green lighter than normal.

The commander arranged transport, since military transports boxed in the rental hover van.

Another thing that always struck Wil as interesting was that no matter what planet they were on, hospitals looked like hospitals. Weird smells, harsh lights. Except Qwazino Three—

their hospitals were more like malls. It was weird.

While the crew was waiting for Bennie, Wil looked at Lyral. "So, what's next?"

She turned. "What?"

He tilted his head. "What's next? For you? We scanned the local newsfeeds on our way in and seems like you went from rising star to wanted criminal to, well, I don't know." He looked around. "Did that commander guy mention if you'd been cleared?"

She opened her mouth, then closed it.

Maxim grunted. "Sounds promising."

She looked at the big Palorian. "I see why Ben-Ari hangs around you all."

Nic hopped off her seat. "I'm going to go get something to eat."

Before she could take more than a few steps, the doors to the treatment area opened. Bennie walked out, his head bandaged.

He was still in his blood spattered, lightly scorched, Knight of Plentallus getup. "Let's suck this poopsicle."

"Not the expression," Wil said, standing.

Bennie looked up at him. "No?"

Wil shook his head. "Nope, not even close." He motioned to the door. "Let's go."

After leaving the hospital, the group retreated to the nearest place to get a drink.

Cynthia looked at Lyral. "So...you didn't really answer. What's next?"

Before she could answer, Nic pointed at one of the entertainment screens over the bar. "Hey, look!"

Everyone turned. On the screen, Mayor Dardle was running, or rather, waddling away from the flock of reporters. The banner at the bottom of the screen was scrolling an update. The mayor was being investigated for his statements regarding the Bol Naar syndicate and the researcher Lyral Adel.

Everyone turned back to Lyral, who released an explosive sigh. She opened her mouth, but before she could answer, Bennie turned to Wil. "You know she's not gonna say, 'I'm going to Dipsey Town.'"

Wil turned, frowning. "It's Disney World. And you never know."

Bennie waved a hand before reaching for his drink. "No, I know."

Maxim turned. "How would she even know what that is?"

Wil shrugged. "Disney is universal."

"Literally, it isn't," Zephyr said before taking a sip of her drink.

The exhausted data scientist shook her head. Clearly, Ben-

Ari was well matched to his team. "I don't know what you're talking about, but not that. I received an offer from a person on the GC Finance Subcommittee, so I'll probably do that for a while. At least until all the Bol Naar syndicate's people have been rooted out." She sighed. "It's too dangerous to stay here. The job is on Tarsis."

Bennie said, "Nic and I can drop you off."

Nic looked over at Bennie. He shrugged. "You still need a lot of training. That means a few more weeks on Nexum. It's sorta on the way. Plus, it'll give us time to work on the *Nontee.*"

"The what?" Wil asked. He took a sip of his drink.

"The *Rocky Nontee.* Like from that old show you made us watch, with the mean old woman in space."

Wil nearly spat his drink out. "It's...Oh man. It's *Rocinante.*" He pronounced it slowly, accentuating each syllable.

"Really?"

Wil nodded, his shoulders shaking from the barely contained laughter. "*Rocinante.*"

"Then what? Back to Fury?" Cynthia asked, trying to bring the conversation back on tracks.

Maxim quickly added, "Not that we've missed you."

Bennie waggled his brow ridges. "You totally did."

Zephyr took a drink and said, "Yeah, the rotten Qwaptar dung smell is fading. Your presence is needed."

Bennie made a rude gesture.

A week later, Lyral safely deposited on Tarsis, Bennie and Nic were moving through some of the more advanced forms on level 27 of the Tower of Plentallus.

Bennie nodded. "You're getting good."

"I've been practicing," Nic admitted with pride.

"I know." He winked.

"You spy on me?" She moved through form 8 into 9 and then 10 smoother than ever before.

"All the time. You're not trustworthy." Bennie smirked.

"I already told you, I didn't know those were yours. You should have put your name on the container."

THE END

THANK YOU

Thank you so much for reading this latest Rogue Enterprises adventure

If you enjoyed it I'd love it if you left a review. Seriously, reviews are a big deal. They help readers find authors. They help authors show how awesome they are.

Reviews are social proof and go a long way to encouraging other readers to take a chance on an unknown author.

OFFER

As they say, there's no harm in asking, so here we go.

If you can help connect me with someone who can get Rogue Enterprises on a screen (Big or Little) I'll cut you in for 10% (Up to $10,000) of whatever advance is paid.

Send me an email and we can discuss.
rights@johnwilker.com

STAY CONNECTED

Want to stay up to date on the happenings in the Galactic Commonwealth?

Sign up for my newsletter at
johnwilker.com/newsletter
You can also join my Patreon page for all
sorts of awesome goodies!

Visit me online at
johnwilker.com

If you like supporting things you love by sporting merch, well you're in luck! I've launched a Space Rogues Shop. Take a look.

ACKNOWLEDGMENTS

I couldn't do this without an amazing group of people who sign up to beta and/or ARC read for me. The Beta readers in particular have to suffer through an early draft to help shape the story.

Below are some of these awesome people (If I missed your name, email me and you'll be in the next one :D)

- Roger Gilmartin
- Rick Lindsay
- Mitchell Schneidkraut
- Alice Clark
- Felix Muller
- Marcus Zarra
- Steve Rakoczy

Thank you so much, all of you!

OTHER BOOKS BY JOHN WILKER

The Space Rogues Series. (If you haven't read it, and want more Wil, Bennie and the others, you're in luck. Space Rogues is set before Rogue Enterprises!) Wil Calder and a bunch of alien misfits somehow keep finding themselves in the thick of it. No one ever checks qualifications when it comes to saving the galaxy!

The Grand Human Empire Series. Jax, Naomi and a pair of droids are just trying to get by. New droid parts ain't cheap after all.